RIOT

Also by Shashi Tharoor

Reasons of State
The Five-Dollar Smile and Other Stories
The Great Indian Novel
Show Business
India: From Midnight to the Millennium

RIOT

Shashi Tharoor

ARCADE PUBLISHING 8 NEW YORK

FIRST EDITION

This is a work of fiction. Names, places, characters, and incidents are either the products of the author's imagination or are used fictitiously.

Though the author works for the United Nations, none of the opinions expressed by the characters in this novel are to be construed as reflecting the views of the author in his official capacity.

Library of Congress Cataloging-in-Publication Data
Tharoor, Shashi, 1956–
    Riot / a novel / by Shashi Tharoor. —1st ed.
      p. cm.
    ISBN 1-55970-605-8
      1. Americans—India—Fiction. 2. Parent and adult child—Fiction. 3. Adult
        children—Death—Fiction. 4. Young women—Death—Fiction. 5. India—
        Fiction. 6. Riots—Fiction. I. Title.
    PR9499.3.T535 R56 2001
    823'.914—dc21   2001033311

Published in the United States by Arcade Publishing, Inc., New York
Distributed by Time Warner Trade Publishing

Visit our Web site at www.arcadepub.com

Visit the author's Web site at www.shashitharoor.com

10   9   8   7   6   5   4   3   2   1

Designed by API

EB

PRINTED IN THE UNITED STATES OF AMERICA

to my mother
Lily Tharoor
tireless seeker
who taught me to value
her divine discontent

"History is a sacred kind of writing, because truth is essential to it, and where truth is, there God himself is, so far as truth is concerned."

—Miguel de Cervantes, *Don Quixote*

"History is nothing but the activity of man in pursuit of his ends."

—Karl Marx, *The Holy Family*

"A truth in art is that whose contradiction is also true."

—Oscar Wilde

RIOT

The New York Journal

Late Edition

MONDAY, OCTOBER 2, 1989

AMERICAN SLAIN IN INDIA

NEW DELHI, India, Oct. 1 (AP) — A rioting mob attacked and killed an American woman in a town east of New Delhi yesterday, a few days before she was to return home, the U.S. embassy announced.

Priscilla Hart, 24, of Manhattan, a volunteer with the nongovernmental organization HELP-US, was beaten and stabbed to death in Zalilgarh town in the state of Uttar Pradesh, where she had volunteered her skills as a public health worker, officials said. It did not appear that she had been targeted because she was American, an embassy source said.

Details of the killing, which occurred during Hindu-Muslim rioting in the town, remain obscure. Ms. Hart had been working and doing research for a doctoral degree at New York University for 10 months.

She was reportedly due to return home on Thursday.

According to a HELP-US spokesman, Ms. Hart was closely involved with developing female population-control awareness programs here as part of a public health project supported by her organization.

No other foreigner has died in the sectarian violence that has killed several hundred Indians in the last three weeks, and Ms. Hart "may simply have been in the wrong place at the wrong time," an embassy spokesman suggested.

The New York Journal

Late Edition

TUESDAY, OCTOBER 3, 1989

DEATH OF AN IDEALIST

By VICTOR GOODMAN

NEW YORK, Oct. 2 — To Priscilla Hart's family, relatives, friends and professors here in New York, the death of the idealistic 24-year-old volunteer and scholar in a riot in India was a heartbreakingly tragic event.

The slim, blond, blue-eyed woman was only a few days away from returning to this city, where she was a doctoral candidate at New York University. During 10 months of field research in the Indian town of Zalilgarh, she had volunteered her time to a population-control program run by the American group HELP-US.

"She loved these people," said Beverley Nichols, an associate professor of sociology at New York University, where she supervised Ms. Hart's dissertation work. "She knew India. Not just the fancy restaurants in Delhi or the diplomatic circles around the embassy. She lived in that little town, among Hindus, Muslims, everybody. Nobody would have had a reason to kill her."

After 10 months in India, Ms. Hart was to have returned to her mother's home in Manhattan next week. "She was planning to write up her research and work as a teaching assistant next semester," Professor Nichols said.

Her parents, who are divorced, and her two brothers gathered today in her mother's apartment and told reporters of their great sense of loss at Ms. Hart's tragic death.

"Priscilla was a gem, an angel, a person brought onto this earth to do good," said her father, Rudyard Hart, 50, a senior marketing executive with the Coca-Cola Company. "She fell in love with India when I was posted there in the late '70s. It was her dream to go back, to do some good for the people there."

Her mother, Katharine Hart, 52, a high school teacher of English, agreed. "Priscilla wanted everyone to work together. She was determined to make a difference in the lives of the women of India. The last time I spoke to her she sounded so fulfilled, so sure of purpose. I can't believe she won't be coming back."

Also present were Priscilla's brothers Kim, 27, and Lance, 23.

"She gave everyone her help, whatever their race or religion," said Kim, a stockbroker.

Ms. Hart's interest in India was sparked during the three years her parents spent there, where her father was involved in an effort to revive the operations of the Coca-Cola Company, which was expelled from the country in 1977. She subsequently wrote her honors thesis at New York University on Indian women. "It was first class," said Professor Nichols, who still receives requests for copies of it.

"She was so committed, so engaged in the problems of India," the professor said. "She was extremely interested in the population question, and in the rights of women. She would have given anything to be able to spend the rest of her life in India."

Ms. Hart had worked for HELP-US, a nongovernmental organization whose initials stand for Health, Education, Literacy, Population – United States, as an intern at their office in New York City during the summers of 1986 and 1987. Throughout her time at graduate school, she remained involved with the group. During her doctoral field research in India, she volunteered to assist in a HELP-US project she had helped design. "She touched a lot of people here with her evident sincerity and compassion," said Lyndon Galbraith, president of HELP-US. "She will be greatly missed."

The New York Journal

Late Edition

Parents Plan to Visit India to View Site of Daughter's Death

By VICTOR GOODMAN

NEW YORK, Oct. 3 — The parents of an American student killed in India announced today that they will travel next week to the town where their daughter was attacked two days ago. They say that the only way to overcome their grief over their daughter's violent death is to confront it. So they are traveling to Zalilgarh, an obscure town in the northern Indian state of Uttar Pradesh, to relive their daughter's last moments.

"We want to talk to her friends and colleagues, the people she worked with, to see where she was," her father, Rudyard Hart, said in a telephone interview from his home in Stamford, Connecticut.

Priscilla Hart, a 24-year-old NYU student and HELP-US volunteer, was killed in a riot. Mr. Hart said she would be cremated in India and her ashes flown back to New York City, where a memorial service will be held next week.

Mr. Hart, a marketing executive, said he and his former wife, Katharine, would fly to India after the service. In the meantime, Mr. Hart said, he hoped the American public would read about his daughter's death and think about the issues that mattered to her.

"I want to make sure Priscilla isn't forgotten," Mr. Hart said. "I want the world to know what she was doing in India, the cause for which she gave her life."

Ms. Hart's mother, Katharine, who is divorced from Mr. Hart, was unavailable for comment.

The New York Journal

Late Edition

AN AMERICAN DEATH IN INDIA

By RANDY DIGGS

ZALILGARH, India, Oct. 15 — It was dusk, that time of the day in rural India when the kerosene lamps are lit and the mosquitoes emerge to prey on the unwary. That Saturday, Sept. 30, Priscilla Hart, 24, had said goodbye to her friends, because in a few days she would be packing her bags to return to New York, where she was a doctoral student at New York University.

The young American woman, a volunteer with a population-control awareness project run by the charity HELP-US, had completed her field research in the small North Indian town of Zalilgarh. That evening, she bicycled to an abandoned fort on the Jamuna River, which flows by the town. Perhaps she hoped for an escape from the crowded and noisy city, where Hindu militants had organized a major religious procession. Perhaps she sought a quiet glimpse of the sunset, a sight she would miss upon her return home.

She would never return. Her body was found a day later. She had been stabbed sixteen times.

In the town she was leaving behind, passions were riding high. The Hindu militants had organized a mammoth procession, some 30,000 strong in a town of just 100,000, to take consecrated bricks through the center of Zalilgarh to a collection point. From there the bricks would be transported to Ayodhya, where the Hindus hoped to use them to construct a temple, the Ram Janmabhoomi, on a disputed site occupied by a disused sixteenth-century mosque, the Babri Masjid.

The procession would wind its way past the town's Muslim quarter, where resistance to the Ram Janmabhoomi agitation was high. The previous night's stabbing, presumably by Muslims, of two Hindu youths putting up banners for the procession had inflamed

Continued on Page 266

from Katharine Hart's diary

October 9, 1989

I cannot believe I am sitting next to him, yet again, on a plane.
How many times we have done this, how many flights, transfers,
holidays, my passport and ticket always with him, even my boarding
card: he was the man, the head of the family, he held the travel documents. And when it was all over, that was among the many rights I
had regained, the right to be myself on an airline. Not an appen-
dage, not a wife, not Mrs. Rudyard Hart, no longer resigned to his
determination to have the aisle seat, no longer waiting for him to
pass me the newspaper when he'd finished it, no longer having to
see the look of irritated long-suffering on his face when I disturbed
him to go to the washroom, or asked him to catch the stewardess's
attention to get something for the kids.

The kids. It's been years since we've all traveled together, as a family.
He enjoyed travel, he often told me, but on his own. He was self-suffi-
cient, he didn't need things all the time like we, the rest of us, did —
juice, or entertainment, or frequent trips to the bathroom. He made it
obvious that being accompanied by us was not his preferred mode of
travel. But we did it often enough, till the kids began to rate airlines
and hotels and transit lounges the way other kids compared baseball
teams. And because of Rudyard's postings, the kids had an unusually
exotic basis for comparison. "Emirates is cool," Kim would say, because
that airline had video monitors on the backs of the seats and a wide
range of channels to choose from. "But they make you fly through
Dubai," Lance would retort, pronouncing it Do-buy, "where it's just
shops, shops, shops everywhere. Schiphol is cooler!" At Schiphol Airport in Amsterdam, his own favorite, Lance would pray for our con-
necting flights to be delayed so that he could have even longer in the
arcade, shooting down monsters and dragons with no regard for jet lag.

How wonderful it is to have your monsters and dragons on a screen in front of you, to be destroyed by the press of a button, and not inside your heart as mine are, hammering away at your soul. Monsters and dragons, not just at an airport arcade between weary flights, but on the plane, in your seat, in the seat next to you.

In the seat next to me sits my monstrous ex-husband. Here we are again on a plane, Rudyard and me together, not husband and wife, merely father and mother. Father and mother with no kids in sight. Kim couldn't get away from work, where he tells me junior stock-brokers are lucky if they can take Thanksgiving weekend. And Lance — Lance, who could never understand why I had to leave his father, Lance is in a world of his own and has no need of other worlds. But I'm not going to worry about Lance today. I've got too much else to think about.

Priscilla.

Priscilla with the baby blue eyes and the straight blond hair and that look of trusting innocence with which she greeted the world. Priscilla with her golden skin, her golden smile that lit up the eyes of anyone she was with. Priscilla with her idealism, her earnestness, her determination to do some good in the world. Priscilla who hated her father because of what he had done to me.

I look at him now, trying to read a magazine and not succeeding, his eyes blurring over the same page he has been staring at since I began writing these words. I look at him, and I see Priscilla: she had his eyes, his nose, his lips, his hair, except that the same features looked so different on her. Where his good looks are bloated by self-indulgence, hers were smoothed and softened by gentleness. And that sullen set of his jaw, that look of a man who has had his own way too easily for too long, set him completely apart from his daughter. There was nothing arrogant or petulant about Priscilla, not even when she was upset about some flagrant injustice. She was just a good human being, and no one would say that about Rudyard.

I look at him, trying to focus on the page, mourning the daughter whose loss he cannot come to terms with. Cannot, because he had already lost her when he lost me, lost her while she was still living. Despite myself, I feel a tug of sorrow for him.

It hurt so much to use the past tense for Priscilla. My baby, my own personal contribution to the future of the world. I would give anything for it to have been me, and not her. Anything.

cable to Randy Diggs

October 9, 1989

FOR DIGGS NY JOURNAL NEW DELHI FROM WASSER-MAN FOREIGN DESK. HAVE BEEN USING MAINLY AGENCY COPY ON HART KILLING. GRATEFUL YOU LOOK INTO STORY IN GREATER DETAIL FOR LONGER FEATURE PIECE. WHO THE GIRL WAS, WHAT SHE WAS DOING, HOW SHE WAS KILLED, WHY. SUGGEST YOU ALSO MEET PARENTS RUDYARD AND KATHARINE HART ARRIVING ON AIR INDIA FLIGHT 101 TOMORROW AND TRAVEL WITH THEM TO ZALILGARH. SHALL WE SAY 1200 WORDS IN A WEEK? AND GET THAT FAX FIXED. THESE CABLES ARE COSTING US A FORTUNE.

from Randy Diggs's notebook

October 10, 1989

Delhi airport. Crowded as usual, even at 4 bloody a.m. Curse of
this New Delhi job is that everyone lands and takes off in the middle
of the effing night. Engines droning, lights flashing, cars roaring, all
at 2-3-4 o'clock. It's only in the 3d World that residents near the
airport would take this crap. But then they don't have a choice, do
they?

Harts emerge from Customs, escorted by clean-cut consular type
from the embassy. Good PR, that. What every traveler needs in India
is an escort through Customs and Immigration. Bad enough to lose
your daughter without having to lose your patience as well in those
interminable queues.

Hart's a striking-looking fellow. Tall, with smooth good looks
now going to seed. Sort of Robert Redford plus thirty pounds,
some of it on his face. Eyes blue, gaze steady, firm handshake. But
there's a weariness there that goes beyond the exhaustion of the
journey.

Mrs. Hart: maternal/intellectual type. Short, heavy-set, with wiry
brown hair and skin too dry and lined for her age. Glasses on a chain
around her neck. Sensible, drab clothes that'll be far too warm in this
heat. (And she's lived in India before: doesn't she remember the
climate?)

She's distinctly unfriendly. Hart seems happy to see me, utters the
predictable thoughts (need to see where it happened — meet the
people who knew and worked with Priscilla — trying to understand — etc) and welcomes the idea of my traveling to Zalilgarh
with them. Mrs. Hart objects: "This is a private visit, Mr. Diggs. I
don't think . . ." But he brushes her aside, as if from habit. They're
divorced, of course.

"Priscilla lived for a cause," Hart tells his wife. "If we don't talk to the press, how are people going to know about her life and her work?"

A couple of agency photographers click at them desultorily. One hack asks all the obvious questions. Not much press interest here. If they're lucky, they'll get an inch or two in one of the Delhi papers. Zalilgarh is too far, the riots yesterday's story.

Hart looks disappointed, as if he'd expected more. A TV crew, perhaps, backing away from him as he strides to the consulate car. He'll learn soon enough that one more death doesn't make that much of a difference in a land of so many deaths. Poor bastard.

transcript of remarks by Shankar Das, Project Director, HELP-US, Zalilgarh, at meeting with Mr. and Mrs. Hart

October 12, 1989

(Owing to a malfunctioning tape recorder, voices of other participants in the meeting were inaudible and could not be properly transcribed.)

Mr. Hart, Mrs. Hart, please come in, please come in. It is my honor to velcome you both to Zalilgarh. Though in such wery sad circumstances. Wery sad circumstances.

Here is chart showing our project. It is population-control awareness project, as you are no doubt knowing. Objective is to inform poor rural women of family planning techniques. Family planning techniques. You are knowing? More importantly, educate them about facts of life. Facts of life. Why have so many children they cannot feed? If they are having fewer children, they are looking after them better.

Miss Priscilla was having so much knowledge. So hard-working. Took so much trouble to get to know local people. Everywhere she went, everywhere, on her cycle. On her cycle. Cycle also destroyed in terrible events. Really terrible.

Please have some tea. No sugar? <u>Bhaiyya, bagair chini ka cha lé aana!</u> Sorry, here habit is to serve tea with milk, sugar, all mixed already. Wery sorry. Wery sorry. New tea coming in just a minute. <u>Bhaiyya, jaldi kar do!</u>

Meanwhile if you vill just look at this wall. Here, you see dimensions of our project. Two thousand, three hundred and forty-three families

12

served. Outreach program to one thousand, one hundred and seventy-five households. Households. Supply of baby powder, you can see figures for yourself. Supply of contraceptive devices. Clinic visits. We are best Indian project. Best.

Normally we are not having Americans working in Zalilgarh project. Policy of HELP is to help people to help themselves, you see. But since Miss Priscilla had been much involved in designing this project when she was in America, it seemed quite natural. Quite natural. She was here for her field research, the project was here, it all fitted in. Fitted in.

You are saying? No, not at all. She was wery popular. Wery modest, wery simple. Not like some big shot person from foreign. Here also, it was always Mr. Das this, Mr. Das that. She was knowing lot about this project, yet she was always asking, not telling. Not telling. You see, Mr. Das, how about if we tried this that way? Or tried that this way? And sometimes I am saying to her, this is wery good idea, Miss Priscilla Hart, but Zalilgarh is not America. Not America. In America you are doing such and such and so and so, but here it is different. And she is always listening. Always listening.

Your tea is all right now? Good, good. She was such a good girl. Such a sweet person. Sweet person. She made friends very easily. Sometimes I am saying to her, you should not be so friendly with all these people. Some of these people not your type. Not your type. And she is laughing and saying, Mr. Das, what is my type, please? Everyone is my type. And I am saying to her, no, you should be choosing more carefully you know, awoid some of these low-class riff-raff. And she is laughing again and saying, oh Mr. Das, are we all high-class riff-raff here, then? Laughing and saying. Laughing and saying.

Excuse me. You see how upset we all are about Miss Priscilla. Wery upset. The day before we had

13

held big farewell party for her. So many people came. We could not have imagined what sort of farewell it would turn out to be. What sort of farewell. Wery sad.

This is Miss Kadambari. She is extension worker with us. She is working a lot with Miss Priscilla. Miss Kadambari will be taking you to where your daughter was staying. I believe you are wishing to see? Wery simple accommodation. Wery simple. But Zalilgarh is not Delhi, isn't it?

We are fixing up appointment for you to meet district magistrate, Mr. Lakshman. He was in charge during riot, you know. He can tell you more details about tragic events of last veek. Wery important man. Wery good friend of Miss Priscilla also. Wery good friend.

Some more tea? No? Thank you very much for honoring us with your visit. I am wishing your goodselves a very comfortable stay in Zalilgarh. Please do not hesitate to call me if you are needing anything. I am always here. Always here.

from Priscilla Hart's scrapbook

December 25, 1988

Christmas in Zalilgarh

Mists of dust on crumbling roadsides,
Cowdung sidewalks, rusting tin roofs.
Bright-painted signboards above dimly lit shops.
The tinkle of bicycle bells, the loud cries
Of hawkers selling vegetables, or peanuts, or scrap.
Red betel-stains on every wall
Compete with angry black slogans
Scrawled by men with a cause.
The dirty white dhotis of dirty brown men
Weaving in and out of traffic, in and out,
In and out of their sad-eyed women
Clad in gaily colored saris, clutching
Babies, baskets, burdens too heavy
For their undernourished bodies.
Here I have come to do good. It's true:
So simple a task in so complex a land.
I wheel my bicycle into their habits,
Tell them what's right, what can be done,
And how to do it. They listen to me,
So ignorant, so knowing, and when they have heard,
They go back to their little huts,
Roll out the chapatis for dinner,
Pour the children drinks of sewer water,
Serve their men first, eat what's left,
If they're lucky, and then submit unprotected
To the heaving thrusts of their protectors,

Abusers, masters. One more baby comes,
To wallow in misery with the rest.

It is God's will. But not my God's.
To their will I oppose my won't.
Give me strength, oh Lord, to make things change.
Give me the time to make a difference.

from Randy Diggs's notebook

October 11, 1989

God, what a dump.

The heat. The dust. The flies. The shit. The crowds. You name it, Zalilgarh has it. Every horrific Western cliché about India turns out to be true here.

letter from Priscilla Hart to Cindy Valeriani

February 2, 1989

. . .

The first time I saw him I didn't really like him. He stepped down from an official car, one of those clunky Ambassadors that look like a steel box on wheels, and he was wearing that awful outfit Indian officials seem to like so much, the safari suit. The shirt was cut too short, its wings stuck absurdly out over his behind, the pants flared too much at the bottom — Indian tailors seem to be stuck with patterns from the '70s, know what I mean? And I thought, Gawd, one more pompous self-important bureaucrat, completely unaware of the impression he makes, coming to throw his weight around our project. I could just imagine Mr. Das bowing and scraping and yes-sirring and no-sirring him to Kingdom Come, all to make sure the government remained happy with us, and I wanted no part of it. But it was too late to slip away, and when you're the only paleface blonde in sight you can't really make yourself inconspicuous. So he walked into the project office, and I was stuck.

And I was soon happy I was stuck. As Mr. Das did the usual spiel — "two thousand, three hundred and forty-three families served. Outreach program to one thousand, one hundred and seventy-five households" — repeating phrases in that odd way he has, I found myself studying our visitor, the new district magistrate. He is dark, my Mr. Lakshman, sort of a Jesse Jackson shade. Fine features, an especially perfect nose, a silken moustache. I was reminded of Omar Sharif in "Lawrence of Arabia" on video. Only Lakshman has a fuller mouth, a really sensuous mouth. I don't believe I just wrote that. (Tear this up when you've read it, Cindy, OK?)

Anyway, all this was nothing more than idle curiosity, until he opened that mouth of his. It was just to ask a question — an

18

unusually perceptive question, in fact, which showed that he'd been listening and actually understood a thing or two about population-control programs — but the words came right out and strummed me deep inside. Not the words themselves, but the sound of the words. Lakshman has a rich, soft voice, not smooth like a radio announcer's but slightly husky, like raw-edged velvet. There was something about his voice that reached out and drew me in, something that was both inviting and yet reassuring. It was a voice like a warm embrace, a voice that was seductive but not a seducer's. Do I make sense? Because if I don't, I can't describe it any better, Cindy. I heard his voice, and the only thing I could care about was hearing that voice again.

And I did, because Mr. Das went on and on, and Lakshman asked him all these gentle, probing questions, and I sat and listened to him, and I saw his sad, gentle eyes, and I knew I had found a kindred spirit.

I know you're going to say, there you go again, Priscilla, you're an incurable romantic, and I suppose I am and I'm not ashamed of it. Because you know what, Cindy, every time I think I've found a kindred spirit I've usually been right, whether it's with you or Professor Nichols or even with Winston, even if that ended badly. And there's no danger of that kind of complication arising here. We've spent loads of time together since that first meeting at the office and he's very correct, very gentle, very proper. Oh, and he's married. OK? So get any wicked thoughts out of your devious little mind, Ms Cindy Valeriani. He's had an arranged marriage, I'll have you know, with all the trimmings, and he has a little daughter he's very proud of, six years old and with dimpled cheeks you can hardly resist wanting to pinch. I know, not just because I've seen her picture in his office, but because she was presented to me when he invited me home to dinner. Little Rekha with the deep dark eyes and the dimples. So there.

The wife's a bit strange, actually, very different from him, reserved and not very communicative. She didn't make much effort to engage me in conversation. In fact, no sooner had the servants served us dinner than she disappeared to attend to Rekha and left me alone with Lakshman. Which was fine with me, of course, but it felt a bit odd, especially when she emerged only when I asked to say goodnight and goodbye.

But in that time we talked and talked, Cindy. I know he only invited me because he wanted to be courteous to the only foreigner in Zalilgarh, and maybe — just maybe — because he liked me when we met at the project and later talked in his office, but we soon connected at a much more, what can I call it, elemental level. As the evening wore on I realized I'm the only person in this back-of-beyond town he can actually talk to — the only person with a comparable frame of reference, who's read the same sorts of books, seen the same movies, heard some of the same music (thank God for elder brothers). These Indian officials lead terribly lonely lives in the districts. He's 33, and he's God as far as the local bureaucracy is concerned. But it also means that he's the only man in Zalilgarh from his sort of background; he's surrounded by people who haven't had his education, haven't thought the same thoughts, can't discuss the same ideas in the same English language. When he's posted in Delhi or even the state capital, Lucknow, it's completely different, of course, but here in Zalilgarh he's It, and he's pretty much alone. Oh, he's constantly being invited to the homes of the local bigwigs, the landlords and caste leaders and contractors and community chiefs with whom he has to be on intimate terms, but he has nothing in common intellectually with any of them. He mentioned one friend, the district superintendent of police, who'd been to the same college, but they're a couple of years apart and hadn't been close then, and in any case I'm not sure their normal work gives them all that much time together. At least that's the impression I had. So when Priscilla Hart comes along, full of stories of life in the Big Apple and knowledgeable as hell about Indian women and their reproductive rights, he sits up and listens. And why not, huh?

Actually, when I said goodnight and left him that night, I realized for the first time how lonely I was. I'd come prepared for the kind of experience I was having before I met him — lots of hard work, conversing with women through interpreters (though my Hindi's getting much better now), some solicitous attention from kindly,

20

hopeless Mr. Das and the helpful if devious extension worker Kadambari (the ones I told you about in my last letter), but with all my spare time spent alone, reading and writing and putting down my notes. And because that's all I expected, that's what I quickly got used to. Until I met Lakshman.

Until I met Lakshman, and talked, and connected with his kindred spirit, and said goodnight, and I found myself flooded with the sense that I was missing something so bad I could taste it. Something I'd taught myself not to miss.

No, I'm not in love or anything like that, Cindy, don't worry. At least I don't think so, and it's all quite impossible, anyway. He's married, and I'm here for ten months, and we inhabit different worlds. But when I came back to my room, with no phone, no TV, with only a few books and erratic light to read them by, I realized how much I'd cut myself off from something I really did have before. Companionship. I could find it with him, I think.

And in the meantime, I'll learn a lot! He's had to educate me from scratch about the whole Hindu-Muslim question. Not just the basics — how the British promoted divisions between Hindus and Muslims as a policy of "divide and rule," how the nationalist movement tried to involve everybody but the Muslim League broke away and called for a state of Pakistan, how the country was partitioned in 1947 to give the Muslims a separate state, etc etc — but on the more recent troubles. I suppose you know, Cin, that 12% of India's eight hundred million people are Muslim, against 82% who're Hindu (I think I've got the numbers right!). For decades since the Partition there've been small-scale problems in many parts of the country, riots pitting one group against the other, usually over some religious procession or festival intruding on the other religious group's space. The Indian government has apparently become rather good at managing these riots, and people like Mr. Lakshman are trained at riot control the way a student is trained to footnote a dissertation. They try to create networks between the two communities, he tells me, using "peace committees" to build bridges between leaders of the two religious groups. It's reassuring to listen to him talk about all this, because the atmosphere here isn't all good. There's a lot of tension in these parts over something called the Ram Janmabhoomi, a temple that some Hindus say was destroyed by the Mughal emperor Babar in 1526. Well, Babar (yes, just like the cartoon elephant!) replaced it with a mosque, apparently, and these Hindus want to reverse history and put the temple back where the mosque now stands. Though Lakshman tells me there's no proof there ever was a temple there. Not that a mere detail like that matters to the Hindu leaders who're busy organizing rallies and demonstrations all around the country and asking their followers to transport bricks to the site so they can build their temple there. . . .

But enough about this place. Cindy, how's your love life? Is Matt still acting as if what happened between you two never happened? . . .

from Priscilla Hart's scrapbook

February 14, 1989

. . .

"No, I'm not particularly young for this job. By the time Jesus Christ was my age, he'd been crucified."

I laughed a little uncertainly, not knowing how to take this. "Do you see your role here as some sort of Messiah to the people?"

"No," he said directly. "Do you?"

I was a bit taken aback at this. "Me? No! Why?"

"Well, you've come to this benighted place, leaving behind all your creature comforts, your microwave ovens and video stores and thirty-one flavors of ice cream, to live in the armpit of India and work in population control. Why do you do it?"

"Population-control <u>awareness</u>," I corrected him. "I'm just teaching — I mean telling — people about their rights, about what's out there, what can help them. That's all," I added, knowing as I said it that I was sounding more defensive than I should.

"Why? Are you pursuing some sort of missionary vocation?"

"Don't be silly. I mean, I am a believing Methodist, but my church didn't send me here. I'm here as a student anyway," I replied, a little more spiritedly. "Doing my field research. It all fits in, and I'm glad to be useful."

"Useful," he murmured, his fingertips touching under his chin, an amused look in his eye. "I think it was Oscar Wilde who said that usefulness is the last refuge of the unappealing. But even a man of his proclivities would have to agree that that last adjective doesn't apply to you."

It took me a second to get his meaning, and then I blushed. So help me God, I blushed.

"I didn't know Indian administrators were required to read Oscar Wilde," I ventured a little lamely, to cover up my confusion.

"God, we read everything," he replied. "What else is there to do in these godforsaken places they post us to? But Wilde, actually, I performed in college. St. Stephen's. 'The Importance of Being Earnest.' My friends and I loved his use of language. 'Arise, sir, from that semirecumbent posture!' 'Truth is rarely pure, and never simple.' 'Really, if the lower orders don't set us a good example, what on earth is the use of them?' For months after the play we went around talking in Wildeisms, some of which we made up ourselves. It got to the point where I could no longer tell the authentic Oscar epigrams from the ones I'd invented on the spur of some particularly opportune moment. I'm afraid the one I just came up with may well have been one of my own. A mere Lakshmanism." He laughed, lightly, softly, and that was the moment I knew I wanted him to kiss me.

"That's an India I've never known," I said.

"The India that performs 'The Importance of Being Earnest'? That makes up Wildean epigrams? That considers the pun to be mightier than the sword? You haven't met many Stephanians, then. The products of St. Stephen's College, the oldest college in Delhi University and the best institution of higher education in India— just ask any Stephanian. The one place where you could actually have a classmate saying, 'I find it harder and harder every day to live up to my silk kurtas.' Mind you, we produce all sorts of Stephanians. I should put you in touch with our chief cop here, Gurinder. No Wildean — quite the opposite, in fact — but in his own way, he's far worse than me." He smiled, dazzlingly, a perfect set of white teeth against the darkness of his face. "Priscilla, my dear, we're just as Indian as the pregnant women in your population-control pro-awareness programs. Unless you think you're somehow less authentically American than the welfare queen from Harlem."

I grimaced inwardly at the last stereotype but saw the point he was making, so just nodded.

A little grinning boy brought in tea. "Ah, Mitha Mohammed," Lakshman greeted him. "His tea is always too sweet. He has a heavy hand with the sugar, which is why we call him Sweet Mohammed. You don't have to drink it if you don't want to." He took a large gulp from his own cup anyway as the boy, still grinning, salaamed and left. "But how come you haven't met many Stephanians? Didn't you say you'd lived three years in Delhi?"

"Yes, but I was a kid then," I replied. "Just fifteen when I — we — left. I was at the American International School the whole time. The only Indians I knew were kids whose parents were working for American companies, or who'd already studied abroad for one reason or another before coming here and so couldn't go back to an Indian school. My parents didn't know that many Indian families, and those who came to the house didn't bring kids. So the only Indians I really got to know were our servants."

"That sounds awful," he said with a grim expression on his face, and I thought I'd caused some terrible offense. But he laughed again. "What a deprived childhood you've had, Priscilla. My poor little rich American kid."

As he said it, he leaned over to pat my hand, which was on my lap, and I felt myself blushing again, a deep shade of crimson this time, I was sure. "We were hardly rich," I retorted. "Middle-class, maybe. My mother taught school."

"Look, Priscilla, by Indian standards an American janitor's rich," he said. "Do you know what salaries are like here? You may think I live like a king here, and in many ways I suppose I do, but my take-home pay would put me below the poverty line in the United States. I'd be eligible for food stamps!" He seemed delighted to be able to make a cultural reference few in India would have understood. He's pretty clued up, I found myself thinking, and then — But that's what he's trying to show me.

"Speaking of food, are you getting hungry?" he asked. "Do you have dinner plans? Because if not, I'm sure Geetha and Rekha would be very happy to see you again."

I began to protest that I couldn't possibly impose, but he waved away my objections. "Look, the servants always cook more than we can eat, so it's really no extra trouble," he said. "But the one thing I should do is to let Geetha know you're coming, so she's not taken by surprise."

He picked up the phone, spoke to an assistant in Hindi, smiled at me as he waited and then spoke again in Hindi, this time, I guessed, to a servant at home. I looked around his office a little uncomfortably:

shabby walls, government-issue furniture with musty files tumbling off the shelves, a calendar with a garish picture of some Hindu gods hanging crooked and forlorn on one side. This was a man blissfully unaware of the importance of appearances. Then his wife came on the phone and any embarrassment I might have felt at intruding on their privacy disappeared, since he spoke to her in a rapid-fire southern language of which I did not know a word. There was a bit of an exchange between them; he seemed insistent, and after a few minutes hung up with a wry smile.

"Look, I really don't want to be any trouble," I began. "Why don't we do this some other time?"

"It's no trouble at all," he assured me. "I just caught Geetha on her way to the temple. I'd forgotten Tuesday is one of her usual temple evenings. But dinner's fine — it'll just be a bit later. Would you mind very much if we had dinner, say, in two hours from now?"

I was still hesitating — not because I didn't want more of his company, but because of the apparent awkwardness of the situation, and also because I wasn't sure how I could put the intervening time to good use — when he spoke again. "Have you seen the Kotli?" he asked suddenly.

I shook my head.

"Then you must!" he replied, grinning with delight. "Zalilgarh's only authentic historic sight. You've been here two months and still haven't seen it?" He tut-tutted theatrically while rising from his desk. "I must take you there. And dusk is the perfect time. You'll see the sunset over the river." He briefly gripped my upper arm as if to lift me from the chair. His grasp was strong, firm, yet light; I didn't want him to remove his hand. "Come. It'll fill the time very nicely until Geetha is ready for us."

He rang a bell. A chaprassi came in to carry his briefcase to the waiting car.

"My bike?" I asked, uncertainly.

"You can leave it here," he said. "My driver will drop you home after dinner, and you can pick up your cycle again in the morning."

Well, I thought, getting into his official Ambassador car, here's a man who thinks of everything.

26

from Randy Diggs's notebook

October 11, 1989

Of course there's no real hotel in Zalilgarh. Why would they need one? Just a few "lodges" for traveling salesmen and whores, dingy rooms above fly-infested restaurants. But the embassy has managed to get the government to give the Harts the use of the official Public Works Department guest house, which is where visiting officials stay when they're touring the district. There is a bit of confusion when it turns out the staff only prepared one bedroom for Mr. and Mrs. Hart. Word of their divorce has apparently failed to penetrate down to the PWD caretakers. Nor have they been told about me. But the guest house is empty except for us. So, after a bit of to-do and some anxious hand-wringing on the part of the main uniformed attendant, not to mention the two twenty-rupee notes I slipped into his folded hands, a couple of additional locked rooms are opened up for our use. They're musty and haven't been dusted in weeks, and the once-white sheets on the beds are rough and stained, but I've no doubt they're better than the alternatives in town. Hart seems glad enough to take my word for it.

After a government-issue dinner (atmosphere strained, soup not), Mrs. Hart retires to her room. Hart must be exhausted too — the jet lag, the courtesy meetings at the embassy, the slow and bumpy ride down from Delhi. His face, his eyes especially, tell the story: he hasn't slept in days. But he wants to talk. We sit on the verandah in reclining wooden chairs whose woven-cane seats have begun to sag, and the mosquitoes buzz around our ears. Hart swats at them irritably until I produce a can of insect-repellent spray. "Thanks. Didn't have the time to think about this stuff," he says shamefacedly.

I always think about this stuff, of course. And also about booze. Hart looks almost pathetically grateful when I extract a bottle of Johnnie Walker Black from my bag and get a couple of plain glass

27

tumblers from the attendant. No ice. Hart doesn't seem to mind. He clutches his glass so hard I'm grateful it's thick PWD issue — a finer glass would have left him with crystal embedded in his palm. So we sit there, the gloom barely dispelled by the dim light of a solitary bulb in a metal lampshade (dipping and flaring alarmingly with the inevitable voltage fluctuations), the buzzing mosquitoes — maddened and repelled by our proximity and our chemicals — swirling around us. And we talk. Or rather, Hart talks, and I listen, letting the tape recorder run discreetly, scrawling the occasional note.

Rudyard Hart to Randy Diggs

October 11, 1989

I asked for India, you know. The office couldn't believe it. "What the hell d'ya want to go down *theah* for?" they asked in Atlanta. Coke had a decent-sized operation in India, but it was headed by an Indian, fellow called Kisan Mehta. Since he took over Coca-Cola India in 1964 the only Americans around had been visiting firemen, you know, checking out one thing or another, basically coming to remind the bottlers and the distributors that they had a big multinational corporation behind them. No American executive had been assigned full-time by Coca-Cola to India since the early 1960s.

But I was so goddamned persistent they relented and let me go after all. Just before Christmas 1976, I was named marketing director for India. I'd argued that a dose of good ol' American energy and marketing technique was all that stood between us and real takeoff. Coke had opened its first plant in India in 1950, and at the time that I was asking to be assigned there, late '76, we had twenty-two plants, with about 200,000 distributors. Not a bad rate of growth, you might think, but I was convinced we could do better. They were selling about 35 million cases of Coke a year in India in those days — a case had twenty-four bottles, seven-ounce bottles, two hundred milliliters in Indian terms. As far as I was concerned, that was nothing. A country with a middle class about a hundred million strong, and we couldn't get each of them to drink just one small Coke a week? I argued that with the right approach, we should be selling 200 million cases in India, not 35 million. And that was a conservative estimate, because a Coke a week per middle-class Indian was really nothing, and I was confident we could exceed my own projections.

Besides, I wanted to go to India. I'd heard so much about the place: my parents had been missionaries there. They'd loved it, the whole schtick, the Taj Mahal, *The Jungle Book*, you name it. They'd even named me Rudyard in honor of Kipling, can you believe it? By the time I was born they had moved to China, but my parents were still so nostalgic for India that they were dreaming Bengal Lancers in the land of Pearl Buck. The missionary life came to an end when China went Communist, and I grew up mainly in the States, but my parents left me with an abiding dream of India that I never shook off.

Much of my working life was spent in companies that had overseas operations everywhere but India. But when I joined Coke I knew this could be my chance. Katharine wasn't thrilled, I'll admit it. I had wanted to take her to India for our honeymoon, but she didn't want to go and we ended up in Niagara Falls instead. She always hated our foreign travels. Always preferred the life she knew in the States, her books, her teaching, to any exotic foreign adventure. She wasn't sure she'd be able to work in India. She was afraid the kids' schooling would be disrupted. She argued long against it, but I wouldn't listen. In the end she gave in and I figured she'd just accepted how much I wanted this for us. For us.

We arrived in Delhi in early 1977. January first week, I believe it was. God, it was great to be there. The weather was fabulous, cool and sunny in January. The government was making all the right noises about opening up the economy to foreign investment. Mrs. Gandhi had been quite hostile to America up to that point, and you remember she'd proclaimed a state of emergency in mid-'75 and darkly claimed the CIA was out to destabilize her government. But with her opponents locked up and the press censored, she thawed quite a bit, and when I was still in Atlanta I'd read about her unexpected appearance at Ambassador Saxbe's for dinner, which everyone interpreted as a major signal that she wanted to really open up to America. And, of course, to American companies. Her younger son, Sanjay, was already talking to McDonald's about coming into India. We, Coke, were already in India, of course, but the possibilities seemed limitless.

Mehta told me soon after I arrived about the earlier warning signs. India had passed a law called FERA, the Foreign Exchange Regulation Act, in 1973, which governed the activities of all companies involved in international trade. One of the provisions of the law, Section 29 I believe it was, required foreign companies doing business in India to apply again to the government for registration, in other words to be reapproved to do business here. We treated this as just another bureaucratic requirement in a country obsessed with forms and procedures — you know these Indians, red tape runs in their veins. So we applied, quite routinely, and the government sat on our application, also quite predictably, and we went on doing business, so nothing was really affected by FERA. Except that, as Kisan Mehta reminded me, our case was still pending with the regulatory bodies, and in the meantime a fair bit of political hostility had been whipped up against us.

It seemed faintly absurd to us in Atlanta or elsewhere in the world that Coke should have become an object of political controversy at all. Sure, there were always people on the hysterical left, whether in Latin America or in India, who would scream that Coca-Cola was a CIA plot, but the attacks on Coke in India were particularly bizarre. People would stand up in Parliament and accuse us of "looting the country" and "destroying the health of Indians." One firebrand socialist, George Fernandes, demanded to know, "What kind of a country is India, where you can get Coke in the cities but not clean drinking water in the villages?" Another of his comrades stood up and asked in Parliament, "Why do we *need* Coca-Cola?" I remember, just before I came out to India, meeting the chairman of the company, Paul Austin, and hearing him marvel that, in a country with so many pressing problems, Indian members of Parliament actually had the time to devote to attacking Coca-Cola! But it didn't faze us. We'd been through worse as a company in France in 1949–50, when attempts to ban Coke nearly led to a trade war. We could handle our share of lefty nationalist hysteria.

Amidst all of this, Mrs. Gandhi ended her state of emergency and called an election. I guess you've done your homework on those days, but it was an incredible time, Randy. She had been a dictator, for all practical purposes, for the twenty-two months she'd ruled under emergency decrees, and here she was, allowing the victims of her dictatorship the right to decide whether she could continue her tyranny! India's an astonishing place, and this was India at its most astonishing. We'd barely unpacked when the election campaign

31

began, and it was as if we'd pitched our tents in a hurricane. Before I had even drawn up my marketing strategy and got moving toward the first phase of my two-hundred-million-cases target, Mrs. Gandhi had been defeated in the elections and a new coalition government, the Janata government, took office. And guess who was named Minister for Industry in the new cabinet? Coke's favorite Indian politician, the socialist George Fernandes. Minister *against* Industry might have been a better title for him.

Kisan Mehta had already urged me not to be too ambitious. Our sales curves in India showed a growth rate comparable to Coke in Japan, he said. This is not the time to rock the boat by trying to double our speed when we should be happy that we're sailing at all. But I didn't listen to him. I thought I knew better.

Now, you've got to understand that Coca-Cola India was actually a wholly owned company, wholly owned by Coca-Cola in the U.S., and what we did was to manufacture and supply Coke concentrates, plus provide the marketing and technical support to our franchisees. The bottlers were all Indian-owned companies that bought the concentrates from us. This way we kept control of the product and of our secret formula, 7X, but we didn't need to employ more than a hundred people in India ourselves. The downside of this was that we were very definitely a foreign company in India.

Well, Mr. Fernandes lost no time in going after foreign companies. IBM and Coke became his first victims. He demanded that we indigenize our operations and that Coke, specifically, should release our secret formula to the authorities as the price of doing business in India. We refused. Paul Austin said at the time, "If India wants Coke, they'll have to have it on our terms." Well, India — at least as represented by this Indian government — didn't want Coke on our terms. In August 1977, eight months after I'd gotten to India, our long-pending application under Section 29 of FERA was rejected by the government. Coke was ordered to wind up in India.

It was a helluva blow, I'll tell you that, Randy. Not just professionally, though that was bad enough. We spent two million dollars grinding up every Coca-Cola bottle in India, and all we got in return was publicity for the sanctity of our secret formula. Big deal. I'd uprooted my family and dragged them halfway across the world and now it seemed the whole reason for doing so had disappeared. It didn't make sense, when they'd just settled down to life and school in India, to uproot them again and drag them back, and frankly it's not as if Coke had something better to offer me back in Atlanta either. Plus there was the question of professional pride. Coke was keeping on a skeleton staff to handle all the liquidation work, including an interminable excise tax case going back decades, so I asked to stay on with them. I felt that if there was a creative way back for Coke in India, I was the man to find it. I wanted desperately to be able to vindicate, one day, my original decision to come to India.

So we stayed on. My eldest son, Kim, was in his last years of high school, and the company agreed I should stay until he'd finished, trying to get Coke back into business here. Katharine had found a job teaching at the American International School. The pay was terrible, but at least it meant she had something to do besides resenting India and me. Lance, the youngest, was just a kid, a bit slow, what they're now beginning to call learning-disabled, and he was happy enough wherever he was. It was Priscilla that India had the greatest impact on. She was twelve when we arrived, just awakening, I suppose, to adolescence and emotional maturity, and it all happened here. I never thought of her in making my decisions, whether to come or to stay, and now I know it was her I should have thought of the most.

Yes, thanks, I'll have another. Didn't have the time to think about getting this stuff. Glad you did. Nah, don't worry about soda. I like the stuff neat. Doesn't do anything to me, really. Except makes me talk.

The professional challenge soon turned out to be a hopeless one. I may as well admit it, though at the time I kept trying to persuade myself and Atlanta that I was on the verge of a breakthrough. With shrewd advice from that old veteran Kisan Mehta, I came up with one clever scheme after another, but nothing worked. I tried to work with the Indian bottlers, who were initially the hardest hit by the government's decision, to generate a change of attitude, pointing out that it was Indians, not just an American company, who'd been hurt by the expulsion of Coke. No dice. And the bottlers figured out soon enough that they could do just as well manufacturing Indian substitutes for Coke, free of the threat of international competition, so that argument lost its force as Thums Up and Campa-Cola were born and thrived in the vacuum we'd left behind. In fact George Fernandes even got the government into the soft drink business, converting a dozen Coke bottling plants to the service of a product called 77. Or maybe it was Spirit of 77. Anyway, it was a rather feeble spirit, and it disappeared pretty quickly from the market. But with all this stuff coming out, I needed another approach to try and bring Coke back into business.

One idea that occurred to me was to take a leaf out of the Pepsi strategy in the Soviet Union. You remember how Pepsi had slipped behind the Iron Curtain while we were still blacklisted there? Their trick was to offer a real quid pro quo — marketing a Soviet product, in their case vodka, in America in exchange for being allowed to market their product, Pepsi, in the USSR. It worked for Pepsi in Moscow, but not for Coke in Delhi. I suggested that we could use Coca-Cola's expertise to set up a chain of stores in the U.S. selling Indian handicrafts, bringing major export revenues to India, in exchange for resuming our sales of Coke in India. The Indian bureaucracy considered it for about three months, then nixed that too.

I kept on trying, Randy. That was the story of my three years in India — trying to get Coke back to a firm foothold in this market, in the face of impossible odds. How ironic it felt, during this time, to be attacked as a tool of Western imperialism! The old imperialists just marched in and took over, or took what they wanted, or both. Here we were desperately trying to court the Indian authorities, inventing new ways to please them, asking to be allowed to bring them the pleasure that our product could provide. This is imperialism?

I'll give you one example. The government had different rules for joint venture companies, so I tried to figure out a way to get those rules to apply to us. Coke itself would have to remain in American hands, of course, so I tried to invent a partnership between Coke and the bottlers that would qualify as a joint venture. But that didn't wash with the Indian regulators. Then I spent an incredible amount of time with a whole bunch of lawyers inventing a scheme under which we'd establish a different Indian company in which Coke would have only a forty-percent stake; we'd manufacture the Coke concentrate ourselves, of course, as before, but we'd transfer it, at cost, to this new company, which would be the company actually selling the product to the bottlers.

I was making some headway in getting the Indian authorities interested in the idea when I found my home base slipping away from under my feet. Atlanta was not interested in pursuing such an unusual strategy for the kinds of rewards India seemed likely to offer. One of the suits in Atlanta wrote me a stern memo: "Coke is a product avidly sought by countries around the world. We shouldn't dilute our own prestige by bending over backwards to accommodate every unreasonable demand of every intransigent government." Every unreasonable demand of every intransigent government. I still remember the phrase. Those words are practically burned into my brain. It was with them, I think, that I began to stop trying.

I was still going to stay on in India till Kim finished school, of course, but increasingly I was just going through the motions. And, I'll admit, I had found other ways to occupy my time. What the hell, it all came out in the divorce proceedings, anyway, so I may as well tell you.

I began an affair, Randy. In the most obviously predictable way possible. With my secretary.

Looking back, I'm ashamed of myself, and I suppose I was ashamed of myself even then, except that I was too blinded by own desires to see my own shame. That's probably the missionary's son talking. My marriage to Katharine had settled into a rut. Sometimes a rut can be a comfortable place to be, but ours was full of too many differences and resentments to be wholly comfortable. I had always had my own way in the marriage — about what we'd do, where we'd do it, when, how. Katharine had always argued, and always given in. In the process she'd become more resentful, I guess, except that I was too busy with my own work to notice. But in turn she was less and less appealing to me. She's a couple of years older than me, I guess you know that, but that wasn't all. Those stolid American middle-class values, her sensible clothes, her sense of responsibility, her moderation in all things — frankly, they bored me. We made love less and less, and she didn't even seem to miss it.

I did.

But I didn't miss making love with her. What I missed, frankly, was sex. The excitement of discovering a woman's body, opening her up to my touch, possessing her as no one like me had possessed her before. That's what I was seeking, and that's what I found with Nandini.

She was exotic, Randy. I mean it — exotic. She shimmered into the office in gorgeous saris, bedecked with jewelry, fragrant with attar of roses, every nail perfectly painted, every hair in place. She smiled dazzlingly at me, her slightly uneven teeth gleaming, and she answered the phone in that convent-educated English with that special lilt only Indian women can manage, and she drove me crazy. I would call her in to dictate some meaningless routine correspondence and ask her to read it back to me just so I could hear her voice lend magic to my words. And also, I'll admit it, so I could look at her.

Have you felt the allure of the exotic yourself, Randy? All right, you don't have to answer that. Just give me some more of your Scotch. Sure you don't want some yourself? Anyway, where was I? Yes, Nandini. Nandini was simply so unlike Katharine, I could have been dallying with another species. She wore little sleeveless blouses that revealed a generous amount of cleavage whenever that front fold of her sari slipped, which it did often enough, whenever she turned, or bent to pick up something, or moved in a dozen different ways. And then, of course, there was the sari itself. What a garment, Randy! There isn't another outfit in the world that balances better the twin feminine urges to conceal and reveal. It outlines the woman's shape but hides the faults a skirt can't — under a sari a heavy behind, unflattering legs are invisible. But it also reveals the midriff, a part of the anatomy most Western women hide all the time. I was mesmerized, Randy, by the mere fact of being able to see her belly button when she walked, the single fold of flesh above the knot of her sari, the curve of her waist toward her hips. That swell of flesh just above a woman's hipbone, Randy, is the sexiest part of the female anatomy to me. And I didn't even have to undress her to see it. I was completely smitten.

And she was attracted to me, too. I could see that. In her smile, in her way of talking, in her eyes when she looked at me. It was not just that she was trying to ingratiate herself with her boss. The signals she sent me were quite clear.

It still took me some time to read them. But one day, late one evening, in my office, when everyone else had gone, it just happened, as these things do.

She was on my side of the desk, standing next to me as she looked over my shoulder at a document I wanted her to retype. As I explained my revisions to her, she looked at the document and took quick notes on her steno pad. Then at one point, she dropped her pencil accidentally, right into my lap. Instinctively, she reached down to pick it up.

My hand closed on hers, keeping it in my lap.

"I like it there," I said.

Don't worry, I'm not drunk. I can handle this stuff. I even used to live on Indian Scotch, if that isn't a contradiction in terms. "Indian-made foreign liquor," they used to call it. Would you believe it! "Indian-made foreign liquor." But it was better than the fake Scotch the bootleggers peddled at four times the price. There was more Johnnie Walker Black Label sold in India than was ever manufactured in Scotland, I can tell you that. Go ahead, pour away.

It's good I can hardly see your face in this light, Randy. I don't have any excuse for myself, and at the time I wasn't really looking for any. I wanted her, it was as simple as that. And at a time when I wasn't able to have much else I wanted, Nandini came as a source of pure, unqualified satisfaction.

When she moved her hand, it was not to extricate herself but to burrow her fingers deeper into my lap. "I like it there, too," she said.

And then she was kneeling by my side and I could smell the fragrance of the attar of roses, I could sense the pressure of those uneven teeth, I felt those elegant fingers on my thigh, and I was in another world, in my office and yet completely outside it, my head swirling with pleasures tangible and imagined. . . .

That was how it began, Randy. And it continued, madly, obsessively, everywhere I could contrive — in hotel rooms booked by the company for visitors who hadn't yet arrived, on official trips where no secretary had been taken before, and of course at the office, mainly on the couch where I received visitors.

And once, thrillingly, on my desk. I came back one day from a particularly frustrating meeting with a smug functionary called the Controller of Capital Issues and Foreign Investments, having heard in tones of complacent arrogance that I was pushing what his government considered an "inessential product." Furious and defeated, I stormed into my office. Nandini walked in behind me, concerned, and closed the door. "Bad meeting?" she asked, gently rubbing the nape of my neck, where a hard knot of tension throbbed.

In response, I turned around and kissed her full on the mouth, holding her so tightly that she almost gasped for breath as I prised her mouth open with an insistent tongue. Without a further word, I pushed her onto the desk, unzipping myself with one hand without releasing my grip on her, then lifting her sari and slip and thrusting myself into her. At that moment, her surrender was total, and for me, that was all that mattered. Her eyes were closed, her bare arms in that sleeveless blouse flung back, her legs splayed as they dangled from the desk, and I was on top, deep inside her, her conqueror. It didn't last very long, but in those few minutes in which I forgot myself, I regained my sense of who I was, and why I was here, and what I had come to do.

I'm sorry, Randy. Do I sound like a shit? Sometimes when I relive those moments I feel I'm reminding myself that I really am the complete asshole Katharine portrayed in divorce court.

In hindsight it's easy to see it inexorably coming to an end. At the time all I could think about was how to make it even better. Nandini was chafing at constantly having to watch out for noises at the office door, constantly having to hurry to vacate a hotel room, constantly having to avoid detection. She wanted, she said, to be alone with me without having to feel tense all the time. Her own place was impossible, not just because she was married, but because she lived with an aged mother who was always in the house. So it had to be mine.

I brought method to my madness. I took a greater interest in my wife's and kids' school schedules than I had ever done before, learning by heart her library hours, Kim's bagpipe lesson schedule, the servants' siesta times. Even allowing for a half-hour's margin of error on either side, the house was completely empty from one to three-thirty on Monday, Wednesday, and Friday afternoons.

On those days I dismissed the driver and took Nandini home myself, confident it was absolutely safe. She loved being there, sinking into the American king-sized bed that Katharine and I had carried around the world with us, seeing us naked together in the full-length mirror, relishing the quiet efficiency of the air-conditioning. And what did I feel, thrashing about with my secretary on the bed in which my wife of twenty years would sleep, her back to me in a flannel nightdress, a few hours later? A twinge of guilt, I'd like to think, but mainly, if I'm honest with myself, excitement, a sense of having reclaimed the conjugal bed for its rightful purpose.

By the time we began trysting at my place, matters were coming to a head anyway. Kim was almost finished at school, and I was ready to admit failure to my bosses and accept a transfer somewhere else. Nandini was beginning to ask about our future and I had not even considered whether we had one. I had embarked on our relationship without thinking beyond the next day. It was clear she had gone much further. Nandini was seeing herself in my marital bed, and convincing herself that's where she belonged. I was beginning to feel trapped.

One night Katharine noticed a suspicious scent on the sheet, and wondered if one of the servants were taking their siesta in her bed. Their injured protestations of innocence made it clear the idea was unthinkable to them. Before long Katharine began to think of another possibility she had considered unthinkable.

You find this embarrassing, Randy? Nah, you journalists have pretty thick skins. You've heard worse, I'm sure. But this is all off the record. You understand that. Fact is, when I've had a few I talk too much. Especially these days. It's all I've got left, Randy. Words.

Yeah, pour the rest. There isn't much left. Might as well finish the bottle.

So Katharine was beginning to get suspicious. But it wasn't my wife who found out. It was Priscilla. And in the worst possible way.

Of all of us, it was Priscilla who led the most Indian life. Kim had his high school friends and his exams; Lance had a small group of American friends with a shared addiction to comics, which they exchanged incessantly; Katharine had her teaching and the household; I had my work and Nandini. Priscilla was the one person with a genuine curiosity about Indians — not the handful of Americanized rich kids she met in her school, but what she called "real Indians." Early on she decided to teach the alphabet to our servants, and was soon giving them reading lessons after dinner. One day she went with the gardener to his home and came back with a horrified account of his family's poverty. I had no choice but to double his wage. Soon everyone who did any work for us wanted her to visit them too.

It was Priscilla who was the most active member of the school social service league, Priscilla who volunteered to read to blind children, Priscilla who helped Sundays at the Catholic orphanage. She didn't know a single Indian with a college degree or a fancy job, but she really cared for the underside of this society.

So inevitably, when the dhobi's young son, who carried the bundles of laundry for his father, came to our home looking feverish and ill one Wednesday, it was Priscilla who insisted he rest instead of continuing with his father's rounds. I was already at the office; I only learned this later. When the father protested that he could not possibly take the boy back home with so many visits left to make, Priscilla declared the child could rest at our place, aspirined and blanketed, and be picked up by his father at the end of the dhobi's day. And it was typical of Priscilla, of course, that she would decide to skip her regular after-school commitments to come home early and make sure her patient had been properly fed by the servants and was doing well.

If I had paid more attention to my daughter, I would have realized all this. And I would not have been at home, buck naked and whooping as I took Nandini doggy-style, slapping her ample behind like a cowboy taming a mare, when Priscilla, puzzled by the noise, opened the door.

She didn't scream. She didn't slam the door. She didn't run away. Instead, she just stood there, her baby blue eyes widening in bewilderment and hurt, not comprehending what was going on, not wanting to comprehend. And as I saw her, I stopped moving, frozen in shame and embarrassment.

"Ruddy, why do you stop?" Nandini clamored, kneeling on the bed on all fours, her breasts still swinging from the momentum of our coition, her eyes shut in ecstasy, oblivious of the intrusion.

That broke the spell in which Priscilla was imprisoned. A solitary tear escaped from one eye and rolled down her cheek. And then she began to sob.

"Priscilla," I said, not knowing what to do. I pulled myself out of Nandini and tried to clamber off the bed while hiding myself, wanting to go to her but anxious to wear something, knowing that she had never seen me naked, let alone in these circumstances.

"Don't come near me!" she screamed then. "I don't want you to touch me! I hate you, Daddy!"

Everything is a blur thereafter. Nandini's little shriek, my pulling on a pair of pants, Priscilla running down the corridor crying, my setting off after her, Priscilla running blindly out of the house toward the street, my chasing her bare-chested and barefoot, trying to hold her in my arms, Priscilla struggling with me on the pavement, raining little blows on my shoulders with her fists, still sobbing. And then Katharine's car screeching to a halt beside us and my wife, also returning early to test her suspicions, leaping out. And my marriage collapsing around me like a tent.

Lakshman to Priscilla Hart

February 27, 1989

I'm an administrator, not a political scientist, but I'd say there are five major sources of division in India — language, region, caste, class, and religion.

Very simply: There are thirty-five languages in India spoken by more than a million people each, fifteen spoken by more than ten million each. The Constitution recognizes seventeen. Take a look at this rupee note: you can see "ten rupees" written out in seventeen languages, different words, different scripts. The speakers of each major language have a natural affinity for each other, and a sense of difference from those who speak the other languages. Hindi is supposed to be the national language, but half the country doesn't speak it and is extremely wary of any attempt to impose it on them. In my part of the country, Tamil Nadu, you'd do better asking for directions in English than in Hindi.

So language divides. And this is compounded by the fact that, within a decade after independence, the government reorganized the states on linguistic lines, so most language groups have their own political entities to look toward to give expression to their linguistic identity. The people of Punjab speak Punjabi, of Bengal Bengali, of Tamil Nadu Tamil, and so on. So we have the twenty-five states in the Indian Union becoming ethnolinguistic entities, helping give rise to strong regional feeling going beyond the states themselves. The "Hindi belt" in the North — overpopulated, illiterate, poor and clamorous — is resented by many in the better-educated, more prosperous South. And both are seen as distant and self-obsessed by the neglected Northeast. There's a real risk of disaffection here, especially as long as power remains concentrated in Delhi and the outlying states find themselves on the periphery, paying tribute to the north.

Next, caste. That's basically a Hindu phenomenon, but caste is hardly unknown amongst converts to other faiths, including egalitarian ones like Sikhism, Christianity, and Islam. There are hundreds of castes and subcastes across the country, but they're broadly grouped into four major castes — the Brahmins, who're the priests and the men of learning (which in the old days was the same thing); the Kshatriyas, who were the warriors and kings; the Vaishyas, who were the farmers and merchants; and the Sudras, who were the artisans and manual workers. Outside the caste system were the untouchables, who did menial and polluting work, scavenging, sweeping streets, removing human waste, cleaning toilets, collecting the ashes from funeral pyres. Mahatma Gandhi tried to uplift them and called them Harijans, or children of God; they soon found that patronizing and now prefer to call themselves the Dalits, the oppressed. One interesting detail that's often overlooked: the top three castes account for fewer than twenty percent of the population. There's a source of division to think about.

Class comes next. It's not the same as caste, because you can be a poor Brahmin or a rich Vaishya, but as with caste, the vast majority of Indians are in the underclass. The privileged elite is, at best, five percent of the country; the middle class accounts for perhaps another twenty percent of the population; the rest of India is lower class. You can understand why the communist parties thought the country was ripe for revolution. Of course they were wrong, and one of the main reasons they were wrong (I'll come to the other main reason in a minute) was the extent to which they underestimated the fatalism of the Indian poor, their willingness to conform to millennia of social conditioning.

This was because of the fifth great source of division in India, religion. Hinduism is great for encouraging social peace, because everyone basically believes their suffering in this life is the result of misdeeds in a past one, and their miseries in this world will be addressed in the next if only they'd shut up and be good and accept things as they are, injustices included. So Hinduism is the best antidote to Marxism. It's interesting, in fact, how many of the leading communists before Partition were Muslims, because of their natural

43

predisposition to egalitarianism. And Brahmins, because they had a natural affinity for dictatorships, even of the proletariat. But religion also breeds what we in this country call "communalism" — the sense of religious chauvinism that transforms itself into bigotry, and sometimes violence, against the followers of other faiths. Now we have practically every religion on earth represented on Indian soil, with the possible exception of Shintoism. So we've seen various kinds of clashes in our history — Hindu-Muslim, Muslim-Sikh, Sikh-Hindu, Hindu-Christian.

Now, you might be forgiven for thinking that with so much dividing us, India was bound to fall apart on one or several of these cleavages. But in fact it hasn't, and it's belied every doomsayer who's predicted its imminent disintegration. The main reason for that is the other thing I said the communists were wrong about. It was that they also underestimated the resilience of Indian democracy, which gave everyone, however underprivileged or disaffected, a chance to pursue his or her hopes and ambitions within the common system. In Tamil Nadu in the South, in Mizoram in the Northeast, yesterday's secessionists are today's chief ministers. Agitations in defense of specific languages or specific tribal groups? No problem, deal with them by creative federalism: give the agitators their own units to rule within the federal Indian state. Naxalites chopping off the heads of landlords in Bengal? No problem, encourage the commies to go to the polls instead, and today the pro-Chinese Communist party celebrates a dozen years in power in Bengal. The untouchables want to undo three thousand years of discrimination? Fine, give them the world's first and farthest-reaching affirmative action program, guaranteeing not just opportunities but outcomes — with reserved places in universities, quotas for government jobs, and even eighty-five seats in Parliament. The Muslims feel like a threatened minority? Tsk tsk, allow them their own Personal Law, do not interfere in any way with their social customs, however retrograde they may be, and even have the state organize and subsidize an annual Haj pilgrimage to Mecca.

Do I make it sound too easy? Believe me, it isn't. Skulls have been broken over each of these issues. But the basic principle is simple indeed. Let everyone feel they are as much Indian as everyone else:

that's the secret. Ensure that democracy protects the multiple identities of Indians, so that people feel you can be a good Muslim and a good Bihari and a good Indian all at once.

It's worked, Priscilla. We have given passports to a dream, a dream of an extraordinary, polyglot, polychrome, polyconfessional country. Democracy will solve the problems we're having with some disaffected Sikhs in Punjab; and democracy, more of it, is the only answer for the frustrations of India's Muslims too.

But who, in all of this, allowed for militant Hinduism to arise, challenging the very basis of the Indianness I've just described to you?

from Priscilla Hart's scrapbook

February 14, 1989

The car stopped where the road ended, at a rusting gate with a sign forbidding entry to unauthorized visitors. The driver took a long stainless steel flashlight out of his glove compartment and got out to open the gate. It creaked painfully. Ahead, there was an overgrown path heading toward the river.

"It's okay," Lakshman told the driver. "You wait at the car. We'll be back soon. Give me the torch." The driver looked relieved, even though Lakshman took the flashlight from him, leaving him alone amid the lengthening shadows.

"He'll probably sleep until we get back," Lakshman assured me cheerfully.

"Tell me more about this place," I said. "Did you say Koti?"

"Kotli," Lakshman replied. "No one quite knows where the term comes from. A 'kot' is a stronghold, a castle; a 'kothi' is a mansion. This wonderful old heap we are about to visit is something in between. People have been calling it the Kotli for generations. It's been a ruin for somewhat longer than anything else that's standing in the Zalilgarh area."

"How old is it?"

"Who knows?" he replied disarmingly. "Some say it goes back to the fifteenth or sixteenth century, and there's probably an Archaeological Survey of India finding that confirms that, though I haven't seen it. But it's old, all right. And deserted."

"Why is it all closed up? Shouldn't you open it for tourists to visit?" I asked.

"Tourists?" Lakshman laughed. "Tourists? In Zalilgarh? My dear girl, I don't think we've had a tourist here since 1543, when Sher Shah Suri camped here while building the Grand Trunk Road. Why

would a tourist come to Zalilgarh? Even you don't qualify as one."
Suddenly his hand was on my upper arm again. "Watch your step
here — there's a lot of rubble on this path. I don't want you twisting
an ankle."

But he released his grip almost instantly as we walked on.

"What happened was that the Kotli sat here undisturbed for generations, like so many ruins elsewhere in India," Lakshman explained.
"The land from here to the river belonged to the old nawab and
then to the government, so nobody could build here, and nobody
wanted to, either. It's quite an isolated place, far away from the town,
near nothing. Plus there was a rumor that it was haunted."

"Haunted?"

"The story goes that the owner of the Kotli was murdered in his
bed by his wife and her lover. But he never let them enjoy the fruits
of their villainy. He haunted the house, wailing and shrieking and
gnashing his teeth, until he had driven them away in terror. No one
would live there after that, so it just fell into disuse."

"Do people still think it's haunted?"

"In India, myths and legends are very slow to die, Priscilla."

"Unlike the human beings," I found myself saying. I was just
trying to be clever, in keeping with his mood, but as soon as I said it
I wished I hadn't.

"Unlike the human beings," he repeated slowly. "Now why
would you say a thing like that, Priscilla? Have you seen so much of
death and dying here? I'd like to think Zalilgarh has been a pretty
peaceful place in recent years. Haven't had so much as a riot since
I've been here. And our infant mortality rates are dropping too."

"I know," I said. "I'm sorry. It was a foolish thing to say."

"No, not foolish," Lakshman said gently. "We've seen more
unnecessary deaths and suffering in my country than I can bear to
recall. It's just that things do get better, you know. And in this
respect, they have."

We walked on in silence for a couple of minutes. Then, silhouet-
ted against the dramatic evening sky — a blue-black canvas splashed
with the angry saffron of the setting sun — I saw the Kotli.

It was a ruin, all right, but it stood strong and solid, its stone rectangular shape a striking contrast to the suppler lines of the foliage-
laden trees, the forlorn weeds, the flowing river beyond it. In the
evening light it seemed to rise from the earth like a fist.

"Come inside," Lakshman said, switching on his flashlight.

I picked my way over the rubble-strewn approach and, predictably, tripped, falling heavily against him. He turned quickly to
hold me, but only for as long as it took to steady me. And then, as he
turned again toward the Kotli, he slipped his free hand into mine.

"Come with me," he said unnecessarily, that voice of his huskier
now, a voice like mulled wine.

I felt the pressure of his hand in mine. It was a soft hand, a hand
that had never wielded any instrument harder than a pen; unlike the
other male hands I had held, it had never mowed a lawn, washed a
dish, carried a pigskin over the touchdown line. It was the hand of a
child of privilege in a land where privilege meant there were always
other hands to do the heavy lifting, the rough work, for you. And yet
in its softness there was a certain strength, something that conveyed
reassurance, and I clung on to that hand, grateful that in the gathering
gloom its owner could not see the color rising to my cheek.

We stepped into the Kotli. There was no floor left, only grass and
pebbles where once thick carpets, perhaps, had covered the stone
tiling. But Lakshman's flashlight danced across the walls and ceilings,
illuminating them for me. "Look," he breathed, and I followed the
torch beam to a patch of marble that still clung to the stone, the
fading lines of an artist's decorative flourish visible across its surface.
The flashlight traced the vaulting lines of a nave, then moved to a
delicate pattern in the stone above a paneless window, then settled
on a niche where a long-ago resident might once have placed his oil
lamp.

"It's marvelous," I said.

"Come upstairs," Lakshman said urgently. "Before the sunset
disappears entirely."

He pulled me to the stairs, his hand insistent in mine. Part of the
roof had long since disappeared, and much of the upper floor was a
long open space, ending in a half-wall, like a battlement. I began to

walk toward it, intending to stand at the edge, the breeze in my hair, and watch the sun set over the river. But Lakshman pulled me back.

"No," he said. "There's a better place."

He walked to the right of the roof floor, the beam of his flashlight dancing, until it caught the dull glint of a padlock. This was attached to a bolted wooden door, clearly a later addition to the premises.

"Only the district magistrate has the key." Lakshman laughed, gaily pulling a bunch from his pocket. He turned the key, extracted the lock, and pulled back the screeching bolt. "Follow me," he said, and pushed the door open.

We stepped into a little room, no larger than a vestry. To the left was a rectangular opening in the wall, a window of sorts, through which the river and the sky were visible, framed as in a painting.

"Come and sit here," Lakshman said.

I sat gingerly where he indicated, on a raised stone slab in an alcove where perhaps a bed had once lain. Lakshman sat beside me, crossing his legs contentedly. There was an expression on his face I hadn't seen before, one of barely suppressed excitement. Anticipation suffused his breathing. "Look," he said, pointing with his flashlight, and then switching it off.

I looked, and felt my blood tingle. Directly across from us a mirror had been hung on the wall. It was pitted black with age in places, but it still served, a silvery glint upon the stone. When Lakshman's beam of light went off, the scene filtering in through the rectangular window was reflected brilliantly in the mirror.

"Now you can watch your first stereo sunset," Lakshman said.

I could not say a word; all sound would have caught in my throat. I looked out through the rectangular window and watched the saffron spread like a stain across the darkening sky, then turned my eyes and saw the colors incandesce in the mirror. Outside the air was thick with the scent of gulmohur and bougainvillea, which seeped in through the opening to mingle with the warmth of Lakshman by my side, his breathing now calm and even, his teeth flashing white beneath a happy smile.

"You like it?" he asked, squeezing my hand.

I wanted to thank him, but the words wouldn't come. My eyes strayed from the scene outside the window to the scene in the mirror. It was simply the most beautiful sunset I had ever seen. I was absurdly conscious that this was Valentine's Day, and that I had never spent it in a more romantic setting. So without really thinking, hardly conscious of what I was doing at all, I pressed myself against him and kissed him on the cheek.

Well, mainly on the cheek. But the edge of my lips touched the edge of his, so that the silken bristles of his moustache grazed my own upper lip, and then it wasn't just a kiss on the cheek anymore. His hands rose to encircle my body in a tight embrace, and both pairs of lips moved with a volition of their own toward each other, and I devoured him hungrily, feeling the faintly spicy taste of his mouth, my tongue exploring the soft moist mystery of him, until the sound that had been trapped inside me emerged at last as a long, low moan.

He pulled his mouth away then, but his hands were still holding me, holding me tight.

"Priscilla," he said huskily, as if he did not know what else to say.

"Lakshman," I replied, tasting the unfamiliarity of those two syllables, as unfamiliar and intimate as the taste at the tip of my tongue.

"I — we — I shouldn't be doing this," he said, and I suddenly felt it was as if a page was being turned back in a book I wanted to continue reading.

I leaned forward then, intending to muzzle my face in his chest, but I never got there. A look crossed his eyes then, a look of both longing and desperation, and I felt his hands seize my face and raise it to his lips, and then I closed my eyes, and let myself be loved.

from Randy Diggs's notebook

October 12, 1989

Met local Hindu chauvinist leader to check out the politics
behind the riot. Man called Ram Charan Gupta.

Indeterminate age — I'd say sixtyish, but could be ten years off
either way. Olive skin, shiny, taut, not much loose flesh about him.
Strong head, topped by a crown of closely cropped white hair
around a sallow bald pate. White kurta-pajamas. Sandals reveal
gnarled toes, but the soles of his feet are smooth: not a man who has
walked much.

Spoke only Hindi, but I suspect understands more English than he
lets on.

Said to be highly respected for his "moderate" and "reasonable"
views and the patience with which he expounds them.

Unsuccessful parliamentary candidate in the last elections; it's
expected that he'll do better next time.

Ram Charan Gupta to Randy Diggs

(translated from Hindi)

October 12, 1989

Yes, that was a glorious day. I remember it well. I can tell you the exact date — it was September fifteenth. That was the day that our leaders launched the Ram Sila Poojan program.

Do you know about our god Ram, the hero of the epic Ramayana? He was a great hero. A king. But because of a scheming stepmother, he suffered banishment in the forest for fourteen years. Such injustice. But Ram bore it nobly. While he was in the forest, his wife Sita was kidnapped by the evil demon Ravana and taken to Lanka. But Ram, with his brother Lakshman and with the help of a monkey army led by the god Hanuman, invaded Lanka, defeated the demon, and brought his wife back. A great hero. I pray to him every day.

Now Lord Ram was born in Ayodhya many thousands of years ago, in the treta-yuga period of our Hindu calendar. Ayodhya is a town in this state, but a bit far from here, more than four hours' journey by train. In Ayodhya there are many temples to Ram. But the most famous temple is not really a temple anymore. It is the Ram Janmabhoomi, the birthplace of Ram. A fit site for a grand temple, you might think. But if you go to Ayodhya, you will see no Ram Janmabhoomi temple there. In olden days a great temple stood there. A magnificent temple. There are legends about how big it was, how glorious. Pilgrims from all over India would come to worship Ram there. But a Muslim king, the Mughal emperor Babar, not an Indian, a foreigner from Central Asia, he knocked it down. And in its place he built a big mosque, which was named after him, the Babri Masjid. Can you imagine? A mosque on our holiest site! Muslims praying to Mecca on the very spot where our divine Lord Ram was born!

Naturally our community was very much hurt by this. Is that so surprising? Would Muslims be happy if some Hindu king had gone and built a temple to Ram in Mecca? But what could we do? For hundreds of years we suffered under the Muslim yoke. Then the British came, and things were no better. We thought then that after independence, everything would change. Most of the Muslims in Ayodhya left to go to Pakistan. The mosque was no longer much needed as a mosque. Then, a miracle occurred. Some devotees found that an idol of Ram had emerged spontaneously in the courtyard of the mosque. It was a clear sign from God. His temple had to be rebuilt on that sacred spot.

But would the courts listen? They are all atheists and communists in power in our country, people who have lost their roots. They forgot that the English had left. It was English law they upheld, not Indian justice. They said no, neither Hindus nor Muslims could worship there. They refused to believe the idol had emerged spontaneously; they claimed someone had put it there. They put a padlock on the gates of the mosque. I ask you, is this fair? Do we Hindus have no rights in our own country?

For years we have tried everything to undo this injustice. The courts will not listen. The government does nothing. My party leaders finally said, we have had enough. It is the people's wish that the birthplace of Ram must be suitably honored. If the government will not do what is necessary, the people will. We will rebuild the temple.

With what, you may ask? With bricks — *sila*. Bricks from every corner, every village, of our holy land. Bricks bearing the name of Ram, each brick consecrated in a special puja, worshipped in its local shrine, and then brought to Ayodhya. This was the Ram Sila Poojan, the veneration of the bricks of Ram. The building bricks of a great new temple, to commemorate the birth of our great and divine king.

What excitement we all felt that day! The announcement of the Ram Sila Poojan was greeted with pride and joy across the country. All of India burst into a frenzy of activity. In every village, young men came out to bake the bricks, to write or carve or paint the name of Ram on them, to venerate them at their local temples. A thrill was in the air. It was a thrill that comes from the prospect of the imminent fulfillment of a long-cherished dream. When the bricks were ready, they were carried through each village in a sacred procession, then to be taken to Ayodhya to rebuild the Ram Janmabhoomi there.

In Zalilgarh too, we were busy with the Ram Sila Poojan. We are not such a small-small town as you people from Delhi may think. Zalilgarh is the district capital, after all. So after days of doing our Ram Sila Poojan in each village of the district, we had planned a big procession in Zalilgarh town on Saturday the thirtieth of September. It was intended to be the climax of all our Ram Sila Poojan work throughout the area. Volunteers from each village in the district would bring their bricks, those from each neighborhood in the town would do the same, and we would all march together in one glorious procession, shouting slogans of celebration. From there we would proceed all the way to Ayodhya, to take the bricks to the spot near this usurper's mosque, where they were being collected for this holy purpose. At last, after centuries of helplessness, we were about to right a great wrong.

We were going to rebuild the temple.

What preparations we made for that day! Young men worked so hard, making flags, printing posters, preparing pennants in holy saffron that we would string along our route. Our women sewed bunting, painted placards for the men to carry. The tailors of Zalilgarh toiled overtime to make shirts and kurtas in saffron for us. And the bricks! They were perfect: red like the blood we would so gladly have spilled for our Lord, with the name of Ram painted on them in bold white Devanagari script. We were going to make it such a great occasion. What do you call it in English? A red-letter day.

But these Muslims are evil people, Mr. Diggs. You have to understand their mentality. They are more loyal to a foreign religion, Islam, than to India. They are all converts from the Hindu faith of their ancestors, but they refuse to acknowledge this, pretending instead that they are all descended from conquerors from Arabia or Persia or Samarkand. Fine — if that is so, let them go back to those places! Why do they stay here if they will not assimilate into our country? They stay together, work together, pray together. It is what you Americans, I know, call a ghetto mentality.

Now these Muslims have already divided our country once, to create their accursed Pakistan on the sacred soil of our civilization. Some of the greatest sites of Hindu civilization — the ancient cities of Harappa and Mohenjo Daro, the world's oldest university at Takshashila, even the river Indus from which India gets its name in your language — are all now in a foreign country. It galls me to say this, but we have swallowed our pride and accepted this vile partition. But is this enough for them? Oh no! The Muslims want more! And we had Muslim-loving rulers, like that brown Englishman Jawaharlal Nehru who was our first prime minister, to give it to them. Muslim men want four wives, whom they can divorce by chanting a phrase three times — so Nehru gives them the right to follow their own Personal Law instead of being subject to the civil code of the rest of the country. Muslims want to go abroad to worship at their Mecca, so the government pays for the ships and planes to take them there every year and the hotels and lodges for them to stay in on the way. I ask you, why should my tax money go to helping Muslims get closer to their foreign god?

I see all this is new to you. It is worse, Mr. Diggs, it is worse! Muslims have their own educational institutions with government subsidies, they have top jobs in the bureaucracy, they have even managed special status for the only Muslim-majority state we have, Kashmir. Do you know a Hindu from anywhere else in the country cannot buy a piece of land in Kashmir?! And worst of all, these Muslims are outbreeding the Hindus. They claim the right to four wives, and they keep them constantly pregnant, I tell you. While Indira Gandhi forcibly dragged our young men away to be vasectomized during her emergency rule a dozen years ago, these Muslims resist even voluntary family planning, saying it is against their religion. They all have dozens of children, Mr. Diggs! You only have to look at the population figures to know what I am talking about. When they broke our country with their treasonous partition, many of them left for their accursed Pakistan. In what was left of India, the Muslims were barely ten percent. By the time of the last census even the government was saying they are twelve percent of the population; and today, believe me, it is fifteen percent. It will not be long before they produce enough Muslims to outnumber us Hindus in our country, Mr. Diggs. You know what their slogan was, back in those days of Partition? They sang, "Ladke liye Pakistan, haske lenge Hindustan": "We fought to take Pakistan, we will laugh as we take Hindustan." That is the grave danger we are facing, Mr. Diggs. And what is the answer of successive Congress Party governments? Nothing but appeasement. Pure and simple appeasement.

Things have declined even more dangerously under Nehru's successors. The latest one, his grandson Rajiv Gandhi, is the worst, I tell you. Have you heard of the Shah Banu case, Mr. Diggs? A Muslim man wants to get rid of his seventy-five-year-old wife, and since it is easy for Muslims, he does so. But he wants to pay her just forty rupees in alimony, because he says that in his religion he is only obliged to return the bride-price that had been given when they got married, sixty years ago. Well, she goes to court, saying how can she live on forty rupees today, and what sort of justice is this after sixty years of marriage? The court upholds her claim, awards her a fair alimony every month, and reminds the government that the Constitution's directive principles call for the establishment of a common civil code for all Indians. You will not believe the outcry from our Muslims! A common civil code — exactly what you have in America, Mr. Diggs — and their leaders acted as if the gas chambers had been prepared for their entire community. So what does the craven Rajiv Gandhi do? He quickly passes a new law, which he cynically calls the Muslim Women (Protection of Rights Upon Divorce) Act, to undo the court's judgment. Muslim women, under the law, will have to abide by their religion's mediaeval rules, and if they are left destitute, there is no protection, no remedy, available to them from our civil courts. They will have to get help from their religion's charitable boards, the waqfs. Can you imagine such a thing? In the twentieth century? And all to accommodate the most obscurantist Muslim leaders! When will this pampering stop?

I'll tell you, Mr. Diggs. Not until we have defeated these so-called secularists who are ruling our country and have brought us to our knees with their corrupt and self-serving ways. Not until we have raised the forces of Hindutva to power. Only then will we be able to teach these Muslims a lesson. Your Lakshman and others accuse us of fomenting violence. What nonsense! It is always others who do it, and then blame us. Sometimes I suspect the so-called secularists start the violence deliberately, just in order to discredit us. Wherever Hindutva governments have come to power — as they have done in four or five states, Mr. Diggs — there has been no communal violence, no rioting under their rule. What do the secularists say about that, hah?

Do you know what my colleague Sadhvi Rithambhara says? The Sadhvi is a famous preacher — a woman, for we are a progressive, modern faith, Mr. Diggs: have you ever heard of a Muslim woman preacher? Anyway, this is what she says: Muslims are like a lemon squirted into the cream of India. They turn it sour. We have to remove the lemon, cut it up into little pieces, squeeze out the pips and throw them away. That is what we have to do, Mr. Diggs. That is what the Vishwa Hindu Parishad, the Bajrang Dal, the Shiv Sena, the Rashtriya Swayamsevak Sangh and all the associated organizations of our political family, the Sangh Parivar, will do one day. And the whole world should be grateful, because these Muslims are evil people, I tell you. Why is it that no Muslim country anywhere in the world is a democracy? Look around you, anywhere on the map, they are all dictatorships, monarchies, tyrannies, military regimes. Take my word for it, it's the only way they know. Muslims are fanatics and terrorists; they only understand the language of force. Where are Muslims in power where they are not oppressing other people? And wherever these Muslims are, they fight with others. Violence against non-Muslims is in their blood, Mr. Diggs! Look at what Muslims are doing in the Middle East, Indonesia, the Philippines. Only in Yugoslavia do Muslims live in peace with non-Muslims. But that is because the Muslims there are the only Muslims in the world who are not fanatic about their faith. Unlike the ones we have here.

But I digress. You asked me about the background to the riot. Our Ram Sila Poojan procession. As I was saying, these Muslims are evil people, Mr. Diggs. They could not abide the thought of us Hindus reasserting our pride. We were peacefully minding our own

57

business — what did it have to do with them? We did not have any great love for these Muslims, it is true, but we would not have attacked them. Why spoil a sacred event with an unnecessary fight? No, it was they who started it. As they always do.

I will tell you what happened. How it happened. It was the eve of the day of the great procession — Friday the twenty-ninth. Yes, yes, Friday is their holy day, but their big prayers were long over and we had not disturbed them. Our volunteers, good Hindu boys, stalwarts of the Bajrang Dal and the Vishwa Hindu Parishad, were doing their work in the evening, preparing for the great day the next day, Saturday the thirtieth. They were putting up posters, tying flags to lamp-posts, stringing the bunting and the pennants across the road. My own son Raghav was amongst them.

The work took time, it became dark, but everyone was in good spirits. Some were singing. It was late, but though they were tired, they were looking forward to the next day. Suddenly, they heard the noise of a motorcycle engine. Out of the darkness it came, two men on a motorcycle, with no light on.

Muslims.

Muslims! Their evil faces were masked with burqas, the black robes their women wear so that no one can see them. The motorcycle slowed down. Some of our boys were standing and working quite far from the road. But two boys, Amit Kumar from Bahraich, and Arup, Makhan Singh's son, good boys from decent families, were painting slogans on a wall near the pavement. The motorcycle neared them. Still the rest of the group didn't realize anything was wrong. Then those burqa-clad cowards raised their arms. Dull steel flashed in the moonlight.

Daggers! Mr. Diggs, they had daggers!

Savagely they slashed at the Hindu boys. The others stared mesmerized for a moment, helpless as the attackers' arms went up and down, again and again, striking our two boys in the back, arms, legs, face. They screamed as they went down, and my son Raghav and his friends rushed towards them. But it was, Raghav tells me, as in a dream, when your legs don't carry you forward as fast as you want to go. The motorcycle engine revved and it was gone, one last flailing of an arm nearly slashing my son's face as he ran towards Amit and Arup.

The poor boys were in a very bad way. They were bleeding from cuts everywhere. Their arms and legs dangled helplessly, Raghav said, like those of a rag doll. They picked them up, rushed them to the Zalilgarh government hospital. They called me. I went straight to the hospital, then to the police. It was terrible. The boys needed many emergency operations. All through the night we waited, rage and prayer mingling in our hearts. Ram be praised, they survived. But Amit would never walk again without a limp. And Arup Singh, a handsome boy who was to get married the next month, was left with a hideously scarred face that he would have to live with for the rest of his days.

There was blackness in our hearts that night, Mr. Diggs. These Muslims could not be allowed to get away with this. We knew what they wanted — to stop our procession the next day. To thwart our Ram Sila Poojan program. To prevent, in the end, the rebuilding of the Ram Janmabhoomi temple itself. This was a victory we were determined they would never be allowed to have.

At dawn that morning, the thirtieth of last month, I was asked to go to the police station. Me? The police station? What wrong had I done? But no, they told me, it was for an emergency meeting of Hindu community leaders. Others would be there — the pramukhs and leaders of the RSS, the VHP, the Bajrang Dal. All the major Hindu groups. So I agreed, though I had no great faith in this young district magistrate or his ally, the superintendent of police. These people, they come to our districts with fancy so-called secular ideas they have learned in English-language colleges, and they try to tell us what to do. They, who do not understand their own culture, their own religion, their own heritage. Such people have no right to call themselves Indians. But they rule over us, you see.

When we assembled at the police station, the DM and the SP were already there. Lakshman, the DM is called. From the South. A good-looking man, if with somewhat feminine features, and rather too dark to have found himself a good bride here. The SP is a turbaned

Sikh, Gurinder Singh. Neither Hindu nor Muslim, though his people have fought the Muslims for centuries. But with people like Lakshman and Gurinder it didn't matter what their religion was. They had both been to the same college, I believe, some fancy-shmancy Christian missionary place in Delhi where they only talk English and eat with forks and knives. So they thought alike. That was our problem.

Lakshman didn't waste any time getting to the point. "I know you are all concerned about the incident last night," he said.

"Concerned?" the Bajrang Dal man, Bhushan Sharma, inter-rupted him, almost screaming. "We're bloody enraged! Those boys were brutally murdered in cold blood!"

"They'll be all right," Lakshman said calmly. "I've spoken to the doctors. There's been no murder in Zalilgarh. Yet."

"No thanks to the Muslims," Sharma was still shouting. "Murder is exactly what they intended. What kind of law and order are you maintaining in this city?"

"We have made some arrests overnight," Gurinder said, smiling. He smiled a lot, especially when he was talking about deadly serious matters. "We will find the perpetrators." He always used words like that. "The perpetrators are absconding." Even when he was supposed to be speaking Hindi. *"Perpetrators abscond kiye hain."* Still, Gurinder had a reputation for being an efficient man. And an honest one, which is rare enough in his profession.

"But I want to ensure that the situation doesn't get out of hand," Lakshman added. "The police will bring these assailants to justice. But I must appeal to you all to stay calm. And above all, to refrain from any action that could inflame the situation."

"Refrain? Us refrain?" Sharma was belligerent. "Are we to sit back and take anything the Muslims fling at us? Especially today, when we have so much at stake?"

"Especially today," Lakshman replied. "In fact, after what has hap-pened last night I wonder about the advisability of proceeding with your march today. I suggest you consider postponing—"

But he could not get the rest of his sentence out before he was drowned in a hubbub of protest from all of us. After everyone had shouted their objections, I stood up, leaned on the table, and looked him squarely in the eyes. "That is exactly what the Muslims want us to do," I said quietly. "They hoped to intimidate us into giving up our plans. And you want us to play into their hands? Never!"

Lakshman tried everything. Oh, what a variety of approaches he tried. Calm reasonableness. Firm advice. Earnest appeal. Passionate entreaty. Tensions were high, he said. Our Ram Sila Poojan program had awakened the fears of the minority community. They were afraid, anxious, easy prey for extremists and hotheads. We had already seen what could happen. If we marched, there was no telling what else could occur. A small spark could ignite a conflagration. Did we want that?

"They attack us, and you tell us *they* are afraid?" Sharma was scathing. "We want to march peacefully, and you tell us *we* are inflaming tensions? This is a strange way of seeing things, District Magistrate–sahib."

After several attempts, he realized we were implacable. The Ram Sila Poojan march through Zalilgarh would go ahead as planned. We were determined not to be diverted from our long-planned course.

He changed tack. "Change your route, then," he suggested, pulling a map out of a folder that Gurinder passed him. "The route you are planning to take for your march is dangerous. It goes right through Muslim mohallas, and in two places passes right in front of Muslim mosques. Some Muslims will see this as provocation, and I must say I can't disagree with them. You will simply incite some of the hotheads into doing something like last night."

"If they do, DM–sahib," I replied, "they will be breaking the law. And it is your job to deal with them. Yours and the SP's." Gurinder did not react, other than to smile again. "We are exercising our democratic rights to take out this procession. You are afraid that some criminal elements will break the law if we do. Well, then, catch them. Prosecute them. Punish them. But don't punish us."

"There are more than thirty thousand young men, volunteers from all over the district, gathered in Zalilgarh for this march," Sharma added. "Are you going to try and stop them, Mr. Lakshman?"

Lakshman and Gurinder exchanged glances, as if to say that this was exactly what they had considered doing. It would have led to violence if they had tried — violence between the volunteers and the police. They had clearly thought better of it.

"No, I am not going to try and stop you," Lakshman replied at last. He did not say "stop them," but "stop you." He was looking at me rather than at Bhushan Sharma. "But I am relying on your good sense to ensure that your volunteers behave. And that nothing is done, especially in the Muslim neighborhoods, that threatens the peace here in Zalilgarh."

"Of course," said someone, trying to be conciliatory, and before we knew it, Lakshman and Gurinder were laying down conditions. We could march, but we must not beat drums or cymbals near the mosques. We could shout slogans, but they had to be moderately phrased, and not inflammatory. We could carry placards, but no weapons. Conditions he was entitled to impose on us by virtue of the power vested in him as district magistrate. We had to agree, or his smiling Sikh accomplice could withdraw the police permission we had to march. Surely they wouldn't dare? We could have called their bluff, but there was nothing to be gained by confronting them. We agreed.

"I want it in writing," Lakshman said, biting a lower lip.

These overeducated college types. They want things in writing, as if the magic of a few words-turds on a page would cast some sort of spell on us peasants. We looked at each other; Sharma shrugged. Gurinder wrote down his rules on a sheet of police stationery, and we all signed.

We knew it would make no difference. Whatever was going to happen, was going to happen.

And we were prepared.

from Priscilla Hart's scrapbook

July 16, 1989

Learned something interesting about the Hindu god Ram, the one all the fuss is about these days. Seems that when he brought his wife Sita back from Lanka and became king, the gossips in the kingdom were whispering that after so many months in Ravana's captivity, she couldn't possibly be chaste anymore. So to stop the tongues wagging, he subjected her to an agni-pariksha, a public ordeal by fire, to prove her innocence. She walked through the flames unscathed. A certified pure woman.

That stopped the gossips for a while, but before long the old rumors surfaced again. It was beginning to affect Ram's credibility as king. So he spoke to her about it. What could Sita do? She willed the earth to open up, literally, and swallow her. That was the end of the gossip. Ram lost the woman he had warred to win back, but he ruled on as a wise and beloved king.

What the hell does this say about India? Appearances are more important than truths. Gossip is more potent than facts. Loyalty is all one way, from the woman to the man. And when society stacks up all the odds against a woman, she'd better not count on the man's support. She has no way out other than to end her own life.

And I'm in love with an Indian. I must be crazy.

Professor Mohammed Sarwar to V. Lakshman

August 26, 1989

Thanks for receiving me. It's flattering to think I made enough of an impact in college that you still remember me.

Yes, I'm at the Univ now, good old Delhi University, teaching in the History Department. Actually, I'll be here for a few weeks. Trying to do some research in my period that seems oddly topical right now. I'm working on the life of a man called Syed Salar Masaud Ghazi, popularly known as Ghazi Miyan, a hugely revered Muslim warrior-saint in these parts. You haven't heard of him? So you see why my research is necessary.

The fact is that we have, especially in North India, an extraordinary tradition of heroes, whether warriors or saints or, in this instance, both, who are worshipped by both communities, Hindu and Muslim. You hear a lot about the "composite culture" of North India, but not enough about what I tend to call its composite religiosity. A number of Muslim religious figures in India are worshipped by Hindus — think of Nizamuddin Auliya, Moinuddin Chishti, Shah Madar, Shaikh Nasiruddin who was known as Chiragh-i-Delhi, or Khwaja Khizr, the patron saint of boatmen, after whom even the British saw fit to name their Kidderpore Docks in Calcutta. Ghazi Miyan is in this league.

But it's not enough to hail composite religiosity, to applaud complacently the syncretism of Hindu–Muslim relations in India. Of course we have to keep reminding people that tolerance is also a tradition in India, that communal crossovers are as common as communal clashes. But we mustn't abdicate the field of religious conflict to the chauvinists on both sides. What we need, as my friend and fellow professor Shahid Amin, whom you knew at college, likes to say, are "nonsectarian histories of sectarian strife."

Ghazi Miyan, according to popular belief, was a great Muslim warrior who was killed on the field of battle in A.D. 1034 fighting a bunch of Hindu rajas not that far from here, a bit to the north, at Bahraich. Soon after his death he was canonized in popular memory; people began gathering regularly at his tomb; ballads of his exploits were composed in both the Awadhi and Bhojpuri languages, and he is mentioned in a number of Persian and Urdu histories, though if I were writing this I'd put "histories" in inverted commas — some of them are little better than unsubstantiated hagiographies. But what's interesting is that the Ghazi Miyan of the historical texts was no apostle of Hindu-Muslim unity. He was a warrior for Islam. In one seventeenth-century text he's even described as the nephew of Mahmud of Ghazni, that notorious invader who destroyed the fabled Somnath temple in the eleventh century. And as a soldier, the texts say, he went about his business slaying infidels and smashing idols with the worst of them. When he died he was a martyr on a jihad, and his soul may be assumed to have gone straight to an Islamic heaven with no vacancies for Hindus.

So why is this same Ghazi Miyan worshipped by the very Hindus he apparently attacked? Why do Hindu women pray at his tomb for a male child of his noble qualities? Why are songs and ballads to him sung by Hindus? And they were — in fact many of these songs were collected by British colonial ethnographers in the late nineteenth century across a wide swath of North India from Delhi to Varanasi. Now, what's interesting about them is that they tell a different story, of a warrior born with the curse that he would die unwed, who was killed on the day of his wedding when he went forth to protect his herds and his herdsmen from the marauding Hindu Raja Sohal Deo.

And what did his herds consist of? Of cows! Now, doesn't that ring any bells for you? Does the youthful warrior defending his cows not remind you of Lord Krishna of Hindu legend, seducer of milkmaids and protector of cows? In fact, in one of the popular ballads, it is Krishna's foster mother, Jashodha, who makes a dramatic entry into the wedding celebrations of Ghazi Miyan, drenched in the blood of cowherds slaughtered by Raja Sohal Deo, and pleads with him to rise to the defense of the cows. Imagine the scene as this young Muslim bridegroom rises, casts aside his wedding finery, begs forgiveness from his mother, straps on his sword, and walks out to do battle against the killer of kine. It's stirring stuff, I tell you, and there's more in the songs and ballads I've collected: tales reinventing episodes from the Ramayana, tales featuring Krishna himself, all wrapped up in the life of Ghazi Miyan, and sometimes in the miraculous powers of his tomb.

What explains these contradictory legends, of the martyred jihadi revered by Muslim fundamentalists and the noble cow-protector worshipped by ordinary Hindus? Extremists of both stripes have sought to discredit the secular appeal of Ghazi Miyan. The Hindu fundamentalists have attacked the ballads as fraudulent tales made up by scheming Muslim tricksters to hoodwink gullible Hindus. They've also given much circulation to the jihadi versions of Ghazi Miyan's story. And as to the episode of the cows, they argue that the cows had actually been earmarked for slaughter at Ghazi Miyan's wedding feast, and that the reason Raja Sohal Deo attacked the Ghazi's cowherds was in order to liberate the cows from certain death at the hands of the Muslims. Hindus, they say, have been duped for centuries into worshipping an oppressor, and a foreign invader at that. The Hindutva types lament that the offerings made by Hindus at the Ghazi's tomb go to support Islamic schools, hospitals, and mosques — the very fact that the secularists hail as evidence of composite religiosity.

Every year for centuries, perhaps indeed since 1034, Ghazi Miyan's wedding ceremony is rescheduled around the supposed date of the real event. It's always interrupted, as the original event was. Hundreds of baraats, marriage parties, converge on the shrine, but always some "unexpected" calamity — a thunderstorm or even the hint of one will do — leads them to abandon the ceremony. The marriage does not take place. That's the ritual. But the baraats, both Hindu and Muslim, will be back next year.

That's the story I want to look into. There's a wealth of material to collect, some of it around Bahraich, but a lot in the Zalilgarh area too. I'm meeting up with some of the Dafali singers who popularize the ballads to the Ghazi. And I'm staying in town with the sadr here, Rauf-bhai — I don't know if you know him? You do? He's a cousin of my mother's, and one gets a sense of Islam as it is practiced in small-town Uttar Pradesh just by waking up every morning in the Muslim basti and talking to the neighbors.

The whole point is that historians like myself, who haven't sold our souls to either side in this wretched ongoing communal argument, have a duty to dig into the myths that divide and unite our people. The Hindutva brigade is busy trying to invent a new past for the nation, fabricating historical wrongs they want to right, dredging up "evidence" of Muslim malfeasance and misappropriation of national glory. They are making us into a large-scale Pakistan; they are vindicating the two-nation theory. They know not what damage they are doing to the fabric of our society. They want to "teach" people like me "a lesson," though they have not learned many lessons themselves. I often think of Mohammed Iqbal, the great Urdu poet who wrote, "Sare jahan se achha Hindustan hamara" — "Better than all the world is our India" — and who is also reviled for his advocacy of Pakistan, though what he wanted was a Muslim homeland within a confederal India. Iqbal-sahib wrote a couplet that is not often quoted these days: "Tumhari tahzeeb khud apne khanjar se khud-khushi karegi / Jo shukh-i-nazuk pe aashiyan banega, napaidar hoga." Oh, I'm sorry, you're a good Southie who doesn't understand much Urdu. What he's saying is that ours is a civilization that will commit suicide out of its own complexity; he who builds a nest on frail branches is doomed to destruction. The problem is that our Hindu chauvinists don't read much Iqbal these days.

letter from Priscilla Hart to Cindy Valeriani

February 16, 1989

. . .

I couldn't face the prospect of going to dinner with his wife after what had happened, so I told him to make some excuse for me — that I had developed a headache, or something. He didn't hide his disappointment, or the fact that he wasn't looking forward to the prospect of his wife's displeasure after he'd rung her and got her to organize the meal. He made me promise to come some other time — and, since I had been to dinner at his place earlier, I said yes.

In the morning a note arrived for me at the office, in a government envelope in the hands of a uniformed messenger (or peon, as they quaintly call them in India). "My dear Priscilla," it began, and I imagined him trying various salutations — "Priscilla" (too abrupt), "Darling Priscilla" (too effusive), "Dear Priscilla" (too routine), maybe even "Dearest Priscilla" (too premature!) — before settling on "My dear." His handwriting was firm, clear, rapid. "It was wonderful being with you yesterday. Please forgive me for this means of communication, but I realize you have no phone at home, and I must see you again. Please ring me if you can — my direct line is 23648. Or send me a note through the peon who is carrying this envelope. Yours, Lakshman." (Again, how long had he hesitated over that closing? "Yours sincerely"? Too formal. "Yours very sincerely"? Too insincere. "Yours ever"? Too presumptuous. So the simple, slightly suggestive "Yours" — I liked it.)

I hesitated for no more than a few seconds. Using the office phone — and we had only one — for a personal conversation was out of the question. So I scrawled on the same sheet of notepaper: "same time, same place, tomorrow?" The peon bowed and salaamed when I gave him the envelope.

Oh, Cindy, I know what you're thinking and it's not so. I wish we could talk. I miss you so much, Cindy. There's nothing I'd rather have more than one of our long sessions curled up on your bed, hugging those monstrously fat and cuddly pillows of yours (you should see the hard thin slab that passes for a pillow in Zalilgarh) and just talking. Writing to you about all of this isn't really the same thing, and I'm so out of practice writing letters that I'm not sure I'm telling you really how I feel. I know the things that would worry you about all this — he's married, he's Indian, I'm far away and lonely and don't know what I'm doing. If I were you, I'd worry about me too! But Lakshman's special, he really is, and I know I want to be with him more than anything in the world. Am I crazy, Cindy? Don't bother replying to that question — by the time your answer arrives I'll know whether I've just been really dumb or whether I've simply found Mr. Right in the wrong place at the wrong time. . . .

transcript of Randy Diggs interview
with District Magistrate V. Lakshman (Part 1)

October 13, 1989

RD: Mr. District Magistrate, thank you for agreeing to see me. I'm Randy Diggs, South Asia correspondent of the <u>New York Journal</u>. Here's my card.

VL: Thanks. Here's mine. But I suppose you know who I am.

RD: I know who you are, Mr. Lakshman.

VL: So what can I do for you?

RD: I'm doing a story on the young American woman who was killed here last month, Priscilla Hart.

VL: Yes. Priscilla.

RD: And I thought I'd find out from you as much as you can tell me about the circumstances of her killing.

VL: The circumstances?

RD: The riot. The events that led to the tragedy. Her own role in those events. Anything that can explain her death.

VL: She had no role in the events. That was the tragedy.

RD: She—

VL: She was here to work on a population project. And study the role of women in Indian society. She had nothing to do with the Hindu-Muslim nonsense.

RD: So she was in the wrong place at the wrong time.

VL: I suppose you could say that. If there is such a thing as the wrong place, or the wrong time. We are where we are at the only time we have. Perhaps it's where we're meant to be.

RD: Well, I—

VL: Don't worry, I'm not going to entrap you in philosophical arguments. You're here to talk to the DM about the riot, and I'll tell you about the riot. Do have some tea.

RD: Thanks. Is this already sugared?

VL: I'm afraid so. That's the way they serve it around here. Is it all right?

RD: That's fine. Tell me about the riot.

VL: You know about the Ram Sila Poojan? On 15 September, the Bharatiya Janata Party and its militant "Hindutva" allies announced the launching of direct action to build a Ram temple at the disputed site of the Babri Masjid at Ayodhya. The legal and political processes they could have resorted to in order to achieve this agenda were abandoned. It was clear from the kind of language their leaders were using that there would be an all-out and, if necessary, violent battle to accomplish their goal.

RD: Sorry, just checking if this is recording properly . . . it's fine. "Accomplish their goal." Please go on.

VL: Okay, where was I? Oh, yes. Trouble started elsewhere before it got here. In the next few days, much of North India was seized by a frenzy unprecedented since Partition. Groups of surcharged young men paraded the streets in every town, morning and evening, day after day, aggressively bearing bricks in the name of Ram, throwing slogans at the Muslims like acid. Slogans which were horrible in their virulence, their crudeness, their naked aggression. The Muslims, huddled in their ghettoes, watched with disbelief and horror, which turned quickly to cold terror and sullen anger.

RD: You couldn't stop them? Ban the Ram Sila Poojan program?

VL: I wished I could. I saw what was happening as nothing less than an assault on the political values of secular India. I asked permission to ban the processions in my district. It was denied. Only West Bengal, where the communists have a pretty firm hold on power, actually banned the Ram Sila Poojan program. The other state governments were trying to have it both ways. They proclaimed their secularism but did nothing to maintain it. They didn't want to alienate the Hindutva types, so they refused to ban the Ram Sila Poojan. They probably thought, to give them some credit, that banning it would simply give the Hindutva movement the aura of martyrdom and so help them attract even more support. So they let it go ahead. There were certainly some in the government who had a sneaking sympathy for the cause of rebuilding the Ram Janmabhoomi temple. Not just sneaking: many expressed it openly. So the government's inaction in the face of all this provocation profoundly alienated the Muslims. For many of them, their faith and hope in Indian secularism, built over four decades of dogged efforts by successive administrations, soured.

RD: So tensions were high among the Muslims that day.

VL: Tensions were high. And not just amongst the Muslims. The Hindu community was in a state of great agitation. Their leaders — or perhaps I should say, those who claimed to speak in their name — were openly whipping up passions on the Ram Janmabhoomi issue. Even the media and intelligentsia were quickly infected by the communal dementia sweeping the land.

RD: And the secular voices?

VL: What secular voices? There was a deafening silence.

RD: Was this a widespread phenomenon or did you have a particular problem on your hands here in Zalilgarh?

VL: It was pretty widespread in this part of the country: U.P. — you know, Uttar Pradesh — Bihar, parts of Madhya Pradesh. Not so much where I come from, in the South. But here, it was pretty bad. In less than ten days after the announcement of the Ram Sila Poojan, riots broke out in town after town — militant processions brandishing Ram bricks, shouting hate-filled slogans day after day, violent retaliation by small Muslim groups, followed by carnage, deaths, arson, and finally curfew. At one point around three weeks after the launching of the program, as many as 108 towns were simultaneously under curfew.

RD: Tell me about Zalilgarh.

VL: Well, you're here, you've seen it. It's a small district town in Uttar Pradesh. Not much to write home about! But like any other small town in these parts, Zalilgarh could hardly remain untouched by the sectarian fever that had infected the land. An undersized, haphazardly planned town of fewer than one lakh persons—

RD: A hundred thousand?

VL: That's right. About a lakh. With an uneasy balance of almost equal strengths of Hindus and Muslims. In fact, I discovered soon after I arrived that Zalilgarh is classified in official files as "communally hypersensitive." The records show that the first communal clash took place as far back as 1921.

RD: When you say "communal," you mean—

VL: Hindu-Muslim. At that time, Zalilgarh suffered a Hindu-Muslim clash even though in much of the country Hindus and Muslims were united in a joint campaign, the Khilafat agitation against the British. These clashes have been repeated with frightening regularity over the following decades.

RD: What causes these communal clashes?

VL: Oh, many things. The issues are mostly local, such as attacks on religious processions, desecration of shrines, illicit relationships between men and women of different communities, and so on. The two communities live separately but near each other in crowded shantytowns or bastis, and any small spark could set ablaze a bloody confrontation. Each skirmish would leave behind its own fresh trail of hostility and suspicion, which offered fertile ground for the next clash.

RD: Knowing all this, wasn't there anything you could do to prevent what happened? You and the police?

VL: I've asked myself a thousand times if I could have done more than I did. Guru — Gurinder — too. You know the superintendent of police?

RD: Gurinder Singh. I'm interviewing him next. A friend of yours, I believe?

VL: Yes. We were at college together. St. Stephen's, in Delhi, a couple of years apart. I didn't know him well there, but we've become very good friends here. A tremendous officer. But such an unlikely cop.

RD: Why?

VL: Oh, he studied history in college, you know. Played hockey and played hookey. Drank a lot, even then. Was known for cracking bad jokes. They called him "the Ab Surd" — Sikhs are "Surds," you see, short for "Sardarji," which is an honorific for them — oh forget it, like most cross-cultural jokes, it's just too complicated to explain. Anyway, he's absurd when he wants to be, especially with a glass in his hand — make that a bottle. And he swears a lot. As I fear you'll find out. "The story of my life," he says, "begins with the words, 'Once a pun a time.'" Today he'd probably say "a fucking time," so be prepared. He took the IAS exams, as so many of us did at St. Stephen's, largely to please his parents. He really wanted to be a farmer — a peasant, he said, but secretly his ambition was to be a big commercial farmer, mechanized agriculture, tractors, irrigation canals, the lot. Simple pleasures, as Wilde said, are the last refuge of the complex. So he didn't try hard enough in the exams. Couldn't get into the Administrative Service, but made it to the police service. He hoped his parents would credit him for the effort and let him go off and work for his grandfather, who had the land but still tilled it the old-fashioned way. But they were horrified at the prospect. The police, they said, was hardly a great career, but it was better than farming. What sort of status would they have in society if their son were a mere flogger of bullocks? It was one thing if he'd failed the exams altogether, but here he had the chance for a real job, with real power. They weren't going to let him waste his life farming. How much money could a farmer make anyway? He gave in. [Pause.] We all do. [Pause.] I wanted to be a writer. My parents had other ideas.

RD: In America, parents have stopped trying to tell their kids what to do in life.

VL: It'll be a long while before we get to be like America.

RD: I'll say. So you were telling me about Zalilgarh. The demographics. The background. Whether there was anything more you could have done to prevent what happened.

VL: Whether we could have done anything more? I honestly don't think so. We did everything. It started the same way, you know, in Zalilgarh as

75

elsewhere. The pattern was the same — daily belligerent processions and slogans of hate. Gurinder and I responded by the book, doing everything we'd been taught to do in such situations — calling meetings of the two communities, advising restraint, registering strong criminal charges against the more rabid processionists, energizing the peace committees, preventive arrests and so on.

RD: Peace committees?

VL: It's something we set up pretty much everywhere where we have a history of communal trouble. Committees bringing together leaders of both communities to work together, sort out their problems. We used every mechanism we had, every trick we knew. These measures might have been enough in normal times.

RD: But these weren't normal times?

VL: No, these weren't normal times. As the Ram Sila Poojan campaign gathered momentum, there was nothing we could do to ebb the raging flood of communal hatred.

RD: Sorry, I just need to change the tape here.

from Lakshman's journal

March 26, 1989

"I suppose I never forgave my father," she said somberly. "Just seeing him — doing it, doing that, with that awful woman from his office. I was barely fifteen, and I felt personally hurt, as if it was me he'd betrayed, and not my mother. He tried to talk to me, to explain, even to beg forgiveness, though he was too proud a man to use the word. I'll never forget the contempt with which, in my fifteen-year-old superiority, spouting some Freudian wisdom I'd picked up God knows where, I told him witheringly, 'You're pathetic, Dad. Don't you realize you were just trying to make up for not being able to penetrate the Indian market?' "

She laughed, quietly, at the recollection of her own words. "I was known in the family as precocious Priscilla," she said. "Dad was particularly fond of the phrase. He stopped using it after I said that."

I stroked her hair, then kissed her tenderly on the cheek. "Precious Priscilla," I said.

"Oh, I prefer that," she replied, kissing me quickly on the lips. But then she turned serious again.

"I was very upset about what happened," she went on. "It sort of crystallized a whole lot of half-formed feelings I'd developed about my father. What was he doing in India, after all? Trying to sell Coke. For God's sake, it's not as if he was bringing in medicines, or new technology, or clean drinking water, or electrification. It was Coke, for crying out loud."

"Indians do drink Coke, sweetheart."

"Well, some Indians do. But it hardly struck me as a noble endeavor. You know, in school there were the kids of diplomats, but there were also the kids of missionaries working in the tribal districts, others whose fathers were in India to construct dams or power stations or even an underground railway — useful things, necessary things. How I used to wish my dad was doing something like that, and not just selling Coke." She shook her head, and her hair fell across her eyes, a curtain across her regret. I gently pushed it aside as she went on. "The irony is that these other kids actually envied me. 'Your Dad works for Coke? Coo-oool.' You know the kind of thing. They thought their parents' professions were boring, while my dad was glamorous because he sold a product they all knew and valued. Strange, huh?"

I nodded, not wanting to contradict her.

"And then when he didn't do so well, and the government threw Coke out, and he was reduced to spending his time trying to explore schemes to get it back into the Indian market, I began to feel really conflicted about him, you know? On the one hand a part of me thought of him as a bit pathetic, and on the other I was kinda glad he was doing it because this meant we could stay on in India, and I loved India. For years I'd worshipped him, you know, the perfect father figure, tall and strong and handsome, with an easy laugh and a habit of throwing me up in the air when I was a little girl and catching me before I fell. And then I got too big to be thrown in the air, and too wise to see perfection in him, and too intelligent not to question what he was doing. Am I boring you?"

"No, of course not," I said, kissing her this time on the forehead. "Go on."

"I was disappointed, too, in how little he saw of the India I loved. He knew the air-conditioned offices and the five-star hotels and the expatriate party-circuit, and he complained about the incompetence of the government and the inefficiency of the postal system and the unpredictability of the water supply, but he never set foot in a bazaar, he never visited the servants' quarters, he never saw the inside of a temple or a mosque, he never saw an Indian movie, he never made a real Indian friend. He thought he was going to conquer India with his Coke, but all he ended up conquering was a pathetic slut on the make."

I held her tightly. "Let it be, Priscilla," I said softly. "It was a long time ago."

"I know that." She shook herself free of my embrace: this was important. "But I can't forgive him. Not just for doing what he did, hurting Mom, destroying the family I'd always taken for granted. But also for being careless enough and thoughtless enough to do it there, in Mom's and his bed, on that afternoon, and letting me find him. I hated finding him like that. For years I wouldn't, I couldn't, let a boy touch me. I would shudder remembering my father, seeing him naked like that, moving in and out of that woman, slapping her behind, I'd remember the noises they made, his whoops, her moans — it was awful."

"I understand," I said, holding her, and this time she did not shake herself free of me.

"But then I decided I couldn't let him ruin the rest of my life too. Mom had brought us back to the States — we were in New York — and you have no idea what the peer pressure is like, if you're halfway decent-looking and not obviously crazy. Every boy in my grade and one or two grades up wanted to take me out, carry my books home, invite me to the movies. When I resisted at first, or when I agreed but wouldn't do anything they wanted me to, it was awful. Kids in school were beginning to whisper that I was a freak, that I wouldn't even let a boy kiss me, that maybe I was a lesbian. I couldn't stay sealed up like that. And then I wanted — I wanted a pair of strong male arms around me again. I wanted to be thrown up in the air again, and caught as I came down. I wanted so much to find someone who'd help me forget Dad, someone who was as different from him as possible so that he couldn't possibly remind me of him."

And then you ended up with me, I couldn't help myself thinking. Another married man cheating on his wife with an exotic foreigner.

But that was not where she was leading: not yet.

"So in my senior year at high school I got involved with a kid in my class. Well, I may as well say it, a black kid in my class. Darryl Smith. He was an athlete, the captain of the basketball team, not particularly bright or anything, but a really nice guy. And God, was he tall: the thing I'll always remember about my first kiss was having to stand on tiptoe like a ballerina to reach his lips, even though he had to bend down a long way to reach mine." A light shone in her eyes like a distant star, pulsing through the clouds. "People started talking at school, of course, and I suppose I should have felt I was doing something daring, something risky. But in fact with Darryl I felt completely safe, completely free of the shadow of my father. When he took his clothes off for the first time, I couldn't keep my eyes off his lean and well-muscled body. It was as if I was soaking every detail into my memory, registering another set of images over the ones of my father that had haunted me for so long." She looked at me, suddenly, as if she was conscious for the first time that it was me she was talking to. "Does this bother you, Lucky? I'll stop if you want me to."

"No," I lied, my voice thickening, because it was beginning to bother me a great deal. "I want to hear what you have to say."

She hugged me tightly. "It's important, for us, don't you see? I want you to know everything that matters to me. I want you to understand."

"I know," I said. "Go on."

"When my parents found out, they were both upset with me. My father was back in Atlanta, working at Coca-Cola headquarters, so I saw him just three or four times a year. But he was furious, just because Darryl was black. 'They're not like us,' he kept saying. And, 'How could you?' To which I couldn't always resist replying, 'That's a question you ought to answer first, don't you think, Dad?' And of course he refused to meet Darryl, not that I particularly wanted him to, anyway. Mom disapproved, too, in that dry way she has, never raising her voice, never even mentioning his color, just saying, 'Priscilla, you know you can do better. What about that nice boy on the debate team? He wanted to take you out, and you never—' And of course the boy on the debate team was smart, and rich, and white, and Darryl fell short on all three counts. Which made me love him all the more." Her voice lightened, as if to take the drama out of her next sentence. "Love in the face of impossible odds. I began to convince myself that Darryl and I would be together forever." She laughed a little, as if at her own naiveté. "But of course it wasn't going to last. And our problem was not that he was black and I was blonde, not even that he was a jock and I was a straight-A

80

student. It was that we didn't talk to each other. Darryl was uncomplicated, and affectionate, and pretty straight with me, but again unlike my father, he was a man of few words. And he didn't particularly want to listen to mine, either. If I tried to tell him about my family, or about India, or about a book I was reading, he would simply smile a big, gleaming smile and shut me up with a kiss. Which would go on to more than a kiss. And afterwards, he'd want to go get a bite, or a drink, or go dancing; but he wouldn't particularly want to talk.

"I just accepted that as part of how we were. I would talk instead with my girlfriends, especially Cindy, who's the closest friend I have, someone I'd known since grade school, since before we went to India. And I thought, well, he doesn't talk much, but I know he cares about me, and that's what matters. I didn't mind his laconic ways till the day he told me, in that happy, direct way he had, that he had received a basketball scholarship from Gonzaga. In the state of Washington, for God's sake. And he was planning to take it.

"'Gonzaga?' I practically yelled. 'You never told me you'd applied to Gonzaga. I thought we were going to stay here, near the City.' And none of the colleges I'd applied to were anywhere near the Pacific Northwest. Well, it turned out that a Gonzaga talent scout had come around to one of the high school games, liked him in action, and arranged the scholarship. We'd gone to a movie that very evening, and he'd forgotten to tell me about the encounter. So I was completely stunned. 'What about us?' I asked at last. And then I realized the question hadn't even crossed his simple mind, that basketball was what, at that point in his life, he lived for, and I was completely incidental. I had spent so much time in his arms, but I had no idea what was going on inside his head."

She turned to me then, looking directly into my eyes. "He was the first boy who'd really kissed me, you know, kissed properly, not just pecked on the cheek after a date, and of course the first man I'd ever slept with. And in all the ten, eleven months we were together, he never once told me he loved me."

"Because he didn't, Priscilla," I said, pricked by jealousy. "He didn't love you."

"He could have said the words," she replied. "They've been said to me by so many guys who never meant them. But Darryl was too honest to mislead me. I'd merely misled myself.

"I turned to Mom after this, and she was there for me, you know? She was patient and loving and nonjudgmental, and she helped me get over the pain. And she said one thing I never forgot. She said my problem was that I saw things in people that they didn't see in themselves.

"But Darryl did one thing for me. He cured me of my father. He went off to Gonzaga, and I wept for a week, and when I stopped weeping I realized he'd freed me. From himself, but also from the distaste and the fear that the thought of sex had evoked in me since the time I saw my father with that — that whore. Through Darryl, I'd sort of become normal again. You know what I'm saying?"

I nodded, not trusting myself to speak.

"After Darryl, it was easier to be a normal, red-blooded American woman," she said matter-of-factly. "I went out with a lot of guys in college, dated a couple of them quite seriously, even, but they just weren't right for me, you know? One of them, a guy from Boston, Winston Everett Holt III, even wanted to marry me. It was in my junior year of college; he was a senior. Win was a Boston Brahmin, very preppy, with that accent only people with his sort of breeding have, y'know, 'cah pahk' and all that — no, of course you don't know, how could you know — anyway, he had it all, name, family, wealth, good looks, good connections, good prospects. This was what my mother wanted for me. And I turned him down."

"Why?"

"Because I didn't love him. Or maybe I should say that I couldn't love him. He was too much like my father."

"This father of yours has a lot to answer for," I said, lightly, but it was not lightness I felt at her revelations. I was troubled, even hurt, strangely, even though intuitively I had known all along that her life must have been something like this, an American life. I tried to gloss over my own feelings, but they would not be contained, and I found myself blurting: "These guys you went out with, did you sleep with them?"

"Some of them," she replied, and then she looked at me curiously, realizing that the question was not a casual one. "Oh Lucky, does it matter to you?"

"I don't know," I said, only half untruthfully, because I really didn't know how much it did, though I could scarcely be oblivious to the emotions seething inside me.

"Lucky, I'm twenty-four," she said, holding me by both shoulders. "You didn't expect me to be a virgin, did you?"

"No," I replied honestly.

"When you made love to me, here, that first time after the sunset . . ."

"I wasn't thinking then," I said defensively.

"Well, you must have been pretty glad I wasn't a virgin then, right?"

"Right," I said in the same tone, but my cheerfulness was strained, unconvincing. "It's not important, Priscilla. Forget it."

She looked at me quizzically, then nestled herself into my body, her head upon my chest. I was silent. "Can I ask you something?" she said at last.

"Of course."

"Your wife. When you met her — was she a virgin?"

"Does the Pope's wife use birth control pills?" I asked in mock disbelief. "Are you kidding? An Indian woman in an arranged marriage? Of course she was a virgin. Forget sex, she hadn't kissed a boy, she hadn't even held hands with one. That's how it is in India. That's what's expected."

"Expected?"

"Expected," I asserted firmly. "If she wasn't a virgin, no one would have married her. No decent woman from a good family would be anything else." I had surprised myself by my own vehemence.

She was very silent, very still, and I realized I'd hurt her by my choice of words. "I'm sorry, Priscilla. I didn't mean that the way it sounded."

"What did you mean, then?"

"Just that things are very different here, in India. I guess we're repressed, after centuries of Muslim rule followed by the bloody

Victorians. And of course there's a lot of hypocrisy involved. But as Wilde would have said, is hypocrisy such a terrible thing? It's merely a method by which we can multiply our personalities." I tried to lighten my tone. "But sex simply isn't something that's acceptable or even widely available outside of marriage. There's still a great deal of store placed on honor here. Women don't sleep around. And if they did, no one would marry them."

"And men?"

"What about them?"

"Were you a virgin when you had your precious arranged marriage?"

"Practically," I said.

"What kind of an answer is that?"

"I hadn't had a girlfriend or anything like that. There were some guys in college who did, but they were a tiny minority, and I'm not even sure how many of their girlfriends actually slept with them. I mean, it wasn't easy — girls and boys weren't allowed into each other's hostels, no one in college could afford a hotel room, you couldn't even hold hands in public without stirring up trouble. But yes, I did lose my virginity the way many of my friends did. We all had the same normal urges as anyone in America, after all, but none of the same opportunities. So, one night, a group of us from college paid a visit to a brothel."

"No," Priscilla breathed, sitting up. "That's disgusting."

"It's the time-honored way," I replied. "Men have to learn what it's all about, and no decent girl will show them, and in the normal course you only meet decent girls. That's why red-light districts exist. A hundred rupees, I think it was, for a dark chunky woman with betel-stained teeth and too much powder on her face. It lasted two minutes: she never took off her blouse, just lifted a crumpled petticoat and let me in. I never went back."

"I hope not," she breathed.

"Oh, some of the fellows did, the ones who could find a hundred bucks from time to time. I couldn't, but I didn't want to. My curiosity was satisfied. And I was repelled."

"So what did you do?"

"Do?"

84

"For sex, of course."

I laughed. "My dear woman," I said in my most Wildean voice, "have you never heard of the sin of Onan?"

She blushed then. This lovely woman, who had just told me so matter-of-factly of having experienced the touch-and-thrust of sex with God knows how many men, was blushing at the thought of my having given myself a helping hand.

"So you understand why, when my parents wanted to arrange my marriage, I didn't protest too much." I smiled. "I was ready. Boy, was I ready!"

"Well, I hope you weren't disappointed," she said, a bit cuttingly, returning her head to my chest.

"Actually, I was," I said very quietly. "Geetha wasn't just a virgin, she was horrified by what I wanted to do to her. Her mother, it seems, had given her the most basic instruction in what to expect. She refused to disrobe completely — she thought the very idea was disgusting. She showed no desire for my body either. So yes, I guess you could say I was disappointed."

Priscilla looked directly at me with those amazing eyes. "I'm sorry, Lucky," she said softly. "That couldn't have been easy for you to tell me."

"It's okay."

"I'll tell you something, too, that I haven't told anyone. There's one thing I've never done. In bed, I mean. I've never let anyone make love to me the way my father was doing it with that woman. From behind."

I looked at her, and she looked back, unblinking, and I was overwhelmed by the desire to seize her in my arms, to turn her around, to do to her exactly what she'd said she'd never do. I touched her gently on the cheek.

"I understand, Priscilla," I said.

from Randy Diggs's notebook

October 12, 1989

Muslim professor I'd met in Delhi, Mohammed Sarwar, came to
see me here at the guest house. He said he was staying with relatives
in Zalilgarh while doing historical research, and it would be more
convenient if he came to me. Unusual for an Indian — they're
always inviting you home. From which I surmise not just that this
isn't his home, but that the people he's staying with are very poor.
Or conservative. Or both? Mustn't ask.

Sarwar arrives, young, slim, moustache, thinning hair, while
I'm sitting on the verandah with Rudyard Hart. There's my first
surprise.

"Don't I know you?" asks Hart, his eyes narrowing. "I'm sure
we've met before."

"We have, Mr. Hart," Sarwar replies, as he mounts the steps and
shakes his hand. "Over ten years ago."

"Ten years . . . of course! I remember you now. You were — what
did they call you? A student leader." He pronounces the words with
exaggerated care, as if they were a rare species of butterfly. Or an
exotic disease.

"That's right." Sarwar is unabashed.

"With the commie student union, if I remember right."

"With one of the commie student unions, Mr. Hart. There are
two at the university."

"Only in India." Hart is cheerful. "Communism is fading away
everywhere else in the world, but in India it sustains two student
unions." He wags a finger at Sarwar. "And you were leading a
demonstration outside my office."

"Down with American imperialism," Sarwar recites. "U.S.
capitalist exploiter murdabad. Coke is a joke on India's poor."

"I liked that one particularly. Coke is a joke. You must have had great fun making those up."

"Not really. We took ourselves very seriously."

"Of course you did. I invited you into my office to discuss your demands."

"That's right."

"And," Hart adds with satisfaction, "I offered you Coke."

"Which I declined."

"Which, as I recall, you accepted. And drank two."

"No, that wasn't me. I refused. I was from the SFI. It was the girl who was with me, from the AISF. Her father was an extremely rich landlord from Calcutta, a member of Parliament for the Communist Party of India. She had grown up on the stuff. She told me later that it wasn't thirst that led her to accept; drinking your Coke was a way of exploiting the exploiter. She was extremely good at rationalizing the indefensible."

Hart laughs. "What's she doing now?"

"Oh, she's teaching at an American university, Emory I believe. Lecturing on postmodernism and feminism. I'm told she has a green card, a tenure-track post, and the best music system on campus. She still contributes articles to the 'Economic and Political Weekly' here critiquing India's dangerous compromises with the forces of global capital."

"And you? Are you still leading demonstrations outside American imperialist institutions?"

"No." It is Sarwar's turn to laugh. "I gave that up a while ago. I'm a professor now."

"A professor? In what subject?"

"A reader, actually, in the Department of History at Delhi University. What you'd call an associate professor."

"History," Hart murmurs. "You have a lot of that in this country."

"Yes," Sarwar agrees. "Unlike yours. When I was at college I wanted to take an optional course in American history. The head of the department dissuaded me. Americans, he said, have no history. We, of course, have both history and mythology. Sometimes we can't tell the difference."

"What sort of history do you teach?"

"I'm specializing in what we call Mediaeval Indian History. Also called by some the Muslim Period. The time when most of India was ruled by various Muslim dynasties, ending with the Mughals."

"An odd choice, for a communist."

"Oh, I gave that up a while ago too. It was a faith, really, and I soon discovered two other faiths that I realized meant more to me."

"And what were those?" Hart asks.

"Democracy," Sarwar replies quietly. "And Islam."

"Sounds like a perfect segue," I chip in. "This long-delayed reunion is marvelous, Rudyard, but do you think I could proceed with my interview with Professor Sarwar now?"

letter from Priscilla Hart to Cindy Valeriani

April 5, 1989

. . .

"How can you love me?" he asked me suddenly. "When you know nothing about my background — my parents, my village, my ancestral home, where I went to school, what I grew up eating, thinking, listening to, dreaming of?"

"But that's the whole point, Lucky," I replied. "I don't care about your background. I don't care whether you lived in a thatched hut with no running water or grew up in a mansion. I don't care if your parents drove a Mercedes or brushed their teeth with twigs. I love you. Not your family, not your village, not your caste, not your background. I love you. And that's all that matters to me."

He seemed taken aback by this, as if it was a new idea. "I love you too, Priscilla," he said, but there was a note of uncertainty in his words I had not heard before. . . .

Did I tell you he's a poet? Even published a few poems in Indian magazines. "The standards aren't very high," he said apologetically, and you can see the rough edges in his work. I'm copying one below that he gave me. "A bit on the earnest side, as Wilde might have said," he joked, "but then you know why it's important to be earnest." He comes up with these dreadful one-liners when he's nervous, which I find really endearing. Anyway, it is earnest, but he means it, I think. Here it is:

Advice to the World's Politicians

How to Sleep at Night

Try to think of nothing.
That's the secret.

Try to think of nothing.
Do not think of work not done,
of promises unkept, calls to return,
or agendas you have failed to prepare for meetings
yet unheld.

Think of nothing.
Do not think of words said and unsaid,
of minor scandals and major investigations,
of humiliations endured, insults suffered,
or retorts that did not spring to mind
in time.

Think of nothing.
Do not think of your forgotten wife,
of lonely children and their reproachful demands,
or the smile of the pretty woman
whose handshake lingered just a shade too long
in your palm.

Think of nothing.
Do not think of newspaper headlines,
of the insistent transience of the shortwave radio,
or the seductive stridency of the TV microphones
thrust so thrillingly
into your face.

Think of nothing.
Do not think of the waif on the foreign sidewalk,
her large eyes open in supplication,
her ragged shift stained by dirt and dust,
stretching her despairing hand towards you
in hope.

No, do not think
of the woman at the building site,
wobbling pan of stones on her head,
walking numb for the thousandth time
from pile to site and site to pile
as her neglected baby scrabbles in the dust,
eats sand and wails,
unheard.

Think of nothing.
Do not think of the starving infant,
parched lips mute in hunger,
sitting slumped in the mud,
his eyes fading before his heart.
Do not think
of the stark ribs of skeletal cattle,
unable to provide milk, or hope,
in drought-dried lands of which
you know nothing.

Think of nothing.
Do not think
of the dead-eyed refugee, dispossessed
of everything he once called home.
Do not think
of the unsmiling girl whose once-sturdy thigh
now ends at the knee, the rest blown off
by a thoughtless mine on her way
to the well.

No, do not think
of the solitary tear, the broken limb,
the rubble-strewn home, the choking scream;
never think
of piled-up bodies, blazing flames,
shattered lives, or sundered souls.
Do not think of the triumph of the torturer,
the wails of the hungry,
the screams of the mutilated,
or the indifferent smirk
of the sleek.

Think of nothing.
Then you will be able
to sleep.

What do you think, Cindy? He's genuinely earnest, discontented
with the state of the world. He was telling me one day about this
elite cadre he belongs to, the Indian Administrative Service, the IAS.
We've got nothing like it Stateside. You won't believe what it takes
to get in: hundreds, thousands of young men and women studying
sixteen hours a day so 150,000 of them can take an annual exam
from which 400 are selected for all the top national government jobs
that year — and maybe 25 of those for the IAS. Lucky says he had to
wake up at 4:30 each morning to "cram," to learn zillions of facts
and figures about all sorts of things, not because you need to know
them to do your job properly but just to prove you're smart enough
to do the job. To many guys, the exams are the be-all and end-all of
their lives; getting through is a passport to power, privilege, clout,
and lifetime job security.

Lucky had had hopes of becoming a writer, but he couldn't
afford to support himself on his writing, and his family put a lot
of pressure on him to take the civil service exams. He says it seemed
a noble aspiration to him: he did the exams because he wanted to
make a difference. "Like Wilde, I've put my genius into my life and
merely my talent into my writing," he says. It's odd to hear him

constantly quoting Wilde, because you can't imagine anyone less like an apostle of aesthetics. He's not at all the stereotyped Victorian dandy with a lily in his hand and a book of verse in the other. He's a bureaucrat, for Chrissake, a government official. And he's an idealist about his work, as well as a traditionalist culturally and socially, the product of a middle-class professional Indian upbringing. The Oscar Wilde part of him is just in his intellect, I think, something from his education that hasn't fully seeped into his life. And look at his life. He has a job with no room for the Wildean witticisms and quips he learned to enjoy at college. Maybe these allusions are a kind of refuge for him, giving him some distance from the daily realities he has to deal with. Maybe I'm another kind of refuge too?

I don't know, Cindy. But the guy's an idealist, and there aren't too many idealists around in the government. "I didn't spend a year of my life sharing a tiny room with three other guys all swotting for the IAS in order to serve slum dwellers," one of his batchmates (colleagues from the same entry year) told him at the training academy in Mussoorie. "I did it so I could be set for life, look after my parents in their old age, and get myself a good wife." I'm not kidding, Cin; all these guys become instantly more desirable marital prospects the moment they pass the IAS exams. In many parts of India a government job is the ultimate accomplishment, and being in the IAS is the government job to end all government jobs. So fathers of eligible daughters double the dowries on offer when an IAS candidate heaves into view. Listen to one story: Lucky tells me a couple of his college friends fell in love and wanted to get married. Problem was, the girl was from a well-off Brahmin family, and the boy was a Naga from the Northeast, a Christian and a "tribal." The girl's father ranted and raved, made the poor girl's life hell, and forbade any further contact between them. The guy then got into the IAS on the Scheduled Tribe quota, a kind of affirmative action program for India's underprivileged, and suddenly the father's objections melted away. They're now married, and the same father who railed against an "accursed [expletive deleted!] tribal" now boasts of his "IAS son-in-law."

But Lucky's really conflicted about his work. On the one hand, he says, he can do good; as district magistrate he has real power here. On the other hand, he says he's frequently disillusioned with the cynicism he sees around him in government, especially the corruption. A lot of his colleagues are on the take — official salaries are modest, and the way they see it, since all their college classmates are busy making money as businessmen, engineers, whatever, why shouldn't the smarter ones, the guys clever enough to get into the IAS, make money too? India's so full of rules and regulations that government officials can make a fortune from the way they exercise their power to permit — the building of a factory here, the grant of a loan there. And then there's the political interference, from the local legislator, the MLA, or from ministers higher up in the state capital, Lucknow. Some of it is for petty favors — hire this person, authorize this action, expedite that approval — and he does it as part of the way things are. But when the politicians ask him to favor a dubious contractor or promote an undeserving officer or improperly allocate government funds, he refuses, and then they make their displeasure clear, even start threatening to transfer him. That's one good thing about his job: he can't be fired, the worst they can do is transfer him if he won't do their bidding. He doesn't, of course, and so one day he may really get to be too much of a pain for the bigwigs in Lucknow and might find himself suddenly made Deputy Commissioner of Inland Waterways or whatever. I can't bear the thought.

Neither can his wife, of course. Lucky tells me that she keeps asking him why he makes such a point of his principles, why can't he just let well enough alone? Why rock the boat? Doesn't he care about her convenience, and the child's? Lucky says rather bitterly that the rank, the house, the car, the servants are all she cares about. "The supreme vice," he quotes Wilde again, the disillusioned Wilde of "De Profundis" (go on, look it up, Cin!), "is shallowness." And Geetha is irremediably shallow. Lucky thinks she should have married the batchmate who drank himself into oblivion the day he got his IAS results, singing "Meri zindagi ban gayee!" ("I'm made for life!") at the top of his voice in the street. There are eight million civil servants in India, if Lucky's right (and he usually is!). The few hundred members of the IAS are the top of that heap, and in places like Zalilgarh they ARE the government. Ordinary people are so dependent on the government here for everything — from food rations to maintaining law and order — that Lucky really has power over the terms of their daily survival. He gave me a sardonic little poem about his own elitism:

I Am an Indian

I am an Indian, dressed in a suit and tie;
The words roll off my lucid tongue in accents long gone by;
I rule, I charm, protest, explain, know every how and why.
What kind of an Indian am I?

I am an Indian, with a roof above my head;
When I've had enough of the working day, I fall upon my bed;
My walls are hard, my carpets soft, my sofa cushions red.
What kind of an Indian? you said.

I am an Indian, with my belly round and full;
When my kid gets up in the morning she is driven to her
    school;
And if she's hot, the a/c's on, or she'll splash into the pool.
What kind of an Indian, fool?

I am an Indian, with friends where friends should be;
Wide are the branches of my extensive family tree;
Big businessmen and bureaucrats all went to school with me.
I'm the best kind of Indian, you see.

from Katharine Hart's diary

October 12, 1989

The HELP-US extension worker, Kadambari — I didn't get the rest of her name, a rather plain woman with a dark sallow face, wearing a white cotton sari with a navy-blue border, her hair severely pulled back and plaited — took us to Priscilla's place today.

Zalilgarh is just as bad as I feared. The heat radiates toward you in waves, as if some celestial oven is being opened and stoked in your face. The traffic is a torrent, raging rivers of vehicles and bodies in constant motion, streams of bicycles wending their way past thin cows, their ribs showing through their dirty skin, carts creaking past drawn by skeletal buffaloes, clangorous buses blaring their horns as they rattle and belch their way across town. And everywhere, people: half-dressed beggars with open sores clamoring for money, ash-smeared sadhus in saffron waist-cloths and matted hair, men in dhotis and men in pants and men in kurta-pajamas, and most strikingly the women, in multicolored saris of cotton and nylon, glittering with golden bangles and silver anklets. Vendors hawk their wares on the street — savories served on dried palm leaves, peanuts in cone-shaped packets made of old newspapers, sugarcane juice pressed into grimy tumblers — as flies buzz around everything. A listless gust of air blows a couple of sheets of paper at us from a hawker's basket, and they turn out to be exam papers, still unread and unmarked, sold by impoverished teachers for the few pennies they will bring, the dreams of schoolchildren reduced to encasing a few grams of spicy fried lentils. Everything is recycled in India, even dreams. Street urchins gambol amid the refuse; a man relieves himself against a wall daubed with the campaign slogans and election symbols of two competing political parties. Above us, a vision of the infinite, as a murder of crows, cawing and wheeling in the brilliantly blue sky, points our way to Priscilla's last home.

We had to walk down a narrow side-street, a gully they call it, to get there. The sidewalk was strewn with moldering rubbish and it was all we could do to avoid stepping on the trash. The stench was unbearable. Stray dogs nibbled at the scattered refuse. The road was no better, its paving cracked and pitted. Dust rose from every passing vehicle, mainly bicycles and reckless yellow-and-black auto-rickshaws, though a couple of bullock carts rolled past too, their riders idly flogging the tired beasts who were pulling them. Loud noise constantly assailed us, the jangling of bicycle bells, the shouting of male voices, the phut-phut-phut of the auto-rickshaw engines, the blaring of Hindi film music from various storefronts. We walked past groceries, their spices impregnating the air; provision shops, with brightly colored plastic buckets on display; photo developers, testimony to Zalilgarh's ascent to modernity. At the entrance to what had been Priscilla's building, Kadambari stopped at a tiny tin shed housing a paan counter, where a grimy little man sat cross-legged in front of an aluminum table as flies buzzed around his wares. He seemed to recognize her, and without much ado expertly daubed lime paste on a bright green leaf before dropping betel nuts and multicolored supari masalas onto it while Rudyard and I watched. The paanwallah folded the bursting leaf into a triangle that Kadambari wedged into her cheek. I refused her offer to have one too, and we trudged up an exterior staircase behind her.

The weather is pleasant in October, cool by Indian standards, but Rudyard was perspiring as we climbed. The whitewashed steps were dirty, the wall splotchy with red stains from the paan juice that the building's inhabitants casually spat on their way up, as Kadambari proceeded to do. Back in the '70s, when I first came across those stains in Delhi, I assumed they were blood, and wondered whether the homicide rate was greater than reported or, worse, whether tubercular Indians were coughing up blood all over the city. The discovery that it was merely a combination of a national addiction and poor hygiene had come as a relief. But today, the red stains made me think again of blood, Priscilla's blood, spilled by an unknown rioter with a knife, and I stumbled, suddenly blinded.

We reached a landing, two floors up, and entered the interior of the building. The corridor was dingy, lit by a single naked bulb dangling from a wire cord. Four identical wooden doors led off it to the apartments within; they were painted a garish blue, though the garishness was dimmed by dirt and assorted scratches visible even in the poor light. Two of the blue doors were closed but not bolted; one was open and a small child, milk dribbling down his chin, stared out at us round-eyed from the doorway until his sari-clad mother swished up from within and dragged him away. The fourth door, bolted and padlocked, was Priscilla's. Kadambari pulled out a large key and let us in.

It was a small room, sparsely furnished, with a stone floor on which my daughter had placed a small throw-rug, and a single bed. It wasn't really a bed in the American sense of the word, but a string-cot, a charpoy, its white strings sagging noticeably in the middle, with a thin cotton mattress on top. The bed was neatly made, with a stiff white cotton sheet, and a gaily colored Indian bedspread on top. I sat down heavily on it, imagining the impress of my daughter's body, and ran a hand over the bedspread, resting it on the lumpy pillow, feeling the lump in my own throat.

Rudyard marched right in and took in the room — the bed, the rudimentary table that served as her desk, the Indian cupboard, or almirah, the solitary chair, the Grateful Dead poster nailed to the wall, the two pieces of luggage on the floor. She lived simply, my daughter, as we had expected. Half a dozen books were stacked on the table. There was a shortwave radio against the sole window, its antenna extended as far as it would go, straining, I imagined, for news and music from home. It was her only luxury: there was no television set, no telephone. A pedestal fan, signs of rust beginning to show on its casing, stood unplugged in a corner; it was all that Priscilla had to keep off the heat whenever Zalilgarh's erratic electricity supply allowed her to run it. The bathroom was tiny, with an Indian-style squatting toilet, and a tap and a bucket on the floor to bathe at. How had she coped, my baby? Never once had she complained about her living conditions.

Rudyard's eyes alighted on the two framed photos on the desk. One was of me, alone, taken a year previously in New York, by her. The other was a much older picture, taken at the Red Fort in Delhi back in 1978, of the five of us as a family. The children are grinning and squinting at the camera and Rudyard has his arm around me. An innocent tourist moment, but I could imagine Priscilla looking at it over the years, seeing it as an icon of what she had cherished and lost.

Rudyard averted his eyes from the photos and walked to the almirah. Once again, Kadambari produced a key and opened the door. Rudyard almost recoiled from the sight of himself, red-eyed and perspiring, in the mirror on the inside of the door. A few cotton dresses hung limply from wooden hangers. Rudyard pulled open a drawer and found himself holding Priscilla's underthings. He withdrew his hands as if scalded.

A fly buzzed around the room. The sounds of the street were fainter here, filtered by the stillness in our hearts.

I got up from the bed and began to look at everything in the room, touching each of her dresses, searching the pockets, emptying the drawers. I didn't know what I was looking for. Clues, perhaps, but to what? The Zalilgarh authorities weren't looking for anything; they knew she'd been killed in a riot, like seven other people, and that was good enough for them. Clues to her life, perhaps, were what I needed, rather than to her death. Something that would help me understand what she was experiencing here in Zalilgarh, something that would help me hear the stories she would never be able to tell me again.

Rudyard, still perspiring, looked numbly at our daughter's personal possessions, the final legacy of her short life. I could see him struggling to contain something within himself, something he had never felt and did not know how to express. It was there in his strained and sweating face, in the way his brow seemed knit in perplexity and pain. He was staring at each book, each garment, as if unable to comprehend what it was doing there, what he was doing with it. We had to pack, of course, take her things away. Where would we take them? For what purpose? Her clothes, in particular, would be pointless to carry to America. Better to give most of them away here, where others would be glad to have them.

But packing gave us something concrete to do. When I supplanted him at the almirah Rudyard sat silently in the chair, staring vacantly at the wall, and Kadambari stood at the door chewing her paan and watching us. As I struggled with Priscilla's suitcase, though, Rudyard got up and heaved it onto the bed. It was half full of papers, research notes, and a few souvenirs she was no doubt planning to bring to America — a decorative brass plate, a hand-carved wooden box, two embroidered cushion covers. These were simple things, pleasing to the eye, bought cheaply at the local bazaar. They would, I decided, travel back with us as Priscilla had intended them to.

We worked in silence. Neither Rudyard nor I could say a word, at this time, in this place, to each other. I did not trust myself to speak and, as always, tried to find strength in focusing on the practical. Housework and relocation had saved my sanity when my marriage ended; packing and sorting would see me through my pain today.

I looked through the contents of Priscilla's drawers before putting them away, and found nothing unusual. I took the bedspread, with its distinctively Indian paisley pattern, but left the coarse white sheet. The clothes Priscilla would never wear I folded into the second piece of luggage. I might have offered them to Kadambari except that she showed not the slightest interest in what I was doing, and I could not imagine her in a dress anyway. I would ask the kind Mr. Das of HELP-US whether he could think of people to give them to. Fortunately Rudyard paid no attention to Priscilla's toilet bag, because he would have been horrified by two things inside it. A vibrator. And a partly used strip of birth-control pills.

The latter surprised me more than the former. I had assumed Priscilla would be alone here, and I knew she had broken up with her last boyfriend before coming to India. I could not imagine why she would need to use birth control in Zalilgarh.

I found no clues among her papers, though I knew I would need to go through them carefully again. There were two letters from me, but none from any of her friends. A couple of sheets of half-done drawings, some scribbled lines of verse: that was all. Everything else was related to her work for HELP-US or her thesis research. I was sure there was more, somewhere. Priscilla would have made jottings, sketched, kept a diary, written poetry. I knew my daughter well enough to be sure there was something else.

Kadambari took the smaller bag and left the room. Rudyard moved to close the suitcase on the bed. I picked up the old photograph on the desk, intending to put it in my handbag along with the picture of myself that had kept my daughter company for the last ten months. But before I could put it away, Rudyard's hand, oddly unfamiliar, fell upon mine.

"Can I have that?" he asked, his voice thickening.

You have no right, Rudyard, I thought. You're the one who destroyed the world that photo depicts.

But I didn't say that. I said, "Of course, Rudyard."

As I gave it to him he slumped onto the bed, and I found myself holding him as he sobbed uncontrollably, his head hot and wet against my ribs, his body racked with regret. I realized then that, in all the years I had known him, and in all the years of our marriage and its collapse, I had never seen him cry.

from Lakshman's journal

May 3, 1989

We meet every Tuesday and Saturday at the Kotli, just before
dusk. She comes on her bicycle, through the gate I showed her; I
have slipped her a copy of the key to the padlock. She always arrives
first, wheels her cycle in, and hides it where I have shown her,
behind some shrubbery. When I arrive in my official car, there is no
sign that anyone is there. This is a sensible precaution, because
though I usually let the driver off, sometimes I have no choice but to
keep him and I don't want him putting two and two together and
coming up with 22. Sometimes my work delays me; Saturday is a
working day for me, ostensibly half-time, but half-time can stretch
well into the afternoon. Fortunately, on Saturdays Geetha always
goes with Rekha for an early evening puja to the Shiva Mandir and
never notices what time I return home.

At one time I had begun to disapprove of Geetha's pujas: there is a
swami resident at the Shiva Mandir who has an unsavory reputation
for dabbling in tantric practices and other activities on the wrong
side of the law. Before I got to Zalilgarh there were rumors of
human sacrifices that could never be proven, and the swami has
henchmen — he calls them disciples — who look as though they
would not think twice before devoutly slitting your throat on his
orders. But tantra is hardly Geetha's thing and the DM's wife can
scarcely be in any danger, so I didn't put a stop to her regular visits.
And now it's convenient. With Geetha at the temple, I don't have to
worry so much about the time. When I am held up at the office and
arrive at the Kotli later than promised, Priscilla is always there, in the
room at the top of the stairs, reading or writing in her scrapbook, or
simply looking out at the river and the sky turning inky as dusk
descends.

She always rises to greet me, with a smile that warms my soul. We embrace, we kiss — long, cool, lingering kisses unlike any I have ever had — and sooner or later we fall onto the makeshift bed and make love. We find more and different ways to make love, experimenting not because we are jaded but because of our delight in discovering new ways of knowing each other. Afterwards we talk, lying side by side or more often on top of each other.

She loves me, she says, and she means it. This is not love as my parents spoke of it, an emotion anchored in family, in a sense of one's place in the world, in bonds of blood so thick one cannot conceive of snapping them. It is instead love as I have read of it in Western books or seen in Western movies, an individual attraction between a man and a woman, a feeling that is independent of social context or familial connections. I cannot explain to Priscilla that I have been brought up to mistrust this kind of love, because it is so difficult to tell apart from lesser emotions of infatuation or lust. My father spoke to me of this before I went off to the University. "You will face many temptations," he said, "and sometimes you will find yourself developing feelings for a girl that you might mistake for love. Such feelings are normal, but do not confuse them with real love, which comes only from the commitment of marriage and the experience of sharing life's challenges together. The West believes that love leads to marriage, which is why so many marriages in the West end when love dies. In India we know that marriage leads to love, which is why divorce is almost unknown here, and love lives on even when the marital partner dies, because it is rooted in something fundamental in our society as well as our psyche. You are going to college to study, to make your future. But if ever you find yourself distracted by other thoughts, remember what I have said to you."

I never forgot.

I do not know what she sees in me, what the kindred spirit is that ignites such a spark of recognition in her. I believe I know, though, what I see in her. I see it in our trysting place, at our favorite hour, as the twilight seeps into our room and illuminates the colors of our bodies, the spreading crimson of dusk soft upon the black and white of our skin. I see it in her body as we are about to make love, her limbs light with unspoken whispers. I see it in her eyes at night, the moonbeams playing with her hair, the shadows across her hips like a flimsy skirt. In the darkness, I raise her chin in my hand and it is as if a flame has lifted itself onto the crevices of her smile. I let myself into her and my spirit slips into her soul, I feel myself taking her like nothing else I have ever possessed, she moans and my pleasure lies upon her skin like a patina of dewdrops, she is mine and I sense myself buckling in triumph and release, and then she trembles, a tug of her pelvis drawing me into the night. And I know that I love her.

But afterwards, as I lie by her side, our hearts full of fragmentary phrases, I look at the little mirror on the wall and see the darkness encroach like a stain across our love. I love her, but what does it mean once we have arisen? She dreams of holding hands on Broadway and rubbing noses on the honeymooners' bench at the Taj Mahal. I think of Geetha and her parents and mine, and of little lost Rekha calling bewildered for her Appa, her eyes wet with unwiped tears. There are moments, of course, when I too fantasize about a new life with a new wife, a new honey-blond wife with skin the color of peaches-and-cream and eyes like diamonds dancing in the sunlight, and I forget, momentarily, my responsibilities, the burdens of guilt and obligation that shackle me to the present.

Sometimes I dream, and the dreams are curious ones, of an America I have never seen, even in the movies, wide and open and inviting and definitely America, but strange, populated by fast cars and large women, or perhaps large cars and fast women, I am unsure which when I awake. The dreams are oddly precise, too, in the ways only dreams can be, so that in one Priscilla beckons me — I know it is Priscilla but in the dream she looks like Marilyn Monroe, like pictures of Marilyn Monroe I have seen in old magazines — this Priscilla/Marilyn beckons me into an estate wagon, and I think, clearly, precisely, I must get in, this is a very safe car, it is famous for being safe, and my mind's eye studies the manufacturer's name on the back of the hatch, and it reads VULVA. Seriously — for in my dream I see nothing odd about this, reading it as another famous Swedish brand name. Or another dream, in which I am teetering at the top of a skyscraper with Geetha and Rekha trying to hold on to me, they are afraid and crying and I am shouting out to them to hold on, but somehow it is I who leans too far off the edge and then I am falling from a great height, falling falling falling with my wife's and daughter's wailing in my ears, and I always wake up before I hit the ground. Of course I can never go back to sleep.

I haven't read much Freud, but it doesn't take a shrink to interpret this kind of dream. And it gets worse. Once I awake from another dream of falling, except this time I have splashed into a great briny foaming brown sea, and as I rise to the surface, choking and spluttering, I feel the unmistakable taste of Coca-Cola in my nose and mouth. I plunge again, flailing, and choke on the liquid. I am drowning in a sea of Coke! When I surface again I see, just out of my reach, my daughter on a raft, absurdly shaped like an Ambassador car. She is dressed in white, the color of mourning, and her limpid eyes are sadly downcast, seemingly unaware of me drowning just beyond her reach. In my dream I call out to her but find myself sinking again, knowing this plunge is the third and final descent into the depths, that as I go under my lungs will be full of that brown-black liquid and my voice will be stilled. I swear I awake with the taste of Coca-Cola on my tongue.

And Priscilla, I wonder what she dreams. She always says she can never remember a single dream; she awakes refreshed from her slumber, her mind blissfully cleansed of the night's wanderings. I envy her unencumbered sleep, the happy transience of her memory.

I have acquired her memories now, and they torment me. I think of her previous lovers, the basketball jock first, and imagine his dark hand on her pale thigh, much like mine, and something dies a little in me. I ask her, with studied casualness, about her old boyfriends, and she replies quite unselfconsciously, in as much detail as I want. And I always want more than is good for me. Sometimes I stop myself in time, preventing my mind from acquiring a detail that I know will come back to haunt me, to diminish my sense of my own worth as her lover. But then the most innocuous details have that power. She itemizes her menagerie at my request, and they tumble out in her recounting like an amatory United Nations — an

Argentine, a Finn, a Chinese. Am I, I find myself wondering, merely the latest in a long line of exotics who have shared Priscilla's bed, the beneficiaries of some missionary urge to bring succor to the underprivileged? But then I remember she has been in WASP arms too, and consider her progression from Boston Brahmin to Tamil Brahmin. Perhaps her predilection is for minorities.

Of course I know these are unworthy thoughts, and the hot flashes of jealousy always pass, sooner or later, cooled by the refreshing candor of her love for me. I sometimes defuse my discomfort by recalling Wilde: "I like men who have a future and women who have a past." So Oscar would have liked us, on both counts. At other times the words of the old song, learned as a callow teenager, come back to me: "Yesterday belongs to someone else, today belongs to me."

And what about tomorrow? Sometimes we speak of the future as if we have one. As if we have one together. I speculate idly about resigning from the service — are you mad, my mother would certainly ask, to give up the IAS career tens of thousands can only dream about? — to accompany her to her American campus, perhaps to do a doctorate myself, perhaps to write. My mother would disapprove thoroughly of her; my father, were he alive, would disown me. She is innocent of such considerations: she speaks of staying on in India, establishing HELP-US projects wherever I should happen to be posted. I forbear from telling her that the service regulations would almost certainly prohibit an official's spouse from undertaking any such activity. The conflict of interest . . . But something always stops me from entering into the practical details. Priscilla is an escape from reality; her magic cannot survive too much realism.

And so I go along as she spins these glorious schemes in the gossamer of her illusions. . . .

from transcript of Randy Diggs interview with Professor Mohammed Sarwar

October 12, 1989

You should know what Maulana Azad said when he became president of the Indian National Congress at Ramgarh in 1940. I'd give you a copy of the speech, Mr. Diggs, but I don't have access to a photocopier in Zalilgarh. It doesn't matter; I know the words by heart. There is no greater testament of the faith of a religious Muslim in a united India.

The Maulana was a religious scholar, born in Mecca, educated in the Koran and the Hadith, fluent in Persian, Arabic, and Urdu, an exemplar of Muslim learning and culture in India. Yet he confessed that "every fiber of my being revolted" against the thought of dividing India on communal lines. "I could not conceive it possible for a Musulman to tolerate this," he declared, "unless he has rooted out the spirit of Islam from every corner of his being." Remember that his principal rival for the allegiance of India's Muslims was Mohammed Ali Jinnah, the leader of the Muslim League, an Oxbridge-educated Lincoln's Inn lawyer who wore Savile Row suits, enjoyed his Scotch and cigars, ate pork, barely spoke Urdu, and married a non-Muslim. There was no question in the Maulana's mind as to who was the better Muslim; yet Jinnah claimed to speak for India's Muslims and to assert their claims to being a separate nation, while the Maulana worked in the secular (Jinnah said Hindu-dominated) Indian National Congress to remind his fellow Muslims where their homeland really was.

"I am a Musulman and proud of the fact," he said in that great speech. Shall I go on? Is your tape recorder working? "Islam's splendid traditions of thirteen hundred years are my inheritance. I am unwilling to lose even the smallest part of this inheritance. In addition, I am proud of being an Indian. I am part of that indivisible unity that is Indian nationality." And then he added—this is the key part—"I am indispensable to this noble edifice. Without me this splendid structure of India is incomplete. I am an essential element which has gone to build India. I can never surrender this claim. It was India's historic destiny that many human races and cultures and religions should flow to her, and that many a caravan should rest here. . . . One of the last of these caravans was that of the followers of Islam. They came here and settled for good. We brought our treasures with us, and India too was full of the riches of her own precious heritage. We gave her what she needed most, the most precious of gifts from Islam's treasury, the message of human equality. Full eleven centuries have passed by since then. Islam has now as great a claim on the soil of India as Hinduism."

It took courage to say this. The Maulana was dismissed by Jinnah as a "Muslim showboy," a token elected by the Congress to advertise its secular credentials. But the Maulana was not immersing his Islam in any woolly notion of Indian secularism, still less was he uncritically swallowing Hindu professions of tolerance and inclusiveness. He was, instead, asserting his pride in his religious identity, in the majesty and richness of Islam, while laying claim to India for India's Muslims. He dismissed talk of partition by arguing that he was entitled—just as any Hindu was—to a stake in all of India, from Kashmir to Kanyakumari, from the Khyber Pass to Khulna; why should he accept the Pakistani idea of a narrower notion of Muslim nationhood that confined Indian Muslims to a truncated share of the heritage of their entire land? He was a far more authentic representative of Indian Islam than Jinnah, and it is part of the great tragedy of this country's Muslims that it was Jinnah who triumphed and not Azad.

Triumph? Partition was less a triumph for Indian Muslims than an abdication. In fact, most of the country's Islamic leaders, and especially those whom you might think of today as "fundamentalists" (people like Maulana Maudoodi, who was to spend years in Pakistani jails), were bitterly opposed to the movement for Pakistan. They felt that Islam should prevail over the world at large and certainly over India as a whole, and they thought it treasonous — both to India and to Islam itself — to advocate that the religion be territorially circumscribed as Jinnah and the Muslim Leaguers did. Pakistan was created by "bad" Muslims, secular Muslims, not by the "good" Muslims in whose name Pakistan now claims to speak.

You can understand why some Indian Muslims are more viscerally anti-Pakistan than many Hindus, especially North Indian Hindus with their romanticized nostalgia for the good old days before Partition. Indian Muslims know what they have lost, what burdens they have to bear as the result of the Jinnah defection, the conversion of brothers into foreigners. Mohammed Currim Chagla, who was India's foreign minister during the 1965 war with Pakistan, made a speech in Parliament during the Bangladesh war of 1971 in which he said that "Pakistan was conceived in sin and is dying in violence." Do you know M. J. Akbar, the editor of the Telegraph? India's brightest young journalist, a real media star, and a Muslim. Well, he famously denounced Jinnah as having "sold the birthright of the Indian Muslims for a bowl of soup." Some of us feel that our birthright cannot be so easily sold, but it is precisely that sense of loss that drives so many of us to rage and sorrow — the feeling that, since the country was divided in our name,

109

we are somehow less entitled to our due in what remains of it. That a part of our birthright has indeed been given away.

Which leads some of my fellow Muslims into a sort of self-inflicted second-class citizenship, a result of our guilt by association with the original sin of Partition. "If you don't like it here in India," say the crassest of the Hindu bigots, "why don't you go to Pakistan?" How can you reply, "Because this is my home, I am as entitled to it as you are," when Jinnah and his followers have given the Hindu bigots their best excuse? When they acted, in the name of all Indian Muslims, to surrender a portion of our entitlement by saying that the homeland of an Indian Muslim is really a foreign country called Pakistan?

These are the feelings that are played upon by the Hindu chauvinists. They build their case on our own concession of failure. And I'm not talking about the extremist crackpots who claim the Taj Mahal was really a Hindu palace, but the seemingly reasonable ones who call on Muslims to "assimilate" properly, to "acknowledge" our Hindu origins and subordinate ourselves to their notion of the Indian ethos. There are always some Muslims who'll submit to this nonsense, who'll accept a notion of the Indian ethos that doesn't include them. But for every Indian Muslim who's vulnerable to such feelings of guilt, there are two who have outgrown it — who assert, like the Maulana, that India is not complete without us, that we are no less Indian than the most chauvinist Hindu.

But who owns India's history? Are there my history and his, and his history about my history? This is, in many ways, what this whole Ram Janmabhoomi agitation is about — about the reclaiming of history by those who feel that they were, at one point, written out of the script. But can they write a new history without doing violence to the inheritors of the old?

Once, when I was in college, a fellow got into an argument with me and lost his temper. "You partitioned the country!" he yelled. I interrupted him. "If I'd partitioned the country, I wouldn't be here. I'd be in Pakistan," I said. "If you mean I'm a Muslim, I plead guilty to the charge of being Muslim. But to no other charge. Muslims didn't partition the country — the British did, the Muslim League did, the Congress Party did. There are more Muslims in India today than in Pakistan. This is where we belong." I said it quietly, but the fight died in him then. He spluttered and walked away. I stood my ground. All Indian Muslims must, or they will soon have no ground to stand on.

Pakistanis will never understand the depth of the disservice Jinnah did us, Indian Muslims as a whole, when he made some of us into non-Indians. There are still so many Indians who — out of ignorance as well as prejudice — think of us as somehow different from them, somehow foreign, "not like us." I was on a train once, with my wife and children, dressed as you see me, in a shirt and trousers, smoking a Wills and reading the States-man, when my neighbor struck up a conversation about something in the paper — I can't remember what it was, but it had nothing to do with the communal question. Anyway, towards the end of the conversation, which we had both enjoyed, he introduced himself and asked me my name. "Mohammed Sarwar?" he repeated incredulously. "A Muslim?" As if Mohammed Sarwar could be anything but a Muslim! "Yes," I replied, tightly, defensively. He waved a sheepish hand, the gesture taking in my garb, my wife in a floral-patterned salwar-kameez, my little boys in shorts and tee-shirts reading Amar Chitra Katha comics. "But you're not like them at all!"

Not like them at all. I began to say something, but was suddenly overcome by the sheer futility of the attempt. It was bad enough that he had labeled me, consigned his erstwhile conversational partner to the social ghetto of minority status. But I had surprised him, perhaps even disappointed him, by failing to conform to his stereotype of my minority-hood. As a Muslim, I had to look different; perhaps my forehead should bear the indentation of banging it on the floor five times a day in namaz; my wife should no doubt be in a burqa, shielded from infidel eyes; my boys should wear the marks of their circumcisions like a badge. Instead there we were, indistinguishable from any other middle-class Indian family on the train. I looked him directly in the eye till he became uncomfortable enough to avert his gaze. I am a Muslim, I wanted to say to him, but I will never allow your kind to define what kind of Muslim I am.

Yes, there's prejudice in this country. I know I've had a privileged upbringing, an elite education, and I'm now in a position of intellectual authority. I've been conscious of how important it is for me never to forget that isn't that way for millions of my fellow Muslims. Indian Muslims suffer disadvantages, even discrimination, in a hundred different ways that I may never personally experience. If I'm ever in danger of forgetting that, there'll be someone like that man on the train to remind me.

And yet, Mr. Diggs, I love this country. I love it not just because I was born here, as my father and mother were, as their parents before them were, not just because their graves have mingled their bones into the soil of this land. I love it because I know it, I have studied its history, I have traveled its geography, I have breathed its polluted air, I have written words to its music. India shaped me, my mind, my tastes, my friend-ships, my passions. The fact that I bow my head towards the Kaaba five times a day — after years in college when I did not pray even three times a year — does not mean I am turning away from my roots. I can eat a masala dosa at the Coffee House,

112

chew a paan afterwards and listen to Ravi Shankar playing raag durbari, and I celebrate the Indian-ness in myself with each note. I hear the Muslim Dagar brothers sing Hindu devotional songs, and then I attend a qawwali performance by one of our country's greatest exponents of this Urdu musical form, who happens to be a Hindu, Shankar Shambhu, and I am transported as he chants the long list of Muslim pirs to whom he pays devotional tribute before his rendition. This is India, Mr. Diggs!

I was a student in 1971 when the Pakistani gener-als proclaimed a jihad, a holy Islamic war, against India. This was in the war that would cre-ate Bangladesh, another Muslim state in what had been East Pakistan. A jihad, they said, but my chest swelled with pride that the Indian Air Force commander in the northern sector was my class-mate's father, Air Marshal Latif, later Air Chief Marshal. What sort of jihad would the Pakistanis conduct against this distinguished Muslim?

I take my children to the latest Bollywood block-buster and laugh as the Muslim hero chases the Hindu heroine around the tinsel tree. I avidly follow Test cricket and cheer for my hero, perhaps the best batsman in the world, Mohammed Azharud-din, and I cheer for him because he is on my team, the Indian team, not because he is Muslim — or at least, not only because he is Muslim. I cannot tell you how much it meant to me when he scored a century for India against Pakistan, in Pakistan. One day he will captain India, Mr. Diggs, and he will make every Indian proud because no one will notice, despite his name, that he is a Muslim.

Or so I hope. In recent years, Mr. Diggs, there's been a change in the dominant ethos of the coun-try, in the attitudes of mind that define what it means to be Indian. We're seeing more and more the demonization of a collectivity. Look at the things they are saying! Muslims are "pampered" for polit-ical ends, they say: look at the Shah Banu case and

113

Muslim Personal Law. Muslims have four wives, they exclaim, and are outbreeding everyone else; soon they will overtake the Hindus! Muslims are disloyal: they set off firecrackers whenever Pakistan beats India at cricket or hockey. I tried to argue the point at first with those Hindus who were willing to raise it with me, but found it almost too simple to do so. The Rajiv Gandhi government's action on Shah Banu was pure political opportunism; it was a sellout to Muslim conservatives, but a betrayal of Muslim women and Muslim reformers. Why stigmatize the community as a whole when many amongst them too lost out in the process? In any case, Personal Law covers only marriage and inheritance and divorce: how does it affect those who are not subject to it? If Muslims have four wives — and not many do — how does that increase the number of reproductive Muslim wombs, which still remains four whether by one husband or many? And by what statistical projection can 115 million Muslims "overtake" 700 million Hindus? If a handful of Muslims are pro-Pakistani, how can one label an entire community? Surely the families of my hero Mohammed Azharuddin, or, for that matter, of the nation's numerous Muslim hockey stars, aren't setting off firecrackers to commemorate Indian defeats by Pakistan? But it doesn't matter — this is not about logic or reasoning. The national mind has been afflicted with the intellectual cancer of thinking of "us" and "them."

Where do Indian Muslims like myself fit in? I've spent my life thinking of myself as part of "us" — now there are Indians, respectable Indians, Indians winning votes, who say that I'm really "them"!

But I'm determined to resist this minority complex that the Hindu chauvinists want to impose upon me and others like me. What makes me a minority? Is it a mathematical concept? Well, mathematically Muslims were always a minority in India, before Partition, even in the mediaeval Muslim period I spend my life researching and teaching. But when the Great Mughals ruled on the throne of Delhi, were Muslims a "minority" then? Mathematically no doubt, but no Indian Muslim thought of himself as a minority. Brahmins are only ten percent of the population of India today — do they see themselves as a minority? No, minorityhood is a state of mind, Mr. Diggs. It is a sense of powerlessness, of being out of the mainstream, of being here on sufferance. I refuse to let others define me that way. I tell my fellow Muslims: <u>No one can make you a minority without your consent</u>.

I beg your pardon? Yes, I've been to Pakistan. Once. For an academic conference, in fact. Where a Pakistani scholar stood up and spoke about the importance, indeed the centrality, of Islam in his country's national identity. "If the Turks cease to be Muslim, they are still Turks," he said at one point, bringing his peroration to a climax. "If the Egyptians cease to be Muslim, they are still Egyptians. If the Iranians cease to be Muslim, they are still Persians. But if we cease to be Muslim, what are we? We're Indians!" I went up to him afterwards. "My name is Mohammed Sarwar," I said, "and I'm Indian." And I simply walked away from his outstretched hand.

Later, back in India, whenever I tell this story to my Muslim friends, I add something: "For me it's the opposite. We're Muslim, but there are Muslims in a hundred countries. If we're not Indian, what are we?"

The danger is that Hindus like Ram Charan Gupta will get Muslims like me thinking differently. This is why the change in the public discourse about Indianness is so dangerous, and why the old ethos must be restored. An India that denies itself to some of us could end up being denied to all of us. This would be a second Partition: and a partition in the Indian soul would be as bad as a partition in the Indian soil. For my sons, the only possible idea of India is that of a nation greater than the sum of its parts. An India neither Hindu nor Muslim, but both. That is the only India that will allow them to continue to call themselves Indians.

Mrs. Hart and Mr. Das

October 12, 1989

"I don't know how to ask you this, Mr. Das, but it's really important to me. You see, I'm trying so hard to understand the circumstances of my daughter's death."

"Of course, Mrs. Hart, of course. Please be asking anything you want. Anything you want. If I am knowing the answer, I shall of course be telling you vithout any hesitation. Any hesitation."

"Well. [*Deep breath.*] Did Priscilla have a special friend here in Zalilgarh?"

"Miss Priscilla was so much popular, Mrs. Hart. Ve were all being her special friends. Special friends."

"No, you don't understand. I mean I haven't made myself clear. Did she have a special personal friend? An intimate friend?"

"I am regrettably not understanding you, Mrs. Hart. Not understanding."

"Did she have a boyfriend here, Mr. Das?"

"Oh dear, Mrs. Hart, what question you are asking! Miss Priscilla was a weritable angel. She was helping poor women, vorking wery hard. Wery hard. Where from she was to find the time for boyfriend-shoyfriend? Chhi!"

"Mr. Das, I have no doubt she worked very hard, but I assume she had some spare time for herself. I found these among her things. They're birth-control pills, Mr. Das, as I'm sure you know. Why was she taking them?"

"Ah, I see. I see. But why must you assume she was taking them herself, Mrs. Hart? You are knowing we are population-control awareness project. Awareness project. She may have been having them to show the poor women. To show the poor women. Please do not imagine the worst of your poor daughter, Mrs. Hart. The worst."

"Oh, for God's sake. . . . Never mind, Mr. Das. Thank you."

117

"Mrs. Hart, I am understanding wery vell your anxiousness to be knowing more about this great tragedy. Great tragedy. And to have reminders of your lovely daughter. Lovely daughter. Alas, this is all I am being able to find for you in the office."

"What is it?"

"A briefing paper, Mrs. Hart. Briefing paper. On population awareness and women."

"It's not exactly what I was looking for, but I do appreciate your kindness, Mr. Das. Thank you."

"You are being most welcome, Mrs. Hart. Most welcome."

"You haven't come across anything of a more personal nature in her desk, have you?"

"You are meaning? Excuse me, I don't follow. Don't follow."

"I've always known Priscilla to keep a sort of scrapbook, with her impressions, poems, sketches. It wasn't at the apartment — the room she rented. No one seems to have seen it."

"Scrapbook? Hmmm — I am not recalling any such thing, Mrs. Hart. Any such thing. If she had a scrapbook, she was not producing it at the office, isn't it? I am truly sorry I am being unable to help, Mrs. Hart. Miss Priscilla was not really having the facilities here to keep anything, only project files. Project files. But we will certainly look again, Mrs. Hart. You are also being most welcome to look anywhere in this office by your goodself. Meanwhile, you are wishing to take this paper of Miss Priscilla's? This paper?"

"Well, I wouldn't want to deprive you of something you need for your work, Mr. Das."

"Oh, that is perfectly all right. It is a spare copy. Spare copy. And so well-written. What a wonderful writer Miss Priscilla was, Mrs. Hart. Here, you must listen:

"'The case for the HELP-US population-control awareness projects is founded on the clear and demonstrable relationship between high fertility rates and the subjugation of women. This is particularly apparent in India, where women are placed under considerable social and family pressure to bear more children, which in turn reduces their autonomy as decisional agents in society. The fact is that women who are largely confined to, and in a real sense shackled by, the repeated bearing and full-time raising of children suffer a loss of free-dom and agency that restricts their abilities to fulfil their life poten-tial. Young women must be a particular target of HELP–US because raising their consciousness can have a much wider impact on their families and on society as a whole. Women who resist repeated child-bearing will exercise greater authority within their family units which, in turn, will reduce fertility rates and thus reduce the strain on the limited economic and environmental resources of a developing country like India. . . .'

"You see, Mrs. Hart? What a vision your daughter was having? What a vision!"

Ram Charan Gupta to Randy Diggs

(translated from Hindi)

October 12, 1989

You look at me politely enough, but I can see you are not convinced. You have doubtless been reading the opinions of these so-called secularists in Delhi who say there is no proof that the Ram Janmabhoomi temple stood where the so-called Babri Masjid now stands. What do they know about proof who only know what Western textbooks have taught them? It has been known for thousands of years that that is the Ram Janmasthan, the exact place of birth of our Lord Ram. Knowledge passed down from generation to generation by word of mouth is how wisdom was transmitted in India, Mr. Diggs. Ours is an oral tradition, and our tradition tells us that this is where Ram was born. In any case, does it not strike you as strange that Ayodhya is full of temples, but the most coveted spot, the most hallowed spot, the spot with the best site on a hill, is occupied by a mosque? Do these secularists think that was an accident, or a simple coincidence? Or might it be, instead, that Babar, the Mughal invader, demolished the biggest, the best, the most important temple of the Hindus and replaced it with a mosque named for himself, just to rub the noses of the conquered in the rubble of their faith?

This is not just supposition, Mr. Diggs. There is plenty of historical evidence for our claims. Joseph Tiffenthaler, an Austrian Jesuit priest who stayed in Awadh between 1776 and 1781, wrote about how the famous temple marking the birth of Ram had been destroyed 250 years earlier and a mosque built with its stones. A British court even pronounced judgment in 1886, and I quote: "It is most unfortunate that a masjid should have been built on land specially held sacred by the Hindus. . . . But as the event occurred 356 years ago it is too late now to remedy the grievance. All that can be done is to maintain the

status quo. . . . Any innovation could cause more harm and derange-
ment of order than benefit." What does that mean, I ask you, Mr.
Diggs? Does it not imply that the British acknowledged that a
mosque had been built on the site of the temple, but they felt they
could do nothing about it because they did not want to risk a law-
and-order problem?

I have no doubt where the truth lies. What is more important, Mr.
Diggs, is that millions of devout Hindus have no doubt either. To
them this accursed mosque occupies the most sacred site in Hinduism, our Ram Janmabhoomi. Who cares what proof these leftist
historians demand when so many believe they know the truth? Our
faith is the only proof we need. What kind of Indian would support a
structure named for a foreigner, Babar, over one consecrated to the
greatest Indian of them all, that divinity in human form, Lord Rama?

And the Ram Janmabhoomi is not the only temple that was
demolished by these marauding invaders and replaced with their
filthy mosques. There are literally dozens more, all over our country.
Do you know the story of the Kashi Vishwanath temple — or, as
they prefer to call it, the Gyan Vapi mosque? No? Then listen: I will
tell you.

It was just over three hundred years ago. The Kashi Vishwanath
temple was one of the finest in Varanasi — what you call Benares, the
city of temples, on the banks of the holy Ganga, the Ganges. It had
been built as the result of a particularly auspicious dream — a dream
by a princess, in which she was urged to consecrate this spot to Shiva,
the god of destruction in our holy trinity. Inside the famed temple,
which attracted millions of devotees from far and near, stood a magnificent shivalingam made of the purest emerald, a glittering phallic
representation of the power of the godhead. Aurangzeb, the evil
Muslim fanatic who reigned on the Mughal throne in Delhi, whose
hatred for what he called idolatry was notorious, lusted for this prize.
In 1669 he sent down one of his most feared generals with orders to
smash the great temple, where he claimed "wicked sciences" were
being practiced, and to bring the emerald lingam back to him.

The general he chose was an Abyssinian in his service who was
known as Black Mountain. The name was apt in more ways than one.

Black Mountain was a terrifying figure, immensely tall and broad-shouldered, black as the night, clad entirely in black, who always rode a black stallion. He marched on Varanasi with thousands of troops and something the defenders of the city had not faced before — dozens of cannons. And yet, despite this terrible adversary, how the Hindus of Varanasi fought! What a fearsome battle raged, Mr. Diggs! The Hindus defended their temple against impossible odds. Hundreds of Hindu soldiers and civilians were killed, but they could not indefinitely resist the overwhelming might of the invaders.

With defeat inevitable and the might of the Mughals about to descend on the temple, its purohit, the chief priest, made the supreme sacrifice. He seized the emerald lingam — which must have weighed much more than the priest himself — and dragged himself over to the temple well, known as the Well of Knowledge. There, with the forces of General Black Mountain almost upon him, the priest plunged into the waters of the well, clutching the lingam to his heart. Of course the weight of the precious object took him to the bottom, guaranteeing his death. His drowned body soon floated to the top, and was pulled out by Black Mountain's men. But of the prized emerald itself there was no sign. A furious Black Mountain had the well dredged, but the lingam was never found. The Muslims said it must have slipped into an estuary and floated into the Ganges. But we Hindus know it was recovered by Shiva himself, taken out of the clutches of the invaders, who smashed his temple in their rage. It will return to Varanasi one day — but only when the vile mosque they have built in place of the fabled temple is replaced by a Shiva temple once again, and the princess's original dream is once again fulfilled.

So you did not know about the Kashi Vishwanath, eh, Mr. Diggs? This time you will not hear those secularists cleverly decrying the lack of proof that there was ever a temple at that spot. For the proof is visible on the walls of the mosque itself — the back wall of the mosque is the wall of the ruined temple, complete with traces of its original Hindu carvings. You want more proof? In 1937, the British themselves examined the facts and concluded — officially, with a formal report — that the Gyan Vapi mosque stands upon the site of an ancient Hindu temple. Why should it have been any different with the Ram Janmabhoomi? You see, Mr. Diggs, it was very simple. Hindu temples were destroyed and replaced by mosques quite deliberately, as part of a conscious imperial strategy by the Muslim rulers to demoralize the local population and humiliate them. It was a way of saying, your Hindu gods are not so powerful, they had to bow before Muslim might, just as you too must subjugate yourselves to your new Mughal masters. That was the message of the Gyan Vapi mosque, and that was the message of the so-called Babri Masjid.

Now tell me, Mr. Diggs, is that a message that has any place in today's free and independent India? Is it not time to restore the pride of the local people in their own traditions, their own gods, their own worth, by rebuilding the Ram Janmabhoomi temple?

These fancy-pants administrators you are going to meet, Lakshman and Gurinder Singh, want us to call off our agitation because of the riot. Call it off? We will never do that, Mr. Diggs. Never! Because if we do, the Muslims will proclaim victory. They will think they have won, they will crow about our humiliation, and then, believe me, they will come and slaughter us in our beds.

There is the old story of the trooper standing guard with two drawn swords, one in each hand. An enemy soldier comes to him and slaps him across the face. The trooper does nothing and the enemy sneeringly walks away. "Why didn't you react when he slapped you?" asks a bystander. "But how could I?" replies the trooper. "Both my hands were occupied."

That trooper, Mr. Diggs, is Hindu India. We have the swords in our hands but we do not use them even when we are repeatedly slapped. Well, those days are over. We know how to fight back now, with what is in our hands.

Guru Golwalkar, the longest serving Hindu leader this century said it very clearly, years ago: "The non-Hindu people in Hindustan must adopt the Hindu culture and language, must learn to respect and hold in reverence Hindu religion, must entertain no ideas but those of the glorification of the Hindu race and culture, i.e., they must not only give up their attitude of intolerance and ungratefulness towards this land and its age-old tradition but must also cultivate the positive attitude of love and devotion instead — in a word, they must cease to be foreigners, or may stay in the country wholly subordinate to the Hindu nation, claiming, deserving no privileges, much less any preferential treatment — not even citizen's rights." That is the message to these evil Muslims. As you say in your country, they better believe it.

No, the Ram Janmabhoomi temple will be built. No matter how many lives have to be sacrificed to ensure it. Our blood will irrigate the dusty soil, our sweat will mix the cement instead of water, but we will build the temple, Mr. Diggs. Mark my words. I have seen the light in the eyes of the young boys in our procession, even the very ones who were stabbed. It is not just religious fervor that makes their eyes shine, Mr. Diggs. It is the look of victory — as if some spark that has been stamped on for forty years has suddenly blazed again. This light will not be easily put out. It will shine, yes, and it will illuminate the whole of India with its flame.

from Randy Diggs's notebook

October 14, 1989

Gurinder Singh: tough cop. Turban, fierce beard, Sikh. Smart.
Honest? Talks straight. Curses (a lot). Drinks (a lot). "I'm Sikh
enough not to smoke and Punjabi enough to drink like an
Ambassador. I don't mean the diplomatic piss-artist: I mean I guzzle
like that steel behemoth of an Ambassador car we make here."

GS and Lakshman make an odd pair at the helm of the district,
but to all appearances a good one. They're old buddies, sort of. This
from an interview, unprintables deleted: "We weren't exactly close
friends in college. You can see the differences. Lucky's an intellectual
type with a sensitive soul. I'm down-to-earth, a man of action. He
reads books in his spare time; I run. At college he studied English; I
did history. He debated and edited the campus rag; I played [field]
hockey. He's vegetarian; I bunked [skipped] the mess hall the one
day of the week they didn't serve meat. He's a teetotaler; I always
had a bottle of rum under my bed. But I liked the fellow for two
reasons: he's smart and he's honest. So when he ran for president of
the College Union against one of my hockey teammates, a fellow
with as much wood between his ears as in his hands on the field, I
supported Lucky. Made me a bit unpopular with the rest of the
hockey team. But he was the better candidate, and the better man.
I'm glad to be working with him in bloody Zalilgarh."

The pair seem to have made the same sets of enemies. Which
suggests they must work well together.

from transcript of Randy Diggs interview with Superintendent of Police Gurinder Singh

October 14, 1989

RD: So you and the district magistrate couldn't stop the procession from going ahead even after the stabbing incident that night?

GS: You're right. We did our damnedest, you know. Of course, the bloody perpetrators were absconding. But I spent the night arresting every Muslim troublemaker I could think of. If you owned a motorcycle and didn't own a foreskin, I locked you up. Then Lucky and I—

RD: Lucky?

GS: Lakshman. Sorry. I call him Lucky. A college nickname. He calls me Guru. Except when he's issuing orders. Anyway, Lucky and I called in the Hindu leaders at dawn. Buggers came in rubbing the sleep from their eyes. Only made them look more bloodshot and murderous, the bastards. Told them we'd made the arrests, pleaded for calm, asked them to forget their little procession. You'd have thought we'd asked them to sell us their daughters. One of them, a fat little runt called Sharma, got so hysterical I thought his eyes would pop right out of his fucking head. No, they were determined to go ahead.

RD: And you couldn't stop them?

GS: Not really. Actually, Lucky had already asked for permission to ban the procession. Well before the bloody stabbing. But he'd been denied by Lucknow. So, without an okay from the state government,

126

that really wasn't an option. In any case, there were already some twenty-five to thirty thousand Hindutva volunteers assembled in Zalilgarh. Buggers were determined and as charged up as the batteries on their megaphones. Lucky and I realized that if we attempted to halt the procession by force at this stage we were doomed to fail. It was a pissing certainty that police action would lead only to large-scale violence and killings. Don't forget that at that point I was also outnumbered — I had a few hundred cops to their thirty thousand motherloving zealots. So we tried persuasion.

RD: And it didn't work.

GS: You're right — it didn't work. They were as stubborn a bunch of bastards as ever smeared ash on their foreheads. Want a refill on that drink?

RD: No, thanks. But you go ahead. So you gave up?

GS: No, dammit, we didn't give up. What the hell do you think we are, a bunch of pansies? We tried to get them to change their route, to avoid Muslim areas and in particular mosques. They wouldn't agree to that either. Finally Lucky and I felt we had no choice. Our only option seemed to be to let the procession pass — but with intensive control and regulation.

RD: Meaning what exactly?

GS: Bloody soda's flatter than a hijra's chest. This is like drinking dog's piss, if you ask me. <u>Jaswinder! Soda hai?</u> Anyway — sorry, what was it? Something else you asked me.

RD: What did your "intensive control and regulation" mean?

GS: Standard stuff, man. We imposed pretty stiff conditions on them. Oh, Lucky was stern and uncompromising that morning. The buggers could march, but they had to forget about beating drums or cymbals near the mosques. They wanted to carry stuff, fine — but they could carry placards, not weapons. None of this brandishing of swords and trishuls — you know, Shiva's trident, which so many of these saffron-robed monks love to wave about the pissing place. And none of their anti-Muslim slogans of hate, calculated to insult the other motherlovers into rash retaliation.

RD: What sort of slogans?

GS: Pretty rabid ones. In fact, there had been a couple of weeks of sustained, offensive sloganeering before the stabbing incident, so we knew how words could inflame passions. Every day as the bastards prepared for their march, hundreds of young Hindu men would gather in the Muslim parts of town and shout slogans, abusing Muslims, taunting them, goading them. Sometimes they'd roar into the mohallas on motorbikes, revving their engines before shouting their provocations. "Mussalmaan ke do hi sthaan / Pakistan ya kabristan" — "There are only two places for a Muslim, Pakistan or the cemetery." It got worse: "Jo kahta hai Ali Ali / Uski ma ko choddo gali gali" — "He who calls out to Ali, fuck his mother in every alley." Of course the bastards did this during the day, when most of the Muslim men were away at work and the women and kids were cowering in their homes. Some of their slogans were aimed at bolstering the courage of the waverers among the Hindus. "Jis Hindu ka khoon na khaule / Khoon nahin hai pani hai" — "The Hindu whose blood doesn't boil has water in his veins." Or "Jo Janmabhoomi ke kaam na aaye / Woh bekaar jawaani hai" — "He who does not work for the Janmabhoomi is a useless youth." And of course the usual affirmations that "Mandir wahin banayenge" — "The temple will be built right there." That is, where the mosque stands. It may not sound like much, but when you hear these words in the throats of a hundred lusty young men on noisy motorbikes, revving their rage between shouts, you understand how maddened with fear the Muslims became. Whichever pissing Englishman wrote "sticks and stones may break my bones, but words can never hurt me" had never been within sniffing distance of a slogan-shouting Indian mob. Words can hurt you, my friend. These words did. I have no doubt they led directly to the stabbing incident the night before the procession.

RD: So Mr. Lakshman tried to ban the slogan-eering?

GS: Along with all the other things I mentioned. Agree to the conditions, he said, or no march; my good friend the stern cop here will withdraw police permission for your procession. And I nodded, giving my sinister smile. It was a bluff, but they couldn't take the chance that it mightn't be. So they agreed. And then Lucky pulled out a sheet of paper and a pen and asked the leaders of all the main Hindu parties to give us these commitments in writing. Bugger-all good that did, as it turned out.

RD: So they didn't keep their promises?

GS: Lucky seemed to think it would make a difference if they signed something. But frankly, I never thought it would amount to a pisspot full of spit. Someone who doesn't intend to keep an oral promise doesn't suddenly become more trustworthy because he puts it in writing. Their signatures weren't worth a rat's fart on a cold day, if you'll pardon my Punjabi. So I planned an extensive police presence anyway. Throughout the route of the bleeding march — cops at every corner and crossing, more in front of the mosques and sensitive neighborhoods, plus pickets of the Provincial Armed Constabulary, called in from neighboring districts where they'd been dealing with the same sort of crap. We really did everything we fucking could, Mr. Diggs. But it wasn't enough.

RD: Tell me what happened.

GS: Well, the procession began as scheduled. And it was bloody apparent that it was going to be a problem. I'd never seen anything like it myself—

RD: You mean in size?

GS: Size, passion, militancy. Lucky and I were there, of course. He was clutching the piece of paper these bastards had all signed. Bhushan Sharma, Ram Charan Gupta, the whole lot of them, bloody hypocrites to a man. All their written assurances weren't worth the cost of that single sheet of paper. They weren't worth the sweat on Lucky's hand that dampened that sheet every time he disbelievingly reread the undertakings they were openly violating. Restraint in sloganeering? Forget it — the most vulgar and vicious slogans were screamed out by the marchers, initiated by some of our precious signatories. No weapons? The procession was swarming with trishuls and naked daggers, which they flashed and pumped up and down as if practicing for a fucking javelin-throwing contest. Tie those bastards to a hydel generator, and you could have powered the pissing town for weeks. All this was bad enough, but then the leaders suddenly tried to steer the procession into the heart of the Muslim bastis. Just to provoke a reaction. Mind you, this was something they had specifically promised not to do, the sons of bitches. But I hadn't trusted their promise anyway, so my men were in place, and we stopped their little attempted detour. We firmly pushed the slimy sisterloving marchers back to the agreed route.

RD: So you were able to keep things under control for a while.

GS: Yeah, for a while. But how the fuck do you control thirty thousand people on a hot September day if they're determined to make trouble? The sun was getting higher, and so was the temper of the mob. By noon our shirts were soaked with sweat.

Here, have another drink. I could certainly use one.

RD: Thanks.

GS: It was tense, man. Tense. Want me to paint a picture for you? A seemingly endless procession, winding its way slowly, tortuously damned slowly, through the narrow lanes. Dust swirling upwards from their tramping feet. Chauvinist slogans rending the bloody air. Get it? Imagine the scene: The heat. The noise. The confusion. The hatred being spewed. The bloody adrenaline flowing. Those blasted blades flashing in the sun. People pumped up, thirsty, hoarse. Shouting.

RD: Then what happened?

GS: As it passed the main mosque, the procession paused, as if to attack. Lucky's executive magistrates and my police had to physically push the frenzied young buggers onward. In case they forgot they were here to march and turned on the mosque instead.

RD: And the Muslims of the town? Where were they while this was going on in their neighborhood?

GS: At this point, they were all barricaded in their bloody homes. No Muslim was seen out of doors. Not even a circumcised mouse.

RD: Go on. What happened next?

GS: By midafternoon about two-thirds of the procession had passed by the Muslim bastis. Lucky and I began to believe we were going to get away with it. Without the explosion we'd both feared. We should have known we were as likely to escape untouched as a whore at a stag party. Ah! — some fresh soda at last.

Where were we? Yes, we were standing at the crossroads before one particular mosque. Not the main one. A smaller mosque, which had been the site

131

of several communal battles in the past. The Mohammed Ali Mosque, I think it's called. Doesn't matter. In fact that was the mosque where we predicted the frenzy of the procession would reach its climax. That's why we were both there. Bloody DM and twice-bloody SP. Pushing the crowd forward. Acutely alert for a clash. That's the damnedest bloody thing, Mr. Diggs. We were there, prepared for the worst. We weren't even taken by surprise.

RD: You can call me Randy.

GS: Only when I've seen you with a woman. But go on, have another. Soda's okay now. You can't let me drink alone.

RD: Thanks. Actually, it's short for Randolph. But please go on.

GS: As I said, we were prepared. We had prevented an attack on the main mosque. We thought we were seeing this through. Then, suddenly, a bunch of young men came running, in absolute panic. Running from the opposite direction, that is, towards our part of the procession. They were shouting. At first we couldn't hear what they were saying. I even thought they might be Muslims charging the marchers. But they were Hindu all right. And the agitation on their faces suggested something else. They were screaming, "They're attacking us! Bomb maar rahen hain!" — they're bombing us. Who? we asked, and of course the answer came, the Muslims. The Muslims had thrown a bomb into the crowd and a Hindu processionist had been killed. Shit — this was it, the moment we'd feared. Lucky and I ran immediately to the spot. It was barely a hundred meters away. The enraged crowd had gathered round a young man who was lying bleeding on the ground. His chest had been torn open by a crude bomb. His life was quickly ebbing away. People were screaming their fear and rage. The mood was uglier than a hijra's crotch. Lucky quickly lifted the youth into his car, which was waiting nearby, and

132

told the driver to rush him to hospital. He died before he got there.

RD: The first victim.

GS: You're bloody right. The first victim. Lucky and I had a job to do. We were confronting an infuriated mob screaming for bleeding vengeance. We knew that if we didn't act immediately, we'd have a lynch mob on our hands. They'd be running wild through the Muslim bastis. We had to deal with the provocation before it got out of control.

RD: Sounds like it already had.

GS: Look, it was one death so far. We were fearing hundreds. It was pretty clear to me, after a couple of questions, <u>where</u> the bomb had been hurled from. There was a small double-storied house in a very narrow by-lane. This lane branched off, as crooked as a beaten mongrel's leg, from the main lane of the Muslim quarter through which the procession was passing. The idiots who'd thrown it had clearly made a stupid little calculation in those twisted little minds they keep up their ass somewhere. They figured the first bomb would bring the procession to a halt. Then the enraged mob would rush the house. Once the crowd was near the house, these stupid buggers would throw their little collection of homemade bombs from above. Kill a lot of the marchers — that was their only thought. If "thought" isn't too strong a word for their stinking little scheme. And they'd have accounted for a few Hindu fanatics, I have to grant them that.

RD: But they'd have been killed too. Their house could have been burned down.

GS: You're right. Though it wasn't their own house. But don't look for rational thinking in communal riots, Randy. These buggers had been at the receiving end of insults and slogans and petty offenses of all sorts for days leading up to the

Ram Sila Poojan. They were maddened like a chained animal that's been regularly prodded. Of course the poor bastards felt it was time to retaliate.

RD: But the Muslims had already taken action, right? With the motorcycle assault? Was there any connection?

GS: Different buggers. But it was the same sort of attitude that prompted the Muslims on the motorcycles the previous night to stab those Hindu boys. You don't think as far as the next step. You just want to do something, now.

RD: Was the crowd already at the house when you got there?

GS: No, Lucky and I had run to the spot as soon as we heard of the incident. People were still in shock, focusing on the wounded boy. Once we got him off in the DM's car, though, we knew the crowd would become a mob. And mobs want only one thing. Revenge.

from Lakshman's journal

June 2, 1989

We speak, inevitably, about writing. I picked up her scrapbook once without asking her, and she snatched it away with a little scream. These Americans and their exaggerated sense of privacy! I paraphrased Wilde: "Everyone should keep a diary — preferably somebody else's." She wouldn't budge. So I needled her enough to get her to show me some things in it. Not the very personal stuff — about me, perhaps? — but her creative musings, poems, sketches. She's not a bad poet. There's one on Zalilgarh, written last Christmas, that's probably good enough to be published. I tell her so, and she blushes. She doesn't write for publication, she tells me, only for herself. Everything in her scrapbook is for herself, and no one else.

"What's the point, then?" I demand. "Ever since college I've been struggling to find the time to write because I have something to say to the world, and here you have the time to write and you want no one to read it."

That gets us onto my own writing — my erratic, disorganized, unfocused writing, my whenever-I-can-find-the-time-and-the-mood writing, my escaping-from-Geetha writing. I am defensive, almost embarrassed, about my poetry; I do not mention my journal. But I think aloud about fiction.

"I'd like to write a novel," I tell her, "that doesn't read like a novel. Novels are too easy — they tell a story, in a linear narrative, from start to finish. They've done that for decades. Centuries, perhaps. I'd do it differently."

She raises herself on an elbow. "You mean, write an epic?"

"No," I reply shortly, "someone's done that already. I've read about this chap who's just reinvented the Mahabharata as a twentieth-century story — epic style, oral tradition, narrative

135

digressions, the lot. No, what I mean is, why can't I write a novel that reads like — like an encyclopedia?"

"An encyclopedia?" She sounds dubious.

"Well, a short one. What I mean is, something in which you can turn to any page and read. You pick up chapter 23, and you get one thread of the plot. Then you go forwards to chapter 37, or backwards to 16, and you get another thread. And they're all interconnected, but you see the interconnections differently depending on the order in which you read them. It's like each bit of reading adds to the sum total of the reader's knowledge, just like an encyclopedia. But to each new bit of reading he brings the knowledge he's acquired up to that point — so that each chapter means more, or less, depending on how much he's learned already."

"What if she," Priscilla asks in pointed feminism, "begins at the end?"

"It won't matter," I respond excitedly. "The beginning foretells the end. Down with the omniscient narrator! It's time for the omniscient reader. Let the reader construct her own novel each time she reads it."

Priscilla bites her lip, as she always does before saying something she's afraid I won't like. "I don't know if this can work," she says slowly.

"Maybe not," I reply with cheerful defiance. "But you know what Wilde said about form being more important than content. But of course I'd have all the classic elements of the novel in it. You know, the ancient Sanskrit text on drama, the Natya Shastra, prescribes the nine essential emotional elements that must go into any work of entertainment: love, hate, joy, sorrow, pity, disgust, courage, pride and compassion. They'd all be there. Every single one of the nine tenets of the sages would be included. But why bother to do it conventionally? Can't you write a novel about, say, religion without describing a single temple or mosque? Why must you burden your readers with the chants of the priests, the orations of the mullahs, the oppressive air of devotion? Let your readers bring themselves to the book they're reading! Let them bring to the page their own memories of love and hate, their own feelings of joy and sorrow, their own reactions of disgust and pity, their own stirrings of courage and pride and compassion. And if they do that, why should

136

form matter? Let the form of the novel change with each reading, and let the content change too."

"But how will any reader understand the truth?"

"The truth! The singular thing about truth, my dear, is that you can only speak of it in the plural. Doesn't your understanding of the truth depend on how you approach it? On how much you know?"

She bites her lip. "Either something is true, or it's not," she says at last.

"Not so, my darling," I declare. "Truth is elusive, subtle, many-sided. You know, Priscilla, there's an old Hindu story about Truth. It seems a brash young warrior sought the hand of a beautiful princess. Her father, the king, thought he was a bit too cocksure and callow. He decreed that the warrior could only marry the princess after he had found Truth. So the warrior set out into the world on a quest for Truth. He went to temples and monasteries, to mountaintops where sages meditated, to remote forests where ascetics scourged themselves, but nowhere could he find Truth. Despairing one day and seeking shelter from a thunderstorm, he took refuge in a musty cave. There was an old crone there, a hag with matted hair and warts on her face, the skin hanging loose from her bony limbs, her teeth yellow and rotting, her breath malodorous. But as he spoke to her, with each question she answered, he realized he had come to the end of his journey: she was Truth. They spoke all night, and when the storm cleared, the warrior told her he had fulfilled his quest. 'Now that I have found Truth,' he said, 'what shall I tell them at the palace about you?' The wizened old creature smiled. 'Tell them,' she said, 'tell them that I am young and beautiful.'"

from Priscilla's scrapbook

June 22, 1989

He gave me another poem today. "You know so little about me,"
he said. "This is something about my high school years, in Calcutta,
the building where my parents lived. It's a bit all over the place, but
then so was I at that time."

Another self-conscious one-liner. The poem must mean a lot to
him.

Minto Park, Calcutta, 1969–71

The road bends still in my outstretched mind
into the narrow lane bounded by grey battlements
looming castle-like above the ground,
disguising their true function
as "servants' quarters," to which
cooks and houseboys would retire
after the last drink was drunk, the last dish washed.

Behind the battlements stood my building — one of two,
    both grey
and stately — set on manicured asphalt,
with the luxury of a garden beneath, where
frangipani and bougainvillea wafted scents into the air
like the shuttlecocks of the badminton players
next door, launched with the confidence that sent cricket balls
blazing from adolescent bats through the wire fence
into another exclusive address, the Bhowanipore Cemetery.

I would search for the balls there, amongst weed-littered graves,
stumbling across a crumbling tombstone to a little English boy
taken away by malaria, aged nine, a hundred years ago;
or hear the jackals cry at night, their howls a faint echo
of the processions down the road from the maidan,
spewing fear and political anger into the sultry air.
We kept them out, behind the fence, outside the battlements.

When power cuts came ("load-shedding" the favored
   euphemism)
to the rest of the smoke-numbed city, we basked in an
oasis of privilege, our electricity connected to the
Alipore Jail, the Shambhu Nath Pandit Hospital, the lunatic
   asylum,
all too dangerous to be plunged into darkness. Hope like a
   lamp
glimmered on our desks. Luck (and good connections)
lit our way into the future.

At the corner of D. L. Khan Road sat the Victoria Memorial,
her marble skirt billowing with complacent majesty,
as potbellied boxwallahs took their constitutionals
in her shade. Young wrestlers performed their morning asanas
on the lawns, their contortions a widow's legacy. Traffic
   belched its way
across Lower Circular Road. The world muddled through.

In my building, the Asian Paints manager, cuckolded by his
   bachelor neighbor,
traveled often, leaving his gangling cricket-mad son to dream
of emigration to Australia. The bosomy nymphet four floors up
kissed me wetly on the lips one night, then took up with a boy
years older, a commerce student. They are now married.
Just above us was the executive who resembled a Bollywood
   star.

My mother's friends swooned if they passed him near the lift.
High up, kind Mr. Luthra, white-haired and gentle, went
    higher still
one night, his last words to his wife "I don't want to die."
He always haunts the building in my mind, fighting to live.

Down the street, the muezzin wails, calling the Muslim faithful
to prayer. They must jostle past the bell-jingling Hindus
trotting to the Ganesh mandir in the middle of the street,
    their devotions
drowned out by the loudspeakers outside the domed
    gurudwara,
chanting verses from the Granth Sahib. My favorite Jesuit priest
cycles to jail, bringing succor to prisoners. The millionaire
    brewer's son
drives by in his open Sunbeam, racing noisily past the
    complacent cow
grazing idly at the corner. Peace flaps in the wind like washing.

The world we lived in was two worlds,
and we spoke both its languages. In the night
we dreamt of school, and exams, and life,
while the day burned slowly like a basti brazier,
blackening the air we breathed. Naxalites drew proletarian
    blood
while refugees poured into our streets,
children of a Bangladesh waiting to be born.
In the distance, the politicians' loudspeakers growled like
    tanks
rumbling across the border to craft another people's destiny.
The sun seared away our patience.

Behind the battlements, we slept, and lived, and studied,
never quite finishing the last drink, nor emptying the last dish.
Poor cousins from the country stayed with us

till shorthand classes and my father's friendships
won them jobs. We raised funds for Mother Teresa.
The future stretched before us like the sea.

At dawn the saffron spread across our fingers,
staining our hearts with light.

Lakshman to Priscilla

July 1, 1989

Isn't it lovely here? I could sit with you and look across the river at the sky as the sun sets completely, feel the darkness settle on our shoulders like a cloak, and forget everything, especially the hatreds that are slowly being stoked in the town even as we speak. It almost moves me to prayer.

Why do I pray? And how? And to whom? So many questions! Well, I'm a Hindu — I was born one, and I've never been attracted to any other faith. I'll tell you why in a minute. How do I pray? Not in any organized form, really; I go to temples sometimes with my family, but they leave me cold. I think of prayer as something intensely personal, a way of reaching my hands out towards my maker. I recite some mantras my parents taught me as a child; there is something reassuring about those ancient words, hallowed by use and repetition over thousands of years. Sacred Sanskrit, a language alive only in heaven and kept from dying here on earth so that we can be understood when we address the gods. But I often supplement the mantras with incantations of my own in Tamil or English, asking for certain kinds of guidance or protection for myself or those I love. These days I mention you a lot in my prayers.

Yes, I pray to Hindu gods. It's not that I believe that there is, somewhere in heaven, a god that looks like a Bombay calendar artist's image of him. It's simply that prayer is a way of acknowledging a divinity beyond human experience; and since no human has had direct sight of God, all visual representations of the divine are merely crutches, helping flawed and limited human beings to imagine the unimaginable. Why not a corpulent elephant-headed god with a broken tusk? Why is that image any less real or inspiring of devotion than a suffering man on a cross? So yes, I pray to Ganapathi, and to Vishnu and Shiva, and to my memory of a faded calendar portrait of

142

Rama and Sita in my parents' prayer room. These are just ways of imagining God, and I pray in order to touch those forces and sources of life that go beyond the human. Human beings, to me, are rather like electrical appliances that need to be charged regularly, and prayer is a way of plugging into that charge.

So I'm not embarrassed to say I'm a believing Hindu. But I don't have anything in common with these so-called Hindu fundamentalists. Actually, it's a bit odd to speak of "Hindu fundamentalism," because Hinduism is a religion without fundamentals: no organized church, no compulsory beliefs or rites of worship, no single sacred book. The name itself denotes something less, and more, than a set of theological beliefs. In many languages — French and Persian amongst them — the word for "Indian" is "Hindu." Originally "Hindu" simply meant the people beyond the river Sindhu, or Indus. But the Indus is now in Islamic Pakistan; and to make matters worse, the word "Hindu" did not exist in any Indian language till its use by foreigners gave Indians a term for self-definition.

My wife's in the Shiva temple right now, praying. In all the chants she's hearing, the word "Hindu" will not be uttered. In fact, Priscilla, "Hinduism" is the name others applied to the indigenous religion of India, which many Hindus simply call Sanatan Dharma, the eternal faith. It embraces an eclectic range of doctrines and practices, from pantheism to agnosticism and from faith in reincarnation to belief in the caste system. But none of these constitutes an obligatory credo for a Hindu: there are none.

You know, I grew up in a Hindu household. Our home (and my father moved a dozen times in his working life) always had a prayer alcove, where paintings and portraits of assorted divinities jostled for shelf and wall space with fading photographs of departed ancestors, all stained by ash scattered from the incense burned daily by my devout parents. Every morning, after his bath, my father would stand in front of the prayer alcove wrapped in his towel, his wet hair still uncombed, and chant his Sanskrit mantras. But he never obliged me to join him; he exemplified the Hindu idea that religion is an intensely personal matter, that prayer is between you and whatever image of your maker you choose to worship. In the Hindu way, I was to find my own truth.

Like most Hindus, I think I have. I am, as I told you, a believer, despite a brief period of schoolboy atheism — of the kind that comes with the discovery of rationality and goes with an acknowledgement of its limitations. And, I suppose, with the realization that the world offers too many wondrous mysteries for which science has no answers. And I am happy to describe myself as a believing Hindu, not just because it is the faith into which I was born, but for a string of other reasons, though faith requires no reason. One is cultural: as a Hindu I belong to a faith that expresses the ancient genius of my own people. Another is, for lack of a better phrase, its intellectual "fit": I am more comfortable with the belief structures of Hinduism than I would be with those of the other faiths of which I know. As a Hindu I claim adherence to a religion without an established church or priestly papacy, a religion whose rituals and customs I am free to reject, a religion that does not oblige me to demonstrate my faith by any visible sign, by subsuming my identity in any collectivity, not even by a specific day or time or frequency of worship. There's no Hindu pope, Priscilla, no Hindu Sunday. As a Hindu I subscribe to a creed that is free of the restrictive dogmas of holy writ, that refuses to be shackled to the limitations of a single holy book.

Above all, as a Hindu I belong to the only major religion in the world that does not claim to be the only true religion. I find it immensely congenial to be able to face my fellow human beings of other faiths without being burdened by the conviction that I am embarked upon a "true path" that they have missed. This dogma lies at the core of religions like Christianity, Islam, and Judaism. Take your faith: "I am the Way, the Truth, and the Life; no man cometh unto the Father, but by me," says the Bible. Book of John, right? chapter 14, verse 6; look it up, I did. Or Islam: "There is no God but Allah and Mohammed is his Prophet," declares the Koran — denying unbelievers all possibility of redemption, let alone of salvation or paradise. Hinduism, however, asserts that all ways of belief are equally valid, and Hindus readily venerate the saints, and the sacred objects, of other faiths. There is no such thing as a Hindu heresy.

How can such a religion lend itself to "fundamentalism"? That devotees of this essentially tolerant faith want to desecrate a shrine, that they're going around assaulting Muslims in its name, is to me a source of shame and sorrow. India has survived the Aryans, the Mughals, the British; it has taken from each — language, art, food, learning — and grown with all of them. To be Indian is to be part of an elusive dream we all share, a dream that fills our minds with sounds, words, flavors from many sources that we cannot easily identify. Muslim invaders may indeed have destroyed Hindu temples, putting mosques in their place, but this did not — could not — destroy the Indian dream. Nor did Hinduism suffer a fatal blow. Large, eclectic, agglomerative, the Hinduism that I know understands that faith is a matter of hearts and minds, not of bricks and stone. "Build Ram in your heart," the Hindu is enjoined; and if Ram is in your heart, it will matter little where else he is, or is not.

Why should today's Muslims have to pay a price for what Muslims may have done four hundred and fifty years ago? It's just politics, Priscilla. The twentieth-century politics of deprivation has eroded the culture's confidence. Hindu chauvinism has emerged from the competition for resources in a contentious democracy. Politicians of all faiths across India seek to mobilize voters by appealing to narrow identities. By seeking votes in the name of religion, caste, and region, they have urged voters to define themselves on these lines. Indians have been made more conscious than ever before of what divides us.

And so these fanatics in Zalilgarh want to tear down the Babri Masjid and construct a Ram Janmabhoomi temple in its place. I am not amongst the Indian secularists who oppose agitation because they reject the historical basis of the claim that the mosque stood on the site of Rama's birth. They may be right, they may be wrong, but to me what matters is what most people believe, for their beliefs offer a sounder basis for public policy than the historians' footnotes. And it would work better. Instead of saying to impassioned Hindus, "You are wrong, there is no proof this was Ram's birthplace, there is no proof that the temple Babar demolished to build this mosque was a temple to Ram, go away and leave the mosque in place," how much more effective might it have been to say, "You may be right, let us assume for a moment that there was a Ram Janmabhoomi temple here that was destroyed to make room for this mosque four hundred and sixty years ago, does that mean we should behave in that way today? If the Muslims of the 1520s acted out of ignorance and fanaticism, should Hindus act the same way in the 1980s? By doing what you propose to do, you will hurt the feelings of the Muslims of today, who did not perpetrate the injustices of the past and who are in no position to inflict injustice upon you today; you will provoke violence and rage against your own kind; you will tarnish the name of the Hindu people across the world; and you will irreparably damage your own cause. Is this worth it?"

That's what I've been trying to say to people like Ram Charan Gupta and Bhushan Sharma and their bigoted ilk. But they don't listen. They look at me as if I'm sort of a deracinated alien being who can't understand how normal people think. Look, I understand Hindus who see a double standard at work here. Muslims say they are proud to be Muslim, Sikhs say they are proud to be Sikh, Christians say they are proud to be Christian, and Hindus say they are proud to be . . . secular. It is easy to see why this sequence should provoke the scorn of those Hindus who declaim, "Garv se kahon hum Hindu hain" — "Say with pride that we are Hindus." Gupta and Sharma never fail to spit that slogan at me. And I *am* proud of my Hinduism. But in what precisely am I, as a Hindu, to take pride? Hinduism is no monolith; its strength is found within each Hindu, not in the collectivity. As a Hindu, I take no pride in wanting to destroy other people's symbols, in hitting others on the head because of the cut of their beard or the cuts of their foreskins. I *am* proud of my Hinduism: I take pride in its diversity, in its openness, in religious freedom. When that great Hindu monk Swami Vivekananda electrified the World Parliament of Religions in Chicago in 1893, he said he was proud of Hinduism's acceptance of all religions as true; of the refuge given to Jews and Zoroastrians when they were persecuted elsewhere. And he quoted an ancient Hindu hymn: "As the different streams having their sources in different places all mingle their water in the sea, so, O lord, the different oaths which men take . . . all lead to thee." My own father taught me the Vedic sloka "Aa no bhadrah kratvo yantu vishwatah" — "Let noble thoughts come to us from all directions of the universe." Every schoolchild knows the motto

146

"Ekam sad viprah bahuda vadanti" — "Truth is one, the sages give it various names." Isn't this all-embracing doctrine worth being proud of?

But that's not what Mr. Gupta is proud of when he says he's proud to be a Hindu. He's speaking of Hinduism as a label of identity, not a set of humane beliefs; he's proud of being Hindu as if it were a team he belongs to, like a British football yob, not what the team stands for. I'll never let the likes of him define for me what being a Hindu means.

Defining a "Hindu" cause may partly be a political reaction to the definition of non-Hindu causes, but it is a foolish one for all that. Mahatma Gandhi was as devout a Rambhakt as you can get — he died from a Hindu assassin's bullet with the words "Hé Ram" on his lips — but he always said that for him, Ram and Rahim were the same deity, and that if Hinduism ever taught hatred of Islam or of non-Hindus, "it is doomed to destruction." The rage of the Hindu mobs being stoked by the bigots is the rage of those who feel themselves supplanted in this competition of identities, who think that they are taking their country back from usurpers of long ago. They want revenge against history, but they do not realize that history is its own revenge.

from transcript of Randy Diggs interview with Superintendent of Police Gurinder Singh

October 14, 1989

RD: I'll accept that drink now, thanks. What happened next?

GS: Lucky and I quickly realized that the only way the mob could be prevented from assembling below the house — the house from which the fucking bomb was thrown — was by getting there first ourselves. I grinned, and said to Lucky: "DM-sahib, time for us to take charge."

RD: They could have thrown their bombs at you.

GS: That was the risk, clearly. But it was an acceptable risk. To prevent a far bigger tragedy.

RD: And did the mob give way?

GS: We had to keep shouting to the pissing processionists that they should stay back. That we were taking charge of the situation. Fortunately their more rabid leaders, people like Bhushan Sharma or Ram Charan Gupta, were not in that part of the crowd. They were in the front of the motherloving procession, leading it for glory, and word had not reached them yet from where we were. Most of the crowd listened to us and stayed at bay. Inevitably, though, some bloody idiots with the brains of a squashed cockroach edged forward behind us as we headed towards the house.

RD: I've met Ram Charan Gupta.

GS: Our next member of Parliament for Zalilgarh. Or so the pissing political pundits tell me. Ironically, considering what we think of each

148

other, he publicly praised my handling of this particular incident.

RD: What did you do?

GS: I opened fire.

RD: What?!

GS: Look, you've got to understand. We not only had to take control of a situation that was on the verge of getting out of control. We also had to be seen by the bloodthirsty mob as taking effective action. What do you think we should have done? Knocked politely on the door and asked them to serve us some tea with their bombs? Once we'd got to the damned house from which the bomb was thrown, the choice was clear. Assert ourselves, or allow the mob to assert themselves. I ordered the ASI — the Assistant Sub-Inspector who accompanied me — to fire a couple of rounds at the house, and I let loose a burst or two myself. This served several purposes. First, the crowd was satisfied that effective action was being taken. So the bloody idiots understood that they did not need to take the law into their own hands. Second, the stream of bullets also intimidated the hotheads in the procession. Nothing like a volley from a good police-issue revolver to make an asshole think twice. This ensured that the crowd did not venture below the house and present easy targets for further bomb-throwing. And last but not least, as we always used to say in our high school debates, the firing also deterred the bombers themselves. Here they were, all poised and ready to throw more bombs, and my bullets come screaming in. What do they do? They were amateurs, Randy, and the first instinct of a frigging amateur when things get too hot is to drop everything and run. It's one thing to plan to chuck some bombs at a howling mob armed with knives and tridents. Quite another to take on policemen with guns.

RD: So what did they do?

GS: They ran away. They ran for their bloody
lives. The bombers were so frightened by our
firing they were pissing in their pants as they
tried to get the hell out of there. I sent a couple
of my men to the rear of the house. They caught one
of the young idiots. Took him down to the thana.
I'll spare you the details, but soon he was
singing like a mynah bird. Don't look so fucking
shocked, Randy. I've seen enough of your American
cop movies. Whatever they did to him to get the
full story, it was a good deal less than the Hindu
mob would have done. So I figure justice was served
all around. And thanks to him my police case was
very quickly closed.

RD: What was his story?

GS: The story? Very simple, very stupid. A small
bunch of young Muslims — eight youths, two of them
petty government servants, a municipal driver and
a patwari — decided that they had to retaliate
against the insults and provocations flung their
way by the Hindu extremists. Sisterloving idiots,
of course. But they felt alienated from the system — none of them was important enough to serve on
any of our bloody peace committees, for instance.
And they felt equally alienated from the mainstream of their own frigging community, which they
felt was too passive. "Don't we have pride?" one
of them asked me in the interrogation room. "Don't
you have brains?" I replied. I mean, just think
about their brilliant plan. They collected whatever money they could, which was not very much, a
few hundred rupees between them. Then one of them
went off to purchase gunpowder from a firecracker
factory in the neighboring district, where firecrackers are a frigging cottage industry. Place
isn't even a real factory. It's a factory the way
Zalilgarh's a town. Half their bloody phatakas
fizzle out at Diwali time. Anyway, this is their
great arsenal. The night before the major procession, Friday night, they stayed up in an abandoned

ruin by the riverside. We call it the Kotli. No one uses it. They ground the gunpowder with pieces of broken glass and old rusted nails, tied these in newspaper with a string, and made seventeen of what are known in local parlance as "soothli bombs." They figured that would account for a few dozen Hindus, and they hoped to run away in the confusion. They hadn't given any pissing thought at all to what would happen to the house they'd have bombed from, to the basti, to the neighbor-hood. Frigging idiots.

RD: Anyway, your tactic worked. Congratulations.

GS: Worked? For about five minutes. We defused one crisis, but we couldn't prevent the riot itself. Mobs were soon running rampant through the town, especially the Muslim quarter. Save your congratulations. I could use another drink.

from Lakshman's journal

July 16, 1989

I look into her eyes, into those eyes so impossibly blue, eyes of a color I have never looked into before, and I know she cannot understand.

How could I, so well-read, so overeducated, so comfortable with her Western culture, have had an arranged marriage? We talk of Updike and Bellow and the Time magazine bestseller list, I play her my tapes of Bob Dylan and Leonard Cohen and the Grateful Dead, she speaks of "Death of a Salesman" and I counter with "Who's Afraid of Virginia Woolf?" and it is as if we so comfortably inhabit the same world. But even as I hold her white hand in my own dark one, I know that for her these cultural references go together with other things, with Saturday dates in oversized Chevrolets and dressing up for the prom, with love and romance and sex before marriage. Not with the way I got married: parents contacting parents through intrusive intermediaries, a brief visit to the others' home for an elaborate tea, a glimpse of an overdressed girl and a conversation so stilted and artificial it could not possibly be the basis of a lifetime commitment, let alone one consecrated by matched horoscopes and gold jewelry and the gift of a house in Madras by her grateful father, proud to have an IAS officer for a son-in-law.

"But how could you?" Priscilla asks inevitably, when, in response to her questions, I tell her the story of my marriage to Geetha. We are in our favorite spot, the sunset room she calls it, at the top of the Kotli, and she is lying on me, the softness of her breasts pressed into my body, her face resting on my shoulder. We have just made love, and I feel she is entitled to anything, even an answer.

"It's just the way it's done," I reply. "It is the way it's always been done. It's how my parents were married."

"But you're different," she exclaims, half thumping me on the chest with her fists in mock exasperation. "You've been educated differently. You're so — so Western."

I imprison her fists in my hands, and it is as if I am praying, with her my votive offering. "I'm Indian," I say simply. "I enjoy the Beatles <u>and</u> Bharata Natyam. I act in Oscar Wilde plays and I eat with my fingers. I read Marx, and I let my parents arrange my marriage."

She raises herself a little to punctuate her reaction. "But didn't you care at all? After all, this was the person you were going to spend the rest of your life with."

I pull her down again, because I want to feel her body against mine, and because I don't want to look into her eyes, not at this point. "I didn't think of marriage that way," I say quietly. "I thought of it as an extension of my obligations to my parents, part of the duties of a good son. You in America think of marriage as two people loving each other and wanting to be together. We in India see marriage as an arrangement between families, a means of perpetuating the social order."

"But don't Indian men and women love one another?" Her voice is muffled against my chest; her long slender finger idly traces a pattern on my rib cage.

"Of course we do," I reply, "but love is supposed to come after marriage. How can you love someone until you know them, and how can you know them properly until after you're married to them?"

She is silent now, but her fingernail moves on, to my side.

"That tickles," I say.

"Shh," she replies. "I'm writing something." And her finger continues its elaborate curls and loops, stopping with a circled flourish. "Tell me what I wrote," she says.

"I don't know," I respond. "I wasn't aware you were writing till just now. The last letter was an O."

She giggles. "It was a period, silly," she says. "I'll write it again. Pay attention now."

She props herself up on me, and I am dazzled by the gold of the sunlight in her hair. Her breasts are round and milky, their small nipples pinkly aureoled. It is difficult to concentrate on the letters she is now tracing across my trunk. But she is determined to make it easy for me, and her finger moves in exaggerated strokes, pausing after each letter to test my comprehension.

"I," I say, and she nods delightedly. "L. O. U — no, V. F? F?" She shakes her head, underscoring the third spoke of the E across my belly. "E. I love — V again. What's this? I love Victor? Who's Victor?" But I am laughing too much, and she tickles me mercilessly, so I am obliged to concede. "Y. Y. I get it." Her exquisite finger draws a parabola that embraces my flabby belly, the hairs on my chest. "O." And then she traces it again, beginning at my right shoulder blade, her finger gliding silken on my skin, rising to my left shoulder, failing only to complete the circle at the top. "U."

"That's right," she says, and she is suddenly very serious, looking at me with that earnestness that struck me from the first as the hallmark of the expression with which she faced the world.

"I love you," I conclude, with a smile.

"I thought you'd never say it," she responds, but she is no longer looking so earnest. I bring her face down upon mine and kiss her so deeply that we are one body, one being, one breath.

"Wait — I have a message too," I say at last. I roll her over on the mat so that she is on her back. The light illuminates her still-startling paleness. As I loom over her she stretches her arms, her fingers entwining behind my neck. "But I'm not going to use my finger."

I bend and kiss each of her nipples. Then, slowly, gently, savoring each stroke, I trace the lines of my love with my tongue across the smooth velvet softness of her body. I cross the top and the bottom of my I, which confuses her at first, so I do it again, until she giggles with delight. My L begins with her right breast and ends at the bone above her left hip; my O takes in both nipples, now taut and redly rising; my V begins where my L had, descends till I have my nose buried in the soft blond down of her womanhood, then rises again, as she sighs, to end at her left breast; my E curves uninterruptedly like a Greek letter, my tongue a lambent caress, the middle prong of the letter quivering in her navel. By the time I am spelling out Y, O, U, she is moaning gently, her eyes closed, her legs parted beneath me, her breath shorter, but I am relentless, adding a T, its lower point plunging like a shaft into her moistness, and I have to do it again, because she is not expecting another word, and then she cries, "T," with a purr of pleasure rarely associated with the enunciation of the alphabet, and I rush through the two Os that follow, because my need is urgent too, and we spell it out in unison, "I love you too," our voices melding huskily with our bodies as I thrust myself into her.

And as I enter her I forget the roughness of the mat on the stone ledge in the alcove, as we move to our own rhythm I forget my wife, my work, my world, as her pelvis rises to meet mine I forget myself, and as she gasps in climax I burst into her like a flood, a flood of forgetting.

For there is so much to forget, as I lie embracing her afterwards, my fingers in her silken hair, my other hand softly caressing the hollow just above her hip, that curve which so delights me in her body. What must I forget? Geetha herself, my wife of nine loveless years, mother of my much-beloved Rekha; my work, waiting for me at my neglected desk, my driver pacing outside the gate, wondering what the Sahib could be doing for so long in the Kotli; and, harder still to ignore, the mounting communal tensions in this benighted town. Priscilla is consolation, she is escape, but she is more than that: she is a fantasy come true, the possibility of an alternative life, as if another planet had flung its doors open for me.

What benevolent God has brought her here to me, in irredeemable Zalilgarh? I could not have invented Priscilla if she did not exist: her luminous beauty, her intelligence and sincerity of purpose, her complete openness to me, the way she gives so fully of herself. She is that rare combination of innocence and sexual freedom that I now think of as peculiarly American. She has come to do good, to bring enlightenment to the poor women of the area, to convert this small corner of India to what she sees as the right way to live, and somewhere in her engagement with this place she has found me.

And I have found her. There is nothing more important in my life than our twice-weekly assignations. Twice weekly, every Tuesday

155

and Saturday just before sunset, as the dusk gathers around the Kotli like a shawl, we meet at the little secret room I had first taken her to (and first taken her in). We have had to agree on specific days and times in advance to reduce the visible communication between us, the peons bearing awkward notes, the stilted phone conversations always within earshot of others. And I look forward to Priscilla with barely suppressed excitement. Yes, excitement; the word is consciously chosen, because I have to admit I feel my anticipation between my legs as much as anywhere. Love has blossomed, too, but do we mean the same thing when we use the word? I cannot stop thinking of her; my days on the job are illuminated by images of her face and body and the memory of her touch. When I am with her I am in a constant state of exhilaration. I greet her with glee as she runs into my arms; I exult as she disrobes for me; I am ecstatic as we make — that word again — love.

Until Priscilla I had never really known the pleasure of sex. Geetha lies stiffly, unmoving, as I go about what she sees as my business; she neither initiates nor welcomes, making it clear that she understands her amatory role as being to endure rather than to enjoy. She is not one for much foreplay, and she is often still dry when I enter her, her eyes tightly shut, her face contorted in something approaching a grimace. When it is over I move quickly off her, lightened by no great sense of satiation. She turns away from me, her duty done. Not surprisingly, we make love less and less frequently. Since Priscilla entered my life, I have slept with Geetha just once. Neither of us misses it.

"Make love" — I used that compound verb again. And yet how absurd to describe sex with Priscilla with the same words I use for Geetha! Sex with Priscilla is joy, it is celebration; she gives as much as she takes; her body moves with as much rhythmic energy as mine. The process of carnal discovery is an endless delight. She is willing to try everything, and I find myself doing things I had only read about in books, only imagined in the daydreams of a masturbatory adolescence. Afterwards we talk, we idly envisage a long-term future, we share poetry, but for all that, our evenings together are suffused with a lingering lust. I think of her at the office, at the dining table, in the field, and I am instantly aroused.

As a good Hindu I should have an instinctive awareness of the power and the pitfalls of sexual pleasure. The Vedas, the Puranas, so many of the ancient sacred texts of my faith emphasize kama, sexual desire; it is the primordial urge, the first seed of human motivation, the progenitor of thought, the first of the four major goals of man — before wealth, religion, and salvation. Kama is even a god because desire is a sort of sacred energy. But it is precisely because Hinduism recognizes the power of kama that it teaches its adherents to suppress it, to store their energy by conserving their semen, to still their urges by turning to abstinence, meditation, and good works. Sexual desire, the old Hindu sages knew, was pleasurable but passing; it was a hindrance, not a help, in the great quest of man to break the eternal cycle of birth and rebirth.

And yet I have come to a point where I can no longer imagine a week without Priscilla, let alone a life. When I think of her returning to her unattainable homeland in October, as she is scheduled to do, and when I contemplate resuming the texture of my life before I knew her, I am seized with a wordless panic. And yet the alternative is equally unimaginable. Abandon my solemn responsibilities to my wife, my parents, my daughter, my extended family, her family, our caste? To run away with another woman? An American! And where will we go? To do what?

These are questions that I do not give voice to, but it is clear Priscilla is already contemplating the answers. I am beginning to worry that, like a careless paan eater, I may have bitten off more than I can chew. The paan eater spits out the residue in a long stream that looks like blood. In my case I am afraid to spit out what I have, and my blood churns inside me, thickening like quicksand.

birthday card for Lakshman

July 22, 1989

HAPY BRITHDAY TO THE BESTEST DADDY IN THE
HOLE WORLD
I LOVE U XXX REKHA

letter from Priscilla Hart to Cindy Valeriani

July 25, 1989

Cin, I don't want you to be alarmed or anything, but something a little disturbing happened to me today. You remember I mentioned a Muslim woman, Fatima Bi, who the extension worker from the Center took me to? The one with the seven kids, all scrawny and malnourished and wallowing in the dust, whose husband was refusing to let her use any protection? Kadambari, the extension worker, took me along to meet her so I could see at first hand the problems we're facing. The woman's exhausted from childbearing and child-rearing; she subsists in a hovel in the Muslim quarter — I nearly wrote "ghetto" — and she basically has no life. She's shut up in this dank shuttered apartment in an enclosed building off a lane that's basically an open sewer. (I thought I knew India from my years in Delhi, Cin, but to know India you've also got to come to a town like Zalilgarh and <u>smell</u> India.) Anyway, she's covered from head to toe in traditional garb — a long robe leaving only her face bare, but she also wears a scarf over her head, and I bet she has to put on a burqa when she goes out, if she ever does, poor thing. Fatima Bi's a thin, bucktoothed little woman with a prominent mole and an expression of chronic anxiety. She lives with her husband and seven kids in a two-room flat, cooks in the corner of one of the rooms on an open stove, uses a communal bathroom, washes their clothes at a public tap, and suffers the demands and the blows of her husband, to judge by a visibly bruised cheek.

Her husband's some sort of government employee, believe it or not, a chauffeur or something in one of the municipal offices here in Zalilgarh. His name's Ali. The man's actually proud of his seven children and says they're a testament to his virility. When poor Fatima Bi suggested that they couldn't afford any more he took that as a personal insult and beat her up. The woman says that what Ali brings home isn't enough to feed and clothe three children properly, let alone seven. So, at my suggestion, Kadambari and I gave her some condoms last week from the Center's demonstration stocks.

Bad idea. Of course he won't wear them — in fact it made him so angry when Fatima offered the package to him that he beat her up again and called her a filthy whore for even knowing that such things existed. Of course he also asked where she'd got them from and when she told him, he forbade all contact between her and the Center. Remember, she's one of the women who'd never be caught dead coming to the Center — that's why the Extension Worker goes to her. But to reinforce the message he came to the Center and demanded to see Kadambari and me. It was Wery unpleasant, as poor Mr. Shankar Das put it. Ali shouted at us, the veins in his throat throbbing in his fury, and told us never to darken his door again. Kadambari was a little scared, I could see that, but I started to say that it was his wife's right to have as much information as she needed to decide how to conduct her life. Boy, was that a dumb thing to do! Ali hit the roof. "I decide how my wife conducts her life!" he screamed. "Not her! And certainly not you!" (adding a few choice epithets in Urdu about me that Mr. Das asked Kadambari not to translate). And then he flung the packet of condoms in my face and stormed out.

It was all very upsetting, Cin, even though Mr. Das and Kadambari and all the others did their best to help me calm down. Women like Fatima are the very reason population-control awareness is so important; it's the whole reason I do what I'm doing. But I think of that poor thin woman being beaten by her husband because of what I told her she could do. I haven't empowered her in any way, and I've probably made things worse for someone whose life is miserable enough as it is. And I haven't done myself any favors either. That look of pure hatred on Ali's face was frankly terrifying. In the instant that he flung those condoms at me, I knew he would have done the same thing if he'd happened to be holding a stone, or a knife.

Oh, don't worry too much, Cindy. I'm probably just being a little melodramatic — the hysterical foreign woman in India, one of the long line starting with E. M. Forster's Adela Quested. I wanted to talk to Lucky about it when I saw him tonight, but all he wanted was to make love! (Which was very pleasant, and helped me feel a lot better. . . .)

transcript of Randy Diggs interview with District Magistrate V. Lakshman (Part 2)

October 13, 1989

It was exactly as we'd feared. The crowd now began to fan out in every direction, and many rushed straight to the Muslim bastis. I immediately ordered curfew. As the mob was running past, I went onto the mobile wireless to instruct the police and the magistrates who were already on duty in pickets at all sensitive points in the town, to impose curfew with a firm hand in the shortest possible time.

"Do I use force if necessary?" one asked.

"You may take whatever measures involving the use of force you deem necessary," I replied firmly, "including resort to firing, if need be."

I repeated that phrase a few more times to others.

Guru — the SP — and I jumped into the SP's jeep and drove straight to the "communally sensitive" bastis, the Muslim quarters. Things were bad already. The SP himself fired several rounds. From reports at the end of the day I learned that the police resorted to firing at three other places. But it worked. Curfew was fully imposed in the town in the brief space of twenty minutes.

However, even in these twenty minutes, seven lives were lost and scores of people injured, about a hundred Muslim houses and commercial establishments set ablaze, three mosques desecrated. Six of the deaths were caused by the daggers and other weapons carried by the mobs assaulting the Muslim bastis, including a country-made rifle. These six dead were all Muslims. One of them was a boy who brought me my tea at the office sometimes. I would always complain that he put in

162

too much sugar. The others used to call him Mitha Mohammed, Sweet Mohammed. He was always grinning, from ear to ear. They slit his throat with a dagger, and when I saw the body, the crooked line across his skin looked like a smile.

One Hindu died, too. He was killed by the bomb thrown by the Muslim extremists who fled, and who were largely arrested within minutes. Several dozen injured were rushed to hospitals.

Seven deaths in total. The figures had been much worse elsewhere; Zalilgarh had escaped relatively unscathed. I suppose I knew I would be congratulated for my handling of the situation. There were forty-seven injured, though, and lakhs of rupees of damaged property. I didn't know about Priscilla yet. But I felt no relief at all at the end of the day.

Oh, there were moments of high drama. At one point Gurinder, the SP, spotted a frenzied young man brandishing a 12-bore rifle. I have no idea whether he was Hindu or Muslim. At that point neither of us cared where the violence was coming from; we just wanted to stop it. The SP jumped off his jeep and walked towards the young man. He screamed at us, pointed his rifle at the SP and threatened to shoot. Undeterred, the SP kept moving, slowly advancing towards him. The young man looked wildly about, and the rifle wavered in his hands, but he did not fire. Tears were streaming down his face as the SP advanced, tears of rage and fear and sorrow, and his hands were trembling, the rifle jerking uncontrollably in his grasp. When the SP reached him he was practically begging to be saved from himself. Gurinder overpowered him, snatched his rifle, and forced him into a nearby house, which he locked from the outside. I never found out who the young man was, or what his story was. I knew he had reason to be out of his mind with fear. We never prosecuted him.

Soon an uneasy calm fell over the city under curfew. Additional force was called from neighboring districts, and permanent pickets established at all sensitive points. I pressed all my executive magistrates into duty, and spent the whole night scouring the city in mobile patrols with the police.

Gurinder was a hero. He cursed, he swore, he joked, he grinned maniacally, but he was everywhere by my side. Together we ordered large-scale preventive arrests and searches: that first night alone, 126 persons were arrested. Forty houses were searched. I remember these facts vividly because this is what running a district is all about. Overkill, perhaps. But better overkill, Gurinder liked to say, than kill over. Over and over again.

We couldn't forget the ones who had been killed — the ones we knew about, again excepting Priscilla. We had to contact their families, help control their grief, and above all ensure that each death didn't lead to five more. Funerals are the perfect excuse for violence; all that grief and rage looking for an outlet. So we talked to the families of the deceased, and organized quiet cremations and burials in the presence only of close family members, and the magistrates and the police. They weren't all that happy about it, but we took advantage of the fact that they were numbed by pain and grief, and we gave them no choice in the matter.

I decided there would be no relaxation of curfew for seventy-two hours. We kept things calm, except that four more mosques were extensively desecrated in the course of the night. The Muslim community leaders insisted that this could not have been possible without police complicity. Even Gurinder could not be sure that some of his own men hadn't connived at what happened.

That had probably been during the brief moments that we finally got some sleep. I felt terribly guilty: if I had stayed awake, continued on patrol, perhaps this wouldn't have happened. Gurinder and I snatched two hours of sleep in the

police station that Saturday night. We slept on
camp cots, fully dressed and ready to rush out at
the report of any clash. In any case, after two
hours' rest, we got up and resumed our patrols.
The people of Zalilgarh were to become deeply
familiar with our white Gypsy and its flashing red
light, endlessly prowling the shadowy and deserted
lanes and by-lanes of the town.

But who could have had time for sleep, or been
able to sleep if we found the time? The control
room we established was deluged by a continuous
barrage of complaints of mob assault, all of which
had to be checked out. Most proved to be untrue;
rumors were rife. The press was called in and
briefed. We made arrangements for the distribution
of newspapers throughout the city beginning the
next day, in order to control the rumors and dis-
information. The peace committee and responsible
leaders of the two communities were called in and
pressed into service. In the days to come, they
helped keep the calm.

I'm not trying to avoid talking about Priscilla
Hart. I just want to complete the picture of this
riot for you, Mr. Diggs, so you understand what we
were dealing with during those days. The damaged
mosques were certain to cause more trouble as soon
as the curfew was relaxed. So I mobilized the services of the Public Works Department to repair and
restore the desecrated mosques, overnight.
Overnight! I did so with the support of moderate
Muslim leaders, who had to be present while the
work was being done, to ensure that nothing sacri-
legious occurred during the repairs. When it was
done I was able to order the first relaxation of
the curfew, for two hours. The Muslims wended
their way straight to the mosques to offer
prayers, but the fresh paint and mortar told their
own story. The settlements that had suffered arson
looked as if they had been bombed. But except for a
solitary explosion just before curfew relaxation
was to end — an explosion in which no one was

injured — there were no major setbacks during this first easing of curfew.

One more thing, while I'm giving you this portrait of the riot. On the second morning of the curfew, I received a flash message on the mobile wireless that over two hundred women and children in a Muslim mohalla had poured onto the streets, defying the curfew. I got Gurinder and rushed there. There was a throng of women, most in veils or burqas, almost all accompanied by wailing children. Amidst the disconsolate weeping, one woman said: "There is now not a grain of food or a drop of milk in our homes. Our men have either been rounded up by the police or have run away and are in hiding. We earn and eat from day to day. It's all very well for you to impose a curfew. But how long can we let our children starve?"

I didn't have a good answer to the woman, but I promised her I would find one. In my heart I had to do something for the sake of Priscilla, who had worked so hard for the Muslim women of Zalilgarh. I went back to the police station and immediately sent for all the senior district officers. "Right," I said. "You've kept the peace. Now you have an additional job. You're in charge of ensuring civil supplies. Get the wholesale traders to open their godowns. Organize mobile vans with essential commodities for each mohalla. We've got to get food to families."

"And what about the curfew?" one fellow asked. "If we lift it to distribute food, we'll soon be back where we started."

"No," I replied. "We'll lift the curfew only for women during the visits of the mobile vans to each mohalla. During this time they can make their purchases. Any man who ventures out will still be in violation of the curfew." This one's for you, Priscilla, I thought.

"What about those who can't afford to make purchases?" another asked. "Many of them are day laborers. They eat when they work. They won't have spare cash sitting around for food. Especially in some of the poorer bastis, and the Dalit areas."

He had a valid point. So I ordered that ten kilograms of grain be distributed free to each poor family, and promised the traders that the district administration would make good the cost by donations later.

I beg your pardon? Of course. I'm sorry I got carried away. You're not really doing a story on how we managed the riot. You're doing a story about Priscilla. I'm sorry.

Of course, I shouldn't have spoken of a total of just seven deaths, should I? There was an eighth one, neither Hindu nor Muslim.

Priscilla's.

from Lakshman's journal

August 3, 1989

He lies back and feels her peel the layers off him. His nakedness is a discovery, a baring of the self. She explores him with her long fingers, her touch opening him like a wound. He stirs. Her tongue caresses him now, a soft furriness on the inside of his thigh. He is in pain but the pain is exquisite and profound. He opens his eyes, seeing her move above him, her hair cascading around her face like a golden cloudburst. Her tongue scurries over his midriff and he makes an involuntary sound, an unfamiliar sound, half gratitude, half interrogation. The air around him seems to crackle with her charge. She has taken possession of him now, drawing his fullness into her mouth. He moves instinctively under her, but her fingers on his hip are firm as she continues, stilling all but the center of his being. He does not think any more of thrust and counterthrust but lets her take him in, her each breath a whisper to his heart. She is moving faster now, her lips surrounding him like the embrace of the ocean, and he is barely conscious of the tremors in his body, the piercing sweet pain of each stroke, until he trembles and gasps into her from every pore of his body. She does not stop as he shudders, feeling his soul empty into her like a confession.

Afterwards the air is quiet, and her cheek rests against his chest. He feels his heartbeat in her hand. Into the emptiness of his body floods a great happiness, a tsunami of joy that sweeps away all the debris in his mind, till he is cleansed of everything but the certitude that this is truth, this is right, this is what was meant to be.

"I love you," she says softly, and his pain is gone.

"Pornography," Gurinder would say if I showed this to him, which is one more reason I never will. "It's a fucking blow job, man. You can't make poetry out of a blow job." That would be authentic

Gurinder. I know, because I've tried to talk to him about Priscilla — I had to, not just because I had to talk to someone and he's my closest friend in Zalilgarh, but because I had to ask him to ensure the cops stayed away from the Kotli when the DM was there.

But I took it too far. I tried to tell him how much Priscilla had begun to matter to me, how I was beginning to think I could not live without her. He was horrified: to him the one thing that matters is our jobs, our noble calling, our role in society. Try telling Gurinder about the power of sexual love. He just doesn't understand.

"Fuckin' hell I understand, yaar," he'd said. "There are ten-rupee rundis on GB Road who'll give you the same, plus a paan afterwards. Don't tell me you're making a philosophy out of that."

I saw no point in wasting my existential crisis on him. "Bugger off, you philistine" was all I could muster.

"Look, I don't know what the hell's got into you, Lakshman. You can fuck the brains out of this blonde for all I care. But don't let it become so important, yaar. Don't forget who you are, where you are, what you're here to do."

"How can I forget?" I asked, surprising myself with the bitterness in my voice. "How can I possibly forget?"

letter from Priscilla Hart to Cindy Valeriani

August 5, 1989

You know what Guru, the cop here, Lucky's friend, said to me last night? We were at dinner at Lucky's place, half a dozen of us, and he'd clearly had too much to drink, but in the middle of a conversation about colonialism he announced, "The Brits came to exploit us, took what they wanted and left, and in the process they changed us." Then he turned to me quite directly and added, "You come to change us but in the process you also take what you want. Isn't that just another form of exploitation?"

I was so astonished I didn't know how to react, but Lucky cleverly made it sound as if Guru was making a general point about foreign nongovernmental aid projects. I wasn't fooled. I sensed he was trying to convey something quite specific to me, and I burned with shame at the thought that it might be about Lucky.

And yet it couldn't be, Cin. There's no way Lucky would betray our secret to anyone. So it must be about my work here. Like so many Indians, Guru's suspicious of my motives in doing what I do.

What do I want? I want to change the lives of these women, the choices they believe they have. I want to see them one day, these women of Zalilgarh and of a thousand other towns and villages like it in India, standing around the well discussing their own lives and hopes and dreams instead of complaining about their mothers-in-law. I want to hear them <u>not</u> say, with a cross between pride and resignation, "My husband, he wants lots of children," but rather, "<u>I</u> will decide when <u>I</u> am ready for a child." I want them, instead of planning to arrange their teenage daughter's marriage, to insist on sending her to high school. I want all this for them, and that's why I'm here. Is that exploitation? How can it be exploitation to make women more aware of what they can be?

"Population-control awareness" seems more and more of a misnomer to me. I see myself as trying to make women aware of their reproductive rights, not just to control population but to give them a sense of their rights as a whole, their rights as women. Being forced to have babies is just one more form of oppression, of subjugation by men. I'd rather die than have an abortion myself, but I want to help these women understand that control of their bodies is a rights issue, it's a health issue, and if they can improve their health and assert their rights, they will have a real future, and they'll give their daughters a real future. Is this all so difficult to understand, Cin?

And yet, whether Guru meant it or not, I can't help being conscious of a terrible irony. I care about Indian women in general, and yet I don't allow myself to think about one Indian woman in particular — Lucky's wife. I sit at her table and eat her rice and sambar, and I know all along that I am wronging her, that what I want will come at her expense, that Lucky's and my true love can only hurt her in the end. You're right, Cin, to remind me of that. And yet, she doesn't love him, and he doesn't love her. What he feels is the tug of duty, especially from his little daughter. Sometimes I wonder what would happen if Lucky and I had a daughter, a nut-brown baby with America in her eyes. She'd be so beautiful, Cin. And then Lucky would see me as family. . . .

But at the end of the day, I'm not all that inconsistent, am I? Because my life and my work are both about the same thing. It's all about women — about our control of our bodies, our right to sleep with the man we choose, with the protection we choose, for an outcome we choose. I want every woman to have that right. Even me.

from transcript of Randy Diggs interview with Superintendent of Police Gurinder Singh

October 14, 1989

RD: I've been interrupting too much. Go ahead and just tell me the story. In your own words. Take your time.

GS: Hell, man, of course I'll tell it in my own words. Whose damned words do you expect me to use? Look, the police force in those days was stretched almost to the breaking point, like the rubber on a Nirodh, the bloody government-made condom. Ever since the Ram Sila Poojan program had been announced a fortnight earlier, the provincial armed constabulary — we call them the PAC — had been on continuous vigil in the neighboring districts. The riot at Zalilgarh meant that they had to be hastily bundled onto buses and trucks and driven overnight to this frigging town. We immediately deputed them to man every tense enclave. They weren't a pretty sight, I can tell you, with bloodshot eyes and three days' growth on their strained faces. It's a miracle they didn't start a riot themselves.

Lucky was magnificent. He and I made it a point during our own night-long rounds to stop at each of the PAC pickets. We'd speak to the men about how difficult, and how important, their mission was. And occasionally share with them a hot cup of tea. Our cops weren't used to the DM-sahib coming to keep their morale up like this. Most of them had never directly spoken to a DM in their frigging lives. As they stood erect and alert at their watch posts, he would pass amongst them, talking to them in his Tamil-inflected Hindi, and the weary faces of the men would light up like Diwali lamps. You know, before the PAC buggers left for the next riot-torn city last week, the DM persuaded the eminent citizens of Zalilgarh to organize a bada khana of thanksgiving for the men. The buggers sat and ate as the city elders served them. Hasn't happened before, I can tell you.

I don't want to pretend my policemen are all piss-perfect. Hell, we know they're not. But when they screw up, we deal with them. The DM received a lot of complaints about excesses committed by the police during the house-to-house searches in the Muslim bastis. We visited some of the houses. It was true. It was as though a frigging cyclone had swept through them. Everything in those houses had been smashed, torn, or burnt by the search teams — the TV and radio, mattresses, furniture, artifacts, everything. An old Muslim woman aged around seventy took off her kameez and salwar to show us deep lathi marks across her body. From the shoulders down to the ankles. I couldn't bear to look. The DM ordered strong action against the guilty policeman. I ensured that it was taken. Such complaints will not recur on my watch.

In riots, all sorts of things happen. People strike first and ask questions later. It's tough to be a cop in a riot.

You can tell I'm a Lakshman fan. Our partnership was natural, and necessary. The policing challenge was intertwined with the administrative challenge. Intimately, like one of those couples in the temple sculptures at Khajuraho. I'll give you an example. The day after the bomb attack, the DM got a telephone call. One of the seriously injured riot victims, a young bugger, a Muslim called Mohammed, Sweet Mohammed they used to call him, had died on the way to the medical college hospital. They'd slit his throat and he'd bled to death in the ambulance. It was the middle of the frigging curfew, and what does the bloody hospital want? To get the district administration to

173

arrange for the disposal of the body double-quick. So Lucky sent for the young man's father, and the sadr or leader of the Muslim community, a humane and gentle old bugger known universally as Rauf-bhai, "Brother Rauf." Rauf-bhai sat there, unblinking behind his thick glasses, his yellowing beard stretching out like a shield, a white cap on his head. But you know what? His bloody presence alone seemed to quiet the distraught father. Thanks to Rauf-bhai, the father agreed to a quiet funeral. After midnight. It was the only way we could prevent a fresh upsurge of violence. If they'd held the bloody funeral during the day, there would have been another fucking riot.

I arranged for the morgue van carrying the body from the medical college hospital to halt at a rural police thana on the outskirts of Zalilgarh, to wait till midnight. Lucky and I went there. You know, to offer solace to the bereaved family. The DM was very quiet the whole way, which meant he was either exhausted or thinking, or both. Either way, I spared him my jokes for once. Sad bloody scene, Randy. Mohammed's mother was weeping desolately near the body of her son. The father and the sadr, Brother Rauf, were grieving nearby. Lucky walked up to them and quietly said: "We cannot bring back your son. But tell us who was responsible for your loss and we will ensure that justice is done."

The mother replied in angry bitterness. "There is no point in telling you the names of the killers. Every time in Zalilgarh when there are riots, the same men lead the mobs, looting and burning and killing, but nothing ever happens to them. During the last riots, we were hopeful because the police even noted down our statements. We waited for four days, but nothing happened. In the end the police did come, but it was we who were arrested. So this time we have nothing to say."

The DM turned to me and then back to them. "I promise you," he said in that quiet way of his, "that this time justice will be done. I was not here during the last riots. This time I am here. Please give me the names."

And they did finally give the frigging names — of some of the most powerful and prestigious men of the bloody district. The DM turned to me and said very calmly, "Let us round them all up before the body of this boy is lowered into the dust."

"Yes, sir," I replied. No "Lucky" this time, not even "Lakshman"; this was an order from the DM. I left the thana immediately in my jeep, roaring out of there like a blast from a buffalo's behind. I broke my own fucking speed limit several times that evening. I knew the DM would also have to leave on his incessant patrols. It was after midnight when I returned to the graveyard. They'd finished digging the boy's grave. I followed the beam of my torch across the cold moonless dark of the cemetery to the burial spot. The DM was back. The body had not yet been lowered into the dust.

I marched up to the DM, who was standing with the bereaved family. "Sir," I said, "they have all been arrested."

You should have seen the expressions on the frigging faces of those Muslim mourners. They didn't know whether to laugh or to cry.

It was around three o'clock in the morning when the DM and I returned to our camp cots in the police station. We wearily stretched out, fully dressed, to catch a little sleep. Two hours later, as dawn was breaking, we were awakened by an uproar at the thana gates. "What the hell is going on?" I demanded of the constable on duty. "It sounds like a pair of hippos making babies on a tin sheet." Lucky was still rubbing the sleep from his eyes when we found that it was indeed a hippo in human shape. The local MLA from the ruling party, member of the state legislative assembly, a generously endowed and utterly charmless specimen of the tribe called Maheshwari Devi, had arrived. She was with a group of her supporters, all banging pots and pans and shouting motherloving slogans. And frigging hell, they were all holding curfew passes.

"Injustice, injustice!" she was crying out, dutifully echoed by her eunuch supporters. "We will not put up with this injustice. We will not allow the arrest of innocent people."

It didn't take long for Lucky to wake up and figure out what the hell had happened. I'd never seen him so furious. "Tell me," he asked her, "are you the representative of just one community, and not of this whole town? The last few days, when hundreds of Muslims were arrested, beaten, dragged by their beards, and placed behind bars, often on mere suspicion, even though many had no criminal records, no complaint against them, I never heard even a whimper of protest from you. But last night, because ten men have been arrested, after complaints in which they were directly named as guilty of murder, you march here within two hours and shout of injustice? How dare you!"

The hippo was so pissing startled by this out-burst you could have heard her veins pop. No mere government official had ever dared to address her this way. She was as much at a loss how to respond as a blind nympho to a wink. "Get out," the DM said, though if you asked him, he'd fucking say he "directed her to leave the premises of the police station immediately and refused to discuss the issue any further." I escorted her out.

Don't give up on me just yet, Randy. Come on, have another drink. You see, that was not the end of the story. The MLA's demonstration was only the beginning — political foreplay. The whole day witnessed more pressure on the DM than he had

176

experienced, he tells me, in a single day on any issue during his career. The chief minister of the state telephoned to inquire why there was so much outrage. The DM replied that it was a matter of basic justice, and he would not change his decision. He was relieved that the CM did not get back to him again. But from the state capital downwards, the pressure continued to mount like a bad case of wind. Then, just as perceptibly, it eased in the afternoon. Once again, we thought we'd weathered the bloody storm.

Late that night — in keeping with our daily pattern since the tension in the town had arisen — we sat together at police headquarters. We were reviewing the arrests and releases of the day — our scorecard, we used to call it. Lucky noted that some of the numbers didn't add up. He summoned the station house officer and asked him to explain.

The bugger was more tight-lipped than a Hindi film actress who's been asked to kiss the villain. But finally the station house officer revealed that the ten men arrested the previous night had been released. By the frigging courts. Late the same bloody morning.

Lucky looked like a cow that had been hit on the head with a trishul. "Released?" he asked incredulously. "But how could they release them?"

Further questioning revealed that the police — my own men, goddamn them — had framed the weakest possible charges against the sisterlovers. Not of murder, arson, and rioting, but of the most minor bloody offense possible: violation of curfew. So the courts had let the detainees off with a fine of fifty rupees each. Just under three dollars at current exchange rates, Randy. No wonder we hadn't been bothered by the screaming politicians all afternoon.

I told you that earlier that morning I'd never seen the DM so furious. This time he exceeded himself. You've seen Lucky; he's a soft-spoken, thoughtful, calm, and restrained individual. Now everyone was stunned to see him explode with all the unpredictable velocity of a soothli bomb. He shouted at the men in the station house. "You're crooks, not police!" he ranted. "You're deceitful, communal-minded bigots, not fit to wear your uniforms!" He was working himself into quite a state. "Go and find the murderers you've released. Go now! I'll personally chase you right up to the gates of hell if the ten released men are not rounded up again within the hour."

"Lucky," I murmured, "I couldn't have done better myself." I took the best of my police officers and rushed back into town. You should have seen the expressions on the faces of some of the ten accused men when they were rearrested. Like society matrons finding a horny hand up their saris. This time Lucky and I personally supervised the filing of the charges — the preparation of documents for the courts.

The charges may or may not stick when they come to trial. But you should know that the Sessions Court released the accused Hindus on bail within a frigging week. The Muslims who had been rounded up in the bomb case are still being refused bail. The DM went to see the fucking district judge and said, "I have never tried to interfere with the judicial process. But here — the same riot, the same offenses, the same sections of the Penal Code — how can there be two such openly different standards for people of two communities? It is not an ordinary case," he added. "It is a question of the faith of a whole community in the system of justice in our country."

But the motherloving district judge refused to even discuss the issue with the DM. We do our job, Randy. I just wish everyone would do theirs as well.

Let me tell you something about these bloody riots — ours, and the others across northern India. They're like a raging flood. When the

178

stormy waters recede, all you will see left behind are corpses and ruins. Corpses, Randy, and fucking ruins.

Priscilla Hart. I knew you wanted to talk about Priscilla. I'm just trying to get you to understand why we don't know much about what happened to her. We had enough on our minds at the time. But I'll tell you what I know, Randy. Let's have another drink first.

from transcript of Randy Diggs interview with Professor Mohammed Sarwar

October 12, 1989

Look, I'm a historian, not a political activist. Though if you asked me, as a Muslim historian, whether I was a Muslim first or a historian first, I would have to tell you that depended on the context. But your question deserves a reply.

Isn't it amazing how these Hindu chauvinist types claim history on their side? The precision, the exactness, of their dating techniques are enough to drive a mere professor like me to distraction. People like me spend years trying to establish the veracity of an event, a date, an inscription, but the likes of Ram Charan Gupta have not the slightest doubt that their Lord Rama was born at the Ram Janmabhoomi, and what's more, at the precise spot they call the Ram Janmasthan — not ten yards away, not ten feet away, but right there. Their own beliefs are that Rama flourished in the treta-yuga of Hindu tradition, which means that their historical exactitude goes back, oh, about a million years. What is a mere historian like me to do in the face of such breathtaking knowledge?

The poor professors, alas, have not been able to establish with any certitude whether Lord Rama was born at all or simply emerged, wholly formed, from the creative and devout mind of the sage Valmiki, the putative author of the great religious epic the Ramayana. But if he was born, as the epic claims, in Ayodhya, there is no certainty that it was the place we today know as Ayodhya, in Uttar Pradesh — just as we can't be sure if the Lanka he conquered to retrieve his kidnapped wife Sita is the Sri

Lanka of today, rather than somewhere in Central India. The Vedas, the old Hindu scriptures, mention Rama as a king of Varanasi, or Benares, not of Ayodhya. One of the Jatakas, the Dasaratha Jataka, also says that Dasaratha and Rama were kings of Varanasi. There's more. The Ramayana actually mentions the Buddha, who lived around 500 B.C., but at that time the capital of the kingdom of Kosala, Rama's kingdom, was Sravasti, not Ayodhya, and the Ayodhya described in the Ramayana could not possibly have existed before the fourth century B.C. There are other inconsistencies, but you get the picture.

Now to the date of his birth. Simple fact: neither the seven-day week nor the division of the months into thirty days was included in the Hindu calendar, the Panchang, until the fourth century A.D. So even if Rama was a historical rather than a mythological figure, you have to get into a lot of guesswork before you date him. The Ramayana has suggestions that Rama lived in the dwapara-yuga, about five thousand years ago, rather than the treta-yuga of traditional belief. There is a Hindu pundit, a learned man, though without a degree in history as far as I know, a man called Sitanath Pradhan, who goes so far as to declare that the great climactic battle for Lanka was fought in 1450 B.C. and that Rama was exactly forty-two years old at the time. On the other hand, historians dating the existing texts of the Ramayana pretty much agree that it was composed sometime between 400 B.C. and A.D. 200, which is also the period in which that other great epic the Mahabharata was written, give or take a couple of hundred years. Confused enough? Your Hindutva types are presuming to know the exact place of birth of a man whose birthdate is historically unverifiable.

I know there are people who'll say, Ignore these pettifogging historians, how does it matter? All that matters is what people believe. But there too, my historian's inconvenient mind asks, when did they start believing it? The Ramayana existed as a text, as an epic, for about a thousand years before anyone began treating it as sacred. There is no evidence of any temple being built to worship Rama anywhere in India before the tenth century A.D. It's ironic, when you see the passions stirred around Rama's name in northern India today, that it was first in the South that Rama became deified. The Tamil Alvars, who were poets and mystics, started idealizing the god-king from around A.D. 900; it was a Tamil poet, Kamban, who started the cult of Ramabhakti, the divinity of Rama. The first community of Rama worshippers, the Ramanandins, came into existence in Kashmir between the fourteenth and the sixteenth centuries. And then the great poet of these parts, Tulsidas, wrote his brilliant, moving Ramcharitmanas in the sixteenth century, sanitizing the deeds of Rama, removing all those aspects of his conduct that had been questioned as less than godlike in the earlier Puranas, and elevating Rama to his present unchallenged supremacy in the Hindu pantheon. Actually Tulsidas's Ramayana, with all its idealizing of Rama as the ideal man and its barely veiled anxieties about women as the objects of lust in need of protection, owes more than a little to the Muslim invasions of India at the time. The Rama cult, and its offshoot the Bhakti movement, rose during the period of the Muslim conquest of North India and the establishment of the Delhi Sultanate, when Hinduism was on the defensive and where the position of women, who had traditionally been quite free, changed for the worse. Women were put into purdah, away from the prying eyes of the Muslim conquerors; Islamic attitudes towards sexuality and male dominance, emerging from a nomadic warrior society, directly influenced the softer, more liberal and tolerant but now effete Hindu society. Someone ought to do a Ph.D. on the role of Islam in the sanctification of Rama, but I wouldn't take a life insurance policy out on him these days.

182

I know the Hindutva types believe that the temples of Ayodhya precede Babar and that he must have destroyed the biggest one because it was the best located. But the problem with this is that there's a lot of evidence for the opposite — for the building of temples in Ayodhya under Muslim rule, well after Babar built his masjid. I don't want to bore you with all the details of the tax-free land grants given by rulers like Safdar Jang, who ruled from 1739 to 1754, but they document support for temple building. It was land that the Muslim nawab provided to a Hindu abbot that led to the construction of the Hanumangarhi, the most important Hindu temple in today's Ayodhya. Many historians, not just me, argue that Ayodhya filled up with temples as a direct result of support from the Muslim nawabs of the area, and that as the nawabi realm expanded, so did Ayodhya gain as a major Hindu pilgrimage center in the eighteenth and nineteenth centuries. This was two hundred years after the Babri Masjid was built.

So that's my historian's answer to your question: There's no evidence for the historicity of the Ram Janmabhoomi claims. Again, does that matter? Isn't this all about faith, not history? Well, the fact is that the Ram Janmabhoomi agitation is profoundly antihistorical. The bigots who spearhead it want to reinvent the past to suit their aspirations for the present. If we allow them to do it now, here, they will turn their attentions to something else, and the whole orgy of hate and violence will start again. If they get away with attacking Muslims today, they'll hit Christians tomorrow. And at a fundamental level, intolerance is the real enemy; intolerance can always shift targets. We've seen it happen in Bombay, where the Shiv Sena was born in the 1960s as a rabid bunch of Marathi chauvinists trying to drive South Indian migrants out of the city. "Sons of the soil" was their slogan in those days; they looted and burned stores with signs in South

Indian languages. That worked for a while, made them popular with some of the local Tukarams, but its appeal was limited; so the Shiv Sena suddenly turned into a Hindu chauvinist party and started denouncing Muslims, a far better target for their brand of homegrown bigotry.

The Shiv Sena leader says his hero is Hitler. And you know what happened under Hitler. As the German theologian Pastor Martin Niemoeller put it: "At first they came for the Jews, and I did not speak out, because I was not a Jew. Then they came for the Communists, and I did not speak out, because I was not a Communist. Then they came for the trade unionists, and I did not speak out, because I was not a trade unionist. Then they came for me — and there was no one left to speak out for me."

They are coming for the Muslims now, and I must speak out. But not because I am a Muslim. Only because I am an Indian, and I do not want them to come for any other Indians. No group of Indians must be allowed to attack another group of Indians because of where they are from, or who they worship, or what language they speak.

That's why your Ram Charan Guptas have to be stopped. Here. Now. Before they set all of India alight.

from Lakshman's journal

August 10, 1989

Gurinder just won't let up. "You, quitting the IAS?" He let fly a choice expletive or two. "You can't be serious, man! You're made for the IAS. You're doing great work, work that makes a real difference to the lives of real human beings. You've got a great career, a great future. I can't believe you're even contemplating such a damn-fool idea. You know what your problem is? You're thinking with your cock."

He brushed aside my feeble protestations. "You've seen the possibility of sexual paradise with this girl, all in Technicolor, and suddenly everything else in life seems prosaic black-and-white. You really think she's worth giving up everything for — your wife, your kid, your job, your country?" He was really frothing now. "Look, however wonderful things have been with her, yaar, you can't forget a few basic facts. Like, she's an American, Lucky, a fucking Yank. They're not like us. It's a different country, a different culture, a different planet, man. You've lived all your life with a definite set of values. You know what's right because it's always been right. I know you're not entirely happy with Geetha, what the hell, it's never been a secret, but come on, yaar, she's been a good wife to you. She runs a good house, serves a great table, gets the best out of the servants — so what if she gives them hell once in a while? — and spends a lot of time with your daughter. You can bring someone home for dinner at practically no notice and she adjusts to your needs. Your work takes you away unexpectedly, keeps you out till no one knows when, man, and she doesn't complain."

She doesn't complain, I want to say, because she doesn't care whether I'm there or not. But Gurinder won't be interrupted; he plunges remorselessly on with his portrait of Indian domestic bliss.

185

"When you're home she ensures you are served first and gives you the choicest portions before she eats herself. And you can be sure she's never looked at another man and never will. If you die she will honor your memory, put a fresh garland round your fucking framed photo every day and do puja before it. These are not small things, man." He thumped a hand into his palm for emphasis. "Not bloody small things. Take it from me, yaar. It's a comfort to know these are things you can take for granted. As you grow older, you can rest assured there are some things you can always rely on."

I nodded. He needed no further encouragement to go on: "What do you have with Priscilla? Sex. Fucking sex, if you'll excuse the tautology. Sure that's important: if my Bunty didn't enjoy a good joust with my personal hockey stick I wouldn't be a happy man. But you of all people know that isn't enough." He looked me evenly in the eye, as if weighing briefly whether to go on. It didn't take him too long to decide. "And doesn't it bother you that you're not the only man who's been in her bed?" He saw the glint of pain in my eyes and drove home his point with the subtlety of a sledgehammer. "Sex means much less to these Americans than it does to us, Lucky. Look, I'll tell you something. Remember the time she reported her handbag stolen and we found the thief? We recovered the handbag and, as you know, we have to do an inventory of the contents. The thief had spent or sold what he could but there was at least one thing he hadn't touched. The constable doing the inventory was at a total loss when he saw it, so he came to me to ask what it was. It was a vibrator, man. A fucking vibrator. I switched it on for him and burst out laughing at his expression. He asked me what it was for and I said it was an American hairdressing tool — a battery-operated hair curler, I explained solemnly. When Priscilla was given the inventory to sign she paused at that item, frowned, then smiled to herself and signed. She must have thought, what ignorant idiots these Indians are. Hair curler indeed. She had no idea of what disgrace I had spared her in the constable's eyes. If I had told him what it really was, she would have been the talk of every male in Zalilgarh. And they would have treated her with contempt ever afterwards. Or worse, some hothead might have tried to act as a personal substitute for her vibrator, whether she'd wanted him to or not. I'm telling you this just so you know. My instinct was to protect her, Lucky. But don't forget this — she's used to a certain amount of physical pleasure and you happen to be the one she's found here to provide it. At least you don't need batteries."

"Bugger off, Guru. You don't know the first thing about this girl."

"Maybe, maybe not. But look, yaar, all I'm saying is: don't confuse bedding well with wedding bell. Look, screw her as much as you like. You're doing it already. Why should you give up your job, your wife, your life, for that? As we say in Punjab, if you're getting milk regularly, why do you need to buy the cow?" He grabbed me by the shoulders. "There's a lot more to what you need in a woman than a good fuck. And there's a lot more to your life than banging a moist you-know-what every once in a while."

"Do you really think I don't know that, Gurinder?" My tone was sad, but I wasn't going to let him know how much his earthy candor had shaken me. "Of course I know what my responsibilities are, to Geetha, to my daughter, to my job, to my career, to this bloody district. But the point is precisely that Priscilla has come to mean so much to me that everything else pales in comparison."

"Well, it damn well shouldn't," came Gurinder's rejoinder. "Everything around you is real, dark, colored. She's the only pale thing around in your life, Lucky. And you're letting her cast a shadow she's too bloody pale to cast."

"Great metaphor, Guru." I smiled tiredly. "And thanks for all your advice. I know it came from somewhere deep down that mudpit you call your heart. Now push off and interrogate some absconders. I need to think."

As a parting gift I quote him the old ditty: "He who loves foolishly and well / Will meet Helen of Troy in Hell. / But she whose love is thin and wise / Will meet John Knox in Paradise."

He's not impressed. "Forget heaven and hell, yaar," he says as he leaves. "It's purgatory I'm concerned about. We call it Earth."

187

from Lakshman's journal

August 14, 1989

It's midnight, and I can't sleep. Tomorrow, though it's a Tuesday, I won't be seeing Priscilla, because it's a public holiday: Independence Day. The day we threw off the yoke of the white man. The day I will be reminded, painfully, of my dependence on a white woman.

I can't sleep because I'm thinking about her. And about myself. About whether I have a future with her. And about what that would mean for me.

What can I think about but the categories I know? We had a family friend, a friend of my parents, though closer to my mother's age than my father's. Uncle Sudhir, I called him, though of course he wasn't really my uncle. He was an executive in a multinational firm, and I remember thinking of him as impossibly good-looking and glamorous, a fair, smooth-shaven demigod in sharp suits and glistening ties, his aquiline features always ready to break into a cheerful laugh. He had a gorgeous wife, too, whom he had met at university, a stunning woman in vivid saris and skimpy blouses. Over the years she became gradually more stately and less svelte, whereas Uncle Sudhir seemed to get younger and louder, favoring me with conspiratorial winks every time a pretty woman crossed his path at one of my parents' parties. Then we moved to another city, and I didn't see Uncle Sudhir for a while, until I heard, in my parents' tones of shocked disapproval, that he'd got divorced. It was said that he was living with a younger woman, herself a divorcee.

Years later, when I was already working and had come to visit my parents on holiday, I met Sudhir again. He came to call on my father, and I saw a slightly jowlier, lower-shouldered version of the Uncle Sudhir I remembered. He was received in an awkward and uncomfortable manner. My mother barely greeted him before disappearing into the kitchen, and my father, who had if anything become garrulous in retirement, was much more taciturn than usual. I tried to make polite conversation but Uncle Sudhir could sense how things were; he made a couple of valiant attempts at joviality before giving up and leaving. When the front door shut behind him my father's first words were: "Sad case."

"Why?" I demanded in my mid-twenties innocence. "He doesn't seem to be doing badly at all."

"So that's what you think," my father said. "This was a man who had everything: a good salary, a beautiful wife, three healthy children, a wonderful home. Then he gave that all up to pursue his lust. He has suffered the diminishment of his status, lost the respect of friends and family, abandoned the sweet familiar comforts of home life, borne the stigma of social shame, and endured court-ordered financial impoverishment. Above all, he knows that in doing what he did he has spurned those in relation to whom he recognized himself. And you think he's doing well?"

Later that week my father suffered the stroke that would kill him. This was almost the last thing he said to me, and it has stayed in my mind ever since, seared into my synapses.

Gurinder to Randy Diggs, over a drink

Saturday night, October 14, 1989

You want to know why I'm a cop? I'll tell you why I'm a bloody cop.

Not why I first became a policeman, because that had more to do with my parents' wishes. I really wanted to be a successful peasant, a modern peasant. But my parents convinced me that taking the IAS exams was the right thing to do, and I didn't do well enough to get into the pissing IAS, so they offered me the IPS, the police service. And I took it. It was a job: it came with a decent salary, perks, buggers saluting me left and right, social status, that extra swagger in my dad's step when he took me to the club on my weekends home. That's why I first became a cop, but that's not why I'm still a cop today.

How long've you been in this bloody country? Two years, huh? So you weren't here for the really big story of the decade. The assassination of Indira Gandhi. And all that preceded it. And all that followed.

Nineteen eighty-four. Orwell's big bad year. It all went buggering smoothly for the rest of the world, didn't it? No great horrors, no Big Brother, no fucking Third World War. Lots of smug frigging articles about how Orwell's dreadful vision of the future of the world had been belied by bloody reality. But not here. Our 1984 was as sisterloving awful a year as we've had since Independence. It's right up there with the worst — with 1947, when the country was fucking ripped apart, and 1962, when the Chinese hammered the crap out of us in the Himalayas. Our 1984 was a bad shit year, all right, a terrible year for the bloody national vintage.

It began with the Punjab troubles going — as the Chandigarh whore said to the poet — from bad to worse. Some of my fellow Sikhs, stupid buggers to a man, were to blame. We had a mad preacher, Sant Jarnail Singh Bhindranwale, holed up in the holiest

Sikh shrine, the Golden Temple in Amritsar, surrounded by assholes with rifles and Kalashnikovs and bombs, ranting about creating a new Sikh state called Khalistan. Motherloving idiots: one of the greatest of Sikh journalists, Khushwant Singh, wrote that if Khalistan were ever created it would be a "duffer state." Bhindranwale was actually a creature of Indira Gandhi and her cronies, who wanted to undermine the moderate Sikh party, the Akali Dal, by encouraging a rival who was more fucking Sikh than they were, and then he'd gone out of control. But what do you care about all that, huh?

Anyway, Bhindranwale and his thugs were sending out goons to assassinate anyone they didn't like, especially Sikhs who'd cut their hair or smoked cigarettes or disagreed with the separatists' frigging agenda. And they were killing newspaper editors who criticized them, government officials, cops, you name it, nobody was safe, and because the killers were in a sacred sanctuary they were beyond the fucking reach of the long arm of the law. A Sikh cop I sort of knew and greatly admired, a deputy inspector general of police, A. S. Atwal, senior man, able, honest, came out of the temple after praying there with his eight-year-old son and was shot in the back. Killed just like that, outside the Golden Temple. Murdered in cold fucking blood, with his boy wailing in uncomprehending grief at his side. I'm a Sikh who's never taken so much as a bloody trimmer to my nasal hair, I've prayed a hundred times at the Golden Temple, but even I could see we couldn't just let them go on like this, in motherloving impunity. Law and order were going down the pissing tubes in my own bloody home state, man. People generally, Sikh and Hindu, didn't feel safe anymore; something had to fucking well be done.

For two years after Atwal's murder — a time when she would have found no shortage of Sikhs from the police and the army ready to volunteer to go in and arrest the murderers — Mrs. Gandhi did bugger-all. She was too busy playing politics, while Bhindranwale and his sisterloving goons continued on their rampage. Then, in 1984, she finally did something. Indira bloody Gandhi, the only man in the cabinet, sent the army into the Golden Temple. She could have besieged the place, cut off the water supply, prevented food from reaching the terrorists, starved them into surrender. But no, she sent in the frigging army and tried to — what's the bullshit word they used? — to extirpate the terrorists from there. That was the term of art. Extirpation. Isn't it wonderful how the English language manages to bureaucratize the savagery out of bloody human violence? And the army did extirpate the terrorists — at a price. Say what you like about that madman Bhindranwale, and I've said a few things myself, but he was a proud Sikh and he wasn't going to cave in at the first whiff of grapeshot. They had to pound the place with artillery. Hundreds of innocent Sikhs, pilgrims, ordinary frigging worshippers, who happened to be in the temple at the time, lost their lives. Bhindranwale fought back like all hell; he and his people went down in the finest bloody Sikh tradition, all guns blazing. And at the end of the army assault the temple stood pockmarked and bloodied, many of its priceless treasures damaged or destroyed, Sikh pride in ruins.

Yes, man, our pride. It wasn't just the masonry of the temple that was shattered that day by the assault they called Operation Bluestar. It was unbearable even for those Sikhs who had despised Bhindranwale and all his works. I mean, if some Mafia gang had taken shelter in the Vatican, would anyone have aimed howitzers at Saint Peter's bloody Cathedral? We felt personally, intimately violated. The same Khushwant Singh who had been so critical of the Khalistanis that he was on the terrorists' hit list himself, Khushwant Singh returned his civilian honors to the government in protest. If he felt that way, you can imagine what the rest of the buggered Sikh community was going through.

No, I didn't immediately think of doing anything similar, resigning or anything. Not at that time. Because I told myself I was on the side of the law enforcers. And the government had made an honest bloody mistake. They had done the right frigging thing in the wrong way — they had ended the Bhindranwale terror, but they had done too much damned damage in the process. It was unjustifiable, but excusable. They had to be forgiven. That was my view, and that of others like me, educated Sikhs, people in the establishment. But feelings were running bloody high in the Sikh community generally, even though the president of India, Giani Zail Singh, was himself a Sikh, and he went on television to explain what the government had

192

had to do and why. The preening bastard had had a hand himself in spawning the frigging Frankenstein's monster that Bhindranwale became, but that's another story.

Anyway, the end of Bhindranwale did bugger-all to end the terrorism — in fact it simply worsened it. A whole new bunch of angry Sikhs were recruited by the motherloving thugs as a result of the Golden Temple tragedy. And a lot of Sikhs vowed revenge on those who had done this, this thing, to their holiest of holies. The prime minister, Mrs. Indira bloody Gandhi, was their primary target.

Now, I was no great fan of Mrs. G, I can tell you, but I'll grant her one thing — she didn't have a bigoted bone in her body. She'd married a Parsi, and her daughters-in-law were an Italian Catholic and a Sikh. So when people told her she should remove the Sikhs from her security detail, she dismissed them with a glare. She had this patrician Kashmiri glare that instantly shriveled your balls, so they didn't dare suggest it again. "Remove my Sikh security men? Nonsense!" She believed in the pissing professionalism of her protectors, and she thought anyway that she had not acted against Sikhs, just against terrorists, so she had nothing to fear. Unfortunately for her, some Sikhs saw it differently. So one cold morning she was walking briskly in her own back garden, heading for a TV interview with Peter bloody Ustinov, when two of her fucking Sikh bodyguards opened fire on her. A dozen bullets each, I've heard it said; some say they emptied their magazines into her, this sixty-seven-year-old woman they had taken an oath to protect. She died instantly, riddled with the exit wounds of their maddened rage. One of her killers was mown down instantly by the other security fuckers, and the other bugger was overpowered, but they'd had their revenge. Sikh honor had been restored.

Hmph. What do they know of honor who have to kill an old widow to restore it?

Unfortunately, revenge is a game any number can play. The reprisals started the same pissing day: some innocent Sikh bugger standing in the crowd outside a newspaper office when the news about Mrs. G was announced — some poor idiot who didn't see any difference between himself and any of his fellow Indians in the same throng, equally shocked by the headlines — well, this poor idiot got beaten up, his shirt ripped, just for being Sikh. He was the first victim of the backlash to the assassination, but he survived with a few bruises. There were similar incidents here and there in scattered parts of Delhi. Spontaneous bursts of anger directed at the most obvious target, the first available bloody Sikh. And initially, that was all. Until the evil bastards took over.

There were enough of those around, man. The thugs, the odious enforcers, the petty motherlovers of Congress Party politics, Indira's fucking foot soldiers, the rent-a-mob sloganeers who had shouted, "India is Indira and Indira is India." They'd been kept under control so far, but this was their chance to have a go. They too had a thirst for revenge. Only Sikh blood could slake it.

Even I cannot describe to you the full horror of what happened thereafter, Randy. I've been trained to deal with riots, but this was mass bloody murder in the nation's capital. The frigging bastards organized mobs of violent lumpens and set them loose on Delhi's Sikhs. There was an orgy of slaughter, of arson, of looting. Sikh neighborhoods were destroyed, families butchered, homes torched. Some of the mobs had lists of addresses showing which homes and businesses were owned by Sikhs. Can you imagine? In other parts of town, any Sikh unlucky enough to be in the wrong fucking street at the wrong fucking time was killed in the most merciless way possible.

I'll tell you something I haven't talked about in years. I had a ten-year-old nephew, my sister's son, Navjyot. He was returning home from a cricket match with his father. He was a great Gavaskar fan, but Gavaskar was playing in Pakistan at the time. Anyway, what could be more bloody bourgeois, more fucking normal, than a man and his son at a game of cricket on a sunlit October in Delhi? They were driving back home in the family's Ambassador car, the frigging epitome of solid Indian middle-class respectability, when they ran into a mob looking for Sikh blood to spill.

The bastards surrounded the car, howling and baying their hate for the assassins of the prime minister. "Khoon ka badla khoon," they chanted. "Blood in revenge for blood."

My brother-in-law quickly rolled up the windows and locked the doors from the inside. What could he do? There were no bloody police in sight: it was as if they had taken a pissing holiday when they were most needed. He had no means to call for help, no CB radio like some of you Yankee buggers have in your cars. I'm sorry; I know I'm shouting. Randy, I try not to think of my little nephew, his mind still full of cricket, suddenly seized with an unutterable panic at a mob of grown motherfucking men trying to hurt him.

The mob pounded on the door, the roof, the thick glass panes, with their accursed fists.

Then someone brought a can of petrol. Or two. I wasn't there, but I have relived that horrible scene a thousand times, so that it is more vivid in my imagination than most things I have actually seen. I can imagine the faceless bastard, his features twisted in hatred and excitement, eyes bloodshot, swinging the can, the colorless liquid pouring out from it, splashing the metal, the glass, the windshield wipers, the rubber of the tires, the fucking petrol flowing in a graceful arc until the car was thoroughly doused with it. And then someone screaming for a match, a match, a motherloving match, and setting the car alight.

The flames must have soared instantly, and these unspeakable motherfuckers watched, cheering, as a decent man and his little boy were roasted alive in their seats. They must have tried to escape, my brother-in-law would have preferred to face the mob than to burn to death, but the locks on the doors must have fused together with the heat of the blaze, and they remained trapped inside, asphyxiating, burning, choking to death.

Ever since that day I have been haunted by the thought of little Navjyot, his hair tied on the top of his head under a navy blue kerchief, a bright little boy whose greatest ambition was to open the batting for India one day like his hero Gavaskar. I was not there, Randy, I was not there, but I imagine his round eyes widening in horror and bewilderment as the mob surrounded his car, I imagine his father trying to reassure him, calmly locking the damned doors, and I imagine his little face pressed to the window, staring in disbelief as the flames consumed him.

When his mother, my sister, heard the news, she quite literally lost her mind.

When I found out what had happened, I was beside myself with grief and rage. That was when I wanted to resign: I could not bear to serve a system that had allowed this to happen. The Delhi police had claimed they were overwhelmed. It took the bloody government three days to bring out the army and suppress the riots; in the meantime hundreds of Sikhs had lost their lives, thousands had lost everything they possessed. Rajiv Gandhi, the new prime minister, even condoned the violence by declaring that "when a mighty tree falls, the earth shakes." The earth of Delhi was soaked in Sikh blood, and it was the bosoms of the Sikh widows that were shaking in grief and despair. I felt that all my training, all my faith in the country and its bloody institutions, had been futile.

But no, I didn't resign. My father, Navjyot's grieving grandfather, the man who was proudest to see me a cop, stopped me.

"Don't be a fool, Gurinder," he said to me, holding me by the shoulders as if he wanted to shake some sense into me. "Sikhs have lost so much already this year; let us not lose more. Your staying on will help prevent such tragedies in the future. What is the point of throwing away your ability to pursue the criminals, to uphold the law, to ensure that some other mob doesn't murder someone else's favorite nephew?"

I wept, I raged, I argued with him, I spoke of the Sikh soldiers who'd mutinied, I told him about a brilliant senior cop, Simranjit Singh Mann, who had quit the fucking police and joined the Khalistanis, and how I wanted to do the same thing. But he kept holding me, his sad brown eyes looking into the depths of my despair, and he shook his head. "Where do you think this will lead them?" he asked. "Will they achieve anything for their community, or for their country, except to cause more destruction and more unnecessary suffering? Do you want to throw away your future? Do you want to throw away India's future?"

I don't care, I said, and he looked at me as if he'd been shot. But you've got to care, he said. You've got to care about this country the way you care about your mother or me.

I don't know, I replied, I don't know if I can think of this country as mine anymore, after what has happened. I told him of overhearing a Hindu officer saying, "Damned good thing, it's time we taught those Sikhs a lesson."

He didn't flinch, my old man. "There will always be people like that," he said, and for the first time I felt the difference in our ages, in what we had lived through, what we had learned. "If I brought you up to believe everything would be easy, that the whole world would act with integrity and honesty and decency and fairness, then I have failed you," he said. "You can only be true to yourself, and to the soil from which you have sprung, and to the oath you have taken." He looked at me then, looked *into* me. Thirty-seven years earlier he had lost everything in the massacres of Partition: his home, his ancestral lands in what had become, by the scratching of a careless British pen, the foreign country of Pakistan. He had worked hard to rebuild, to build himself the life he now led: the car, the servants, the club, the son in the Indian Police Service. He had sweated to build his share of India; he was not going to let me throw it away for bugger-all. "You say you do not know if this country is yours anymore? Don't be a fool, Gurinder. Whose country is this if not yours? Since the days of Gandhi, we have tried to build a country that is everyone's and no one's, a country that excludes nobody, a country that no one group can claim is exclusively theirs. When Jinnah and the Muslim League wanted to create a country for Muslims, their Pakistan, did the Congress leaders say fine, we will create a country for Hindus? The whole point about India is that this is a country for everybody, and everybody has the duty, the obligation, to work to keep it that way. To fight to keep it that way. I did not bring you up to give up so easily, Gurinder. You have a job to do. You have sworn an oath of office to do it. A Sikh's oath is his sacred duty, Gurinder. You don't have the right to give up on your country."

And Navjyot, I asked, but feebly, because he had won me already. And because I realized I had wanted him to.

Because of Navjyot, he replied without hesitation. Because that should never have happened, and because you have a share of the responsibility to ensure that it never happens again.

He turned me to the photograph of Navjyot that stood on the dresser, a picture of an innocent little face, tender parted lips, shining eyes that had not yet seen the horror that would shut them forever. "That boy will always live in my heart," he said softly. "But somewhere in India there is another grandfather like me whose only hope for the safety of his grandson lies in the trust that he places in you and the policemen under your command. Do not, Gurinder, do not ever betray that trust."

And so I stayed. And that's why I'm still a cop: because a sad, quiet, neatly dressed man in a white beard, my blessed father, had more fucking faith in me than I had in myself. And because, for all the corruption and venality and inefficiency that assails this bloody profession, it is still the last bastion of civility and order in our racked and torn society. And because I want to ensure that, as far as I can help it, no other family has to endure what my sister had to.

And because I am haunted by the face of a little ten-year-old boy enveloped in flames, a boy who loved cricket and called me Uncle.

I want to save that boy. I want to save other children like him. I want to put out the fires.

letter from Priscilla Hart to Cindy Valeriani

August 15, 1989

Cindy dear, it's Independence Day today. India's. I'm sitting at my desk in my loosest cotton shift as my rickety fan totters on its pedestal and blows hot air into my face. August is murderous in Zalilgarh, but it's not as bad as May or June, before the monsoon, when you step into the street and think you've walked into an oven. It'll start cooling down in October, but as it gets colder you'll have the pollution to cope with — the smoke from hundreds of charcoal braziers on the sidewalks, thousands of buses and cars and auto-rickshaws, and God knows how many factories, all rising to be trapped under the winter mist rising from the river. Gurinder said the other day that just breathing Zalilgarh's air is the equivalent of smoking a pack of Charminars a day. And he picked an unfiltered brand to make his point!

I'm alone at home today, the office is closed, Lucky's probably officiating at some flag-raising ceremony this morning, surrounded by self-important functionaries. I imagine him stiff in his safari suit, saluting a foreign flag, a flag without stars or stripes — heck, I don't even know if they salute the flag at these things — and I tell myself, he's a <u>foreigner</u>. But Cin, the word doesn't mean anything to me anymore when I think of him. I know him so well — the strength of his long arms around me, the two crooked front teeth when he smiles, the slightly spicy smell of his sweat when we've made love, the little tilt at the corner of his mouth when I lie on his chest and look up at his face. He's no foreigner. He's more familiar to me, more intimate to me, than any American I've ever known.

Here I am, on Independence Day, wanting to give up my independence for him, knowing he has to win his own independence first. I can't believe he's even hesitating to leave a loveless marriage he hates for the woman he says he loves. It's when

199

he talks about his conflicted feelings, his obligations, that I begin to believe he really is a foreigner after all. . . .

Anyway, speaking of foreigners, I've just had another reminder that I'm one. I went to the bazaar on the weekend, just to see what I could pick up to bring home, you know? It's crazy, these places, stores spilling out on the sidewalks, the shopkeepers openly importuning you to come and buy their wares, the flies buzzing about, the heat so oppressive that you think of going to the nearest Bollywood movie just for the air-conditioning. Anyway, I spotted a couple of embroidered cushion covers I thought you'd like. How much? I asked. "Two hundred each, but for you, three hundred the pair," said the greasy man in the shop. Now, I've been here long enough to know about bargaining, so I promptly said, "No, two hundred for the pair." I was appalled at the alacrity with which he accepted my offer. Sure enough, I show the cushion covers to the wretched Kadambari, and she says, "How much did you pay? Sixty?" Even making allowances for her bitchy nastiness, it's clear I've been ripped off again. I guess it's part of the price you've got to pay for being a foreigner in India. But why must I, of all people, have to pay that price? I'm not some tourist in a five-star hotel — I'm me! And that ought to count for <u>something</u>. . . .

from Lakshman's journal

August 19, 1989

Can't sleep, so am up at 3 a.m. writing this. Geetha is sleeping soundly as usual, her face swollen in unwitting complacency. I can't bear to see that face every time I wake up, and I always wake up before she does. How the hell did I like that face enough to agree to marry her?

Despite myself, I looked in on Rekha in her room. I didn't switch on the light but the moon was bright enough for me to see her angelic face, calm in repose on the oversized pillow. I gently brushed away a curling strand of hair that had fallen over one eye. In her sleep, she smiled at me.

It's Rekha, of course, that I think about all the time now. Priscilla's supposed to leave Zalilgarh in less than two months, and she thinks it's decision time. Do I want to go with her? She has to return to the States, at least for now, and the prospect of escaping with her has its temptations. She showed me, only half jokingly, an ad in an American magazine: "Unemployment is lower in Switzerland. Owning a home is easier in Australia. Going to college is more likely in Canada. Vacations are longer in Denmark. And crime rates are lower in England. But more dreams come true in America."

An alluring prospect, if I had those dreams. But do I, really? Is it freedom I want, or Priscilla? I know I could get her to change her plans and stay on in India, for me. She'll do it — but only on one condition. Only if I tell her I'm leaving my wife for her. That's what she wants. And she wants it now. I can understand her impatience, but I'm not sure I'm ready for anything quite so . . . cataclysmic. How can I explain to her that I'm not even sure I have the right to do that to Geetha, to abdicate my husbandhood? I didn't choose to start my marriage in the first place; how can I choose to end it? My role as a husband and father is central to who I am; it concerns my rootedness in the world; it is inextricably bound up with my sense of my place in the cosmos. I have been brought up to believe that such things — marriage, family — are beyond individual will, that they transcend an individual's freedom of action. Priscilla'll never understand that.

And what about little Rekha, who did not ask to be born into my life but who is there, whose world is circumscribed by the pairing of Geetha and me? How can I ever explain what she means to me to Priscilla? "What's the matter, Lucky?" Priscilla asked me this evening.

> You ask, my love, what the matter is.
> Why do I sound fatigued? stressed? torn?
> The matter is that I am as I sound.
> I, who have accepted your soul's gift of love,
> Am a soul in torment, fearing as I love.
> I give you, my darling, the best part of myself:
> The part that feels most profoundly as a man,
> That knows the warm rush of passion
> At every sight of your smiling body,
> That rejoices in your warm embrace,
> And belongs to you in total surrender.
> That part is yours, my love, forever:
> It can never know again the exaltation,
> The exultation, the poignant sweetness of
> Such flooding love as I bear for you.
>
> That part is yours; but it is a part,
> For I am, in rendering it, rent;
> Having your love, yet not having it;
> Giving my love, yet not parting with it;
> Withholding, as I give, for a prior creditor.
> I have, as you know, an earlier love,
> One for a little soul, first glimpsed
> Tadpole-like in a nurse's arms,

Pink, precious, and premature:
The child I had prayed for, who did not seek
To be mine, but is, and whose life
Ennobles mine. I have loved her
Without reservation, without selfishness,
Without condition, as I could never
Love a woman. Even you.

Now I look at her each day,
Wake her in the morning, give her breakfast,
Do homework with her, take her to the library
And the movies, and I know I fear nothing more
Than I fear not being there for her.
When she cries out, "Daddy, am I as tall
As you were when you were six?"
I am there in the evening to confirm it;
When she tells me of news from school,
Or asks about God, or geography,
I am there as the question occurs to her.
I teach her Tamil songs, passing on a heritage
She traces in her genes; I trim her hair,
Cut her nails, quiz her over breakfast
On the oceans of the world.

Now I look at her and I ask myself,
Can I deny her that?
Can I deprive myself of her?
Can I absent myself from the rest of her childhood?
When she first meets a boy whose easy charm
Starts flutters in her heart,
Will Daddy be the one she tells of her confusions?
Can I ever be happy knowing that I
Have pulled from under the secure carapace of her life
The struts that held her up?
But can I be happy either,
Knowing that you are no longer mine,

That you have returned to America,
That I have shut my eyes to the one true glimpse of happiness
I have ever had as a man?

You ask, my love, what the matter is.
And I can only say, everything is the matter.

Deep emotion and lack of sleep make for unconvincing poetry.
Fifteen lines a stanza: is there such a form anywhere in the canon? I
know I should thrust it aside; in an hour now dawn will break across
my torment like a twig. But this is what I feel, and it's at a level quite
different from what Guru was trying to make me feel. Truth, Wilde
wrote, is just "one's last mood." Is this mood of tormented despair
the one truth that counts now? How will Priscilla understand that
my agonizing is not about her, not about us? But if she loves me,
mustn't I help her understand? Perhaps I ought to give her this
poem. I'd title it "The Heart of the Matter." Or perhaps "A Matter
of the Heart." Or, more originally, both?

I'm too tired to think. And too full of thoughts to sleep.

Rudyard Hart to Mohammed Sarwar

October 14, 1989

You know, I stopped at a cold-drink place this morning. Guess what they're selling? Pepsi. Bloody Pepsi. Except that they call it Lehar Pepsi here. Some Indian rule against foreign brand names.

Despite myself, I bought it. Took a swig. And tasted defeat. Pepsi didn't exist in the Indian market when I was here last. Now they're here and we're not. We could have been ten years ahead of them if we'd played our cards right.

You know, when we see a population without Coke we see an untapped market for the finest beverage invented by man. Not being here is an indescribable waste all around. Indians are being deprived of a wonderful product, and we're being deprived of a chance to lead in this country too, as we do in so many countries.

We've got to come back to India. And we will. It's the way the world is going. You'll have American products, American ideas, American values all spreading throughout the land. And you'll have to have Coke.

I'll tell you what your problem is in India. You have too much history. Far more than you can use peacefully. So you end up wielding history like a battleaxe, against each other. Whereas we at Coke don't care about history. We'll sell you our drinks whatever your history is. We don't worry too much about the past. It's your future we want to be a part of.

My daughter believed in your future too. You know, I went through hell asking God why she had to be killed in a quarrel she had no part of. But now I realize it was her choice to be caught up in this country's passions. She wanted to change India for the better. She was working for the future when she was struck down by the past.

It's something I've been thinking about a lot. Can't say it makes me feel a whole lot better, though. But I now think I'll ask Coke to send me back to India. Give it another try. I think Priscilla would have wanted me to.

note from Priscilla Hart to Lakshman

August 21, 1989

I've read the poem you asked Mitha Mohammed to bring to me at the office. I don't know why you sent it to me, except to make me see our relationship in a different light. Maybe you too need to see things differently, Lucky.

You haven't taken a risk in this relationship. At all. But I have. It was my risk to take, to fall in love with a married man, and I did, and I take full responsibility for it. I'm sorry about that ink splotch; I'm crying as I write this. But I don't want you to feel sorry for me. I want your love, not your pity.

Your poem reduced me to a "smiling body" and a "warm embrace." I thought I was more than that to you, Lucky. When you're dealing with someone else's life, you have to be a lot more careful with your words than that.

I love you with all my heart and soul, but I don't want a relationship with a man who doesn't feel the same way as I do. I want a man who loves me, and a relationship where I can rely on the fact that he loves me. Not my body, not my embrace, ME.

You write of your daughter needing you to be there. I need you to be there for me, too, Lucky. But you don't see that, do you?

You're so good at understanding everyone else's claims on you — your family's, your daughter's, your job's. Do I have no claims on you, Lucky? Am I just a convenient outlet for your passion, your escape from humdrum reality? I know where I am in this relationship. You don't really know where you are, do you?

On Saturday night, I felt such pain for you, looking at your sad and confused face. I believe in us completely, but I don't know what to do. I don't want anything from you that you don't want to give me. And I can't show my needs to you if you don't know how to respond, or if you believe you can't respond because of your "prior creditor."

I know, as a woman, that I've got to do better than this. Your poem frightened me, Lucky. After six months of this relationship I should know where I am, and what I can expect from you. I love you very deeply, but I'm in pain too, Lucky. I'll be at the Kotli tomorrow as I've always been, every Tuesday and Saturday, available at your convenience when your wife is away at the temple. But I'm no longer sure this is good enough for me, Lucky. When we meet, I'll need some definite answers from you.

Gurinder to Lakshman

Monday morning, August 21, 1989

Hey, lover-boy, since you keep going on and on about the pleasures of fucking sexual love — pardon my Sanskrit — do you know
what I did last weekend? For your sake? I read the fucking Kama
Sutra, that's what. Indian civilization's greatest tribute to the pleasures
of sexual congress. In the classic translation by Sir Richard Burton
and F. F. fucking Arbuthnot, no less. I never thought sex could be
made so boring, yaar! Page after page of clinical detail — the nine
types of sexual union, the sixty-four arts, the definitions of the different types of marks a woman can make with her bloody nails, the
classifications of the female yoni as marelike or elephantine. How
does it bugger-all matter, man, whether a woman's embrace is like
"the twining of a creeper" or "the climbing of a tree"? And have you
ever heard anything more pissing ridiculous than Vatsyayana's categories of the sounds women make when being stropped — Phut,
Phat, Sut, Plat? Plat, I ask you! Anyway, the point I was going to
make is, okay, I grant you that sexual love is a fine thing, and sexual
pleasure may even be the finest of pleasures afforded to man, who am
I to argue? But its greatest advocate, this third-century guru of sex,
the immortal Vatsyayana, even he says, and I quote, "A girl who has
already been joined with others, that is, one who is no longer a
maiden, should never be loved, for it would be reproachable to do
such a thing." Look it up if you don't believe me — part 2, chapter 1.
Fucking reproachable, you understand?

And that's why I reproach you, Lucky. I've always admired you,
yaar. Admired you like hell. You've done great work in this town.
You're one guy who puts in all the hours at work you need to even if
your bloody wife is waiting for you to go out to a party. You're a man
who stands up for principle, against politicians, contractors, bosses,
staff. You believe in the job you're doing and you do it honestly and

effectively and well. Okay, so you've found something you didn't have before — so what? Enjoy it while you have it, and then move on, man! The way you move from posting to posting. You don't turn your life upside down for sex, man. Or even sexual love, if that's what you think it is. You don't give up everything you've spent your life living for because your cock tells you it's having a great time.

Don't just take it from me, Lucky. Take it from the bloody Kama Sutra.

letter from Priscilla Hart to Cindy Valeriani

August 22, 1989

Cin, dear Cin, how I wish you were here in Zalilgarh! I don't know how I can cope with all that's going on without you to talk to, to give me a hug and tell me I'm going to be all right. I'm seeing Lucky tonight and I'm scared it's all going to go wrong, that I've asked him for something he's not going to be able to give me. And I don't want to lose him, Cin. He's everything I've ever wanted in a man — doesn't that sound ridiculous? But it's true, and I do love him, Cin, I love him so much it hurts. And I don't know if he loves me enough to risk everything he knows for a life with me. . . .

And to add to everything, as if I don't have enough to deal with, you'll never believe what happened this morning. A little fellow who I know because he delivers tea and takes messages to and from Lucky's office, a boy known to everyone as Sweet Mohammed, came to the Center today. Turns out he's a neighbor or nephew or something of the Muslim woman I've told you about, Fatima Bi, remember? The one with the seven kids. Anyway, they all live on top of each other in the Muslim basti, and he said Fatima Bi had called him and given him an important message for me — she wanted to see me urgently. This from the same woman who'd been beaten up by her husband and told never to contact the Center again! Kadambari, the extension worker, was very nervous about venturing there again (she's Hindu, by the way, which doesn't help in the present charged circumstances, and of course I stick out like a sore thumb wherever I go, so there was no question of going to see Fatima Bi unnoticed). Kadambari was all for saying we couldn't do anything, but that made me mad. "This is what we're supposed to be here for," I said, rather shrilly I'm afraid. "If this woman has the courage to ask us to help, despite the terrible risks she's running, how can we let her down? We have to go!"

So we went, and guess what? Poor Fatima Bi, mother of seven, which is about six more than she can handle, had just discovered she's pregnant again. For the eighth blessed time.

She was beside herself, but she had found a certain steely determination. She asked us what she could do. Kadambari and I explained her options, and told her about the abortion services at the government hospital. "You mean, remove the child? Destroy it?" She flinched slightly as she asked, and when we answered yes, she closed her eyes tightly for a minute. But when she opened them again it was to ask a practical question: Did she need her husband's consent to go to the hospital for an abortion?

No, we told her. She was a free and responsible adult. Under the law, it was her body, and her decision. She didn't need anyone's permission.

Then, she said, she was going to do it.

She looked at us, and it was a new woman I saw, Cin. Not the scared and beaten woman of the previous encounters. Her face was calm. This worm had turned.

Could we help, she asked. Kadambari was about to answer no, that all we could do was to provide the address and telephone number of the abortion clinic, but I interrupted. I knew Fatima'd never be able to get to a telephone, let alone go to the clinic in person to set things up. "We'll make the appointment for you," I said. It was stretching our mandate a bit, but I felt that Fatima Bi had gone so far toward taking control of her own body, her own life, that we needed to give her just that little extra bit of support.

Kadambari didn't like it one bit. The woman's got no real commitment to the cause; for her it's just a job. She looked at me, with her inscrutably dark and sallow face, the black hair pulled tightly back from her forehead, and I knew she thought I was a foreign busybody interfering in something that was none of my business, making things more difficult for her. But I was having none of it. "You're an extension worker," I reminded her. "It's time to extend yourself and work." I don't think she'll ever forgive me for that.

Of course I asked Fatima if she wasn't afraid of her husband's reaction to our visit. Surely he might hear from the neighbors, from someone in this promiscuously crowded basti, that we'd come calling? And when she finally went to the clinic, might he not hear of it? I didn't want Fatima to go ahead without having thought it all through.

It turned out that her husband, Ali, had gone out of town for three days. By the time he was back, she wanted it to be over.

"And then?" I asked. "Won't he be angry?"

"He'll be angry," Fatima replied, her voice flat in the noontime stillness. "But by then it'll be too late. It won't matter anymore."

Lakshman and Priscilla

August 22, 1989

— I love you.

[*Silence.*]

— I said I love you.

— I heard you.

— Is that all you have to say?

— What does it mean?

— What do you mean, what does it mean?

— I know what I mean when I say I love you. I don't say it often. I don't say it lightly. What does it mean when you say it?

— It means I love you. I love the sound of your voice. I love the way your hair tumbles down your face. I love the way you move, the way you arrange your limbs when you sit, or lie, or stand. I love your habit of writing poetry and hiding it away in your scrapbook. I love making love to you. I love the way your face looks when I am moving inside you. I love the sounds you make on our little mat in this magical room. I love being loved by you.

— I know you love me. I just don't know how much.

— I love you! Isn't that enough? I don't think it's possible to love anyone more than I love you.

— Those are just words. Words are just words until you act on them.

— I am acting on them. I'm with you, aren't I?

— Yes, but that's for now. You'll be gone in an hour, more or less. Back to your wife, your daughter. To a home you don't share with me.

— You know what my situation is. I have never misled you.

— I know your situation. But that doesn't make it any easier.

— I know it's not easy for you. It's not easy for me.

— It's easy enough. A woman who's available at your convenience, two evenings a week. You don't have to give up anything. Your work, your social life, your family, your official commitments. You have it all. Including me.

— You make it sound so simple. As if there were no effort, no commitment involved in carving out the you-shaped space in my life, a space that has grown and spread through every part of my being. I didn't have room for you in my life, Priscilla. I didn't need you in my life. I had trained myself to live without love. I told you when we first became involved: This is crazy. For you. For me. Do you remember my words, the second time we met at the Kotli, when you sent me that note and I came here? I said, "I'm overworked, overweight, and married." And you said, I don't care.

— I still don't care.

— But you do. You do care. And you've reminded me of it again today.

— How can I not remind you of it? I live with it every day. With knowing that the man I love has no room for me in his day, unless it happens to be a Tuesday or Saturday. That he will leave an evening with me for a dinner with his wife. That if he's with me, it's for an hour, at most two, and then he'll be off, leaving me to hug my own loneliness.

— Wouldn't you have been lonelier without me? Look, I know how you feel. I live with my own guilt.

— I know you do. But what have you had to give up for me?

— My peace of mind.

— That comes with the territory. If you want peace of mind, don't fall in love.

— I didn't intend to fall in love. When I try and juggle the hundred things in my life, when I feel the guilt of neglecting my daughter, of letting my work pile up in my in-tray, of putting a couple of hours with you ahead of going to the temple with my family, of fearing I will be missed precisely when I cannot explain my absence, I feel that falling in love was the most irresponsible thing I could possibly have done.

— What a curious word to use about love. Irresponsible! So you're suffering guilt about being irresponsible. That doesn't sound much like sacrifice. Other men would give up worlds to have the woman they love. You've given up nothing.

— Why must it be necessary to have given up something?
[*Silence.*]

— Anyway, I have. I've given up my certitudes.

— Your certitudes.

— I have. I've given up the carefully circumscribed order of my life, with its assumptions, its compromises, its predictabilities. I've given up the sense a Brahmin strives all his life to attain, the sense of being anchored to the world. Loving you, I'm adrift. Everything around me is turbulence. I do not know whether I'll sail to a new and sunny paradise with you or crash foundering on the rocks. To me, at my stage in life, that's a lot to give up.

— I've given up a few things too. Do you know what it's like to have a man you can't speak to when you need him? To feel the ache of needing you and knowing you're beyond reach? To not be able to acknowledge you in public, not to go out openly together, not to be able to see you across a crowded room and know that we belong together and I'm leaving with you?

— Do you think I don't feel the same need? Don't you think that every fiber of my being is clamoring to shout to the world, "She's mine, I love her, she loves me"?

— But you can't. You've got too much to lose.

— Yes.

— Or perhaps you just aren't sure enough of your love.

— That's nonsense. You know I love you.

— There's a French saying, "There is no love, there are only proofs of love."

— You've had plenty of proofs of my love.

— What proof? In our lovemaking? I've been made love to just as passionately by men who did not love me.

— You don't have to remind me of that.

— Lucky, you can never prove your love enough. Until you really give up your comfortable other life for me. Until you say to me, "Be mine forever. In the eyes of the world."

— You're mine forever. In my eyes. In my heart. You know that.

— I don't know that I do. Sometimes I think I'm just some romantic fantasy for you. You say I'm in your heart. But you have really no

216

idea where that is. Your heart is just a compartment of your mind. I occupy a space in it, walled off from your work, your writing, your family. When you're with me, you live in that space. I have no reality outside it.

— That's simply not fair. I think of you, love you, breathe you, wherever I am. You accompany me in my heart to meetings, to official dinners, to encounters with ministers. You join arguments you haven't even heard. I imagine you sitting next to me at places you've never been to. You're not just in some compartment of my mind. You permeate my life.

— As I told you. I'm a fantasy.

— I promise you you're not.

— You've promised me nothing, Lucky. You expect my love, unconditionally, but you give me nothing in exchange.

— Nothing?

— I didn't mean that. You give me your affection, you give me your poems, you give me little gifts, you give me dinners, you help me here in all sorts of ways. But you haven't given me the assurance of a future. Sometimes you talk about us being together in America, in India, and it *is* fantasy, that's all it is, except that I've been slow in catching on.

— That's not fair. I've meant it every time we've talked about the future. I've contemplated turning my life upside down. I've agonized over the pain and disruption this would cause, to my family, my daughter, my work, my place in the world. But I've also told myself that all this would be worthwhile because you love me and I love you and I would have a new chance of "being beloved in the world" — something I had felt I would never experience in my life. And then, I think of my daughter, the most vulnerable and innocent victim of my future happiness, and I can't go on.

— You can't go on. And you keep saying you love me.

— Of course I love you. I'll love you as long as I live.

— But you won't give me any assurances we'll be together.

— I don't want to lie to you. I want only to give you a certainty I myself feel. I feel certain of my love. I don't feel certain that I can risk destroying my daughter to fulfil my love. Don't you see?

— Aren't you afraid you could lose me?

— More afraid of it than of anything else, except losing my daughter.

— But you don't have to lose either of us. Your daughter'll always be your daughter, Lucky. And you don't have to lose me. You could have me so easily. Just by committing yourself, clearly, now.

— I can't. Not now.

— I understand you're scared. About your daughter.

— I am scared. But not only about my daughter. About you too.

— About me? Why?

— Look, this is difficult to say without hurting you, and I don't intend to hurt you.

— Go on.

— It's not easy. You're from a different world, Priscilla. There are a lot of adjustments I'd have to make to be part of that world as your — husband.

— It's not that difficult, Lucky. You're more Western than you think you are. You'll adjust pretty easily.

— It's not that kind of adjustment I'm talking about. I mean adjusting within myself. Look, let me explain. It's something that troubled me from the start, but I kept pushing it aside, telling myself it didn't matter. In my culture, no man with any self-respect gives his mangalsutra, his ring, his name, to a woman who's been with other men before. I never thought that in my life I would ever be in a position where another man could even think, "I have slept with his wife. I have seen his wife naked. His wife has pleasured me."

— You're sick.

— I'm Indian. As far as I know, that's the way the vast majority of the world thinks: The woman you marry is the repository of your honor.

— I don't believe I'm hearing this, from an educated man in 1989.

— That's the point. I learned. I became an educated man of 1989. I trained myself not to let it matter. I learned to love you without letting the shadows of the others fall between my love and your body. Oh, I suppose that, without thinking about it, I had sort of shared the general belief here that there are the women you sleep with, and the women you marry. I've grown out of that belief, quite consciously. I had started off sleeping with you, not even thinking of anything permanent, let alone marrying you. Then I fell in love. Now I found myself wanting to marry the woman I was sleeping with.

— How convenient.

— Spare me the irony, Priscilla. My knowledge of your past has tormented me far more than I let on. But I told myself I had to understand the culture you came from. That by the standards of your peers you're practically virginal. And above all, that what mattered was that you loved me.

— Yes.

— I told myself, how does it matter who she's been with before? What matters is that she's with me now. I have her. These other men don't.

— Exactly.

— I want so much for it not to matter, don't you see? But can you blame me for being scared? How can I know that a woman who has slept with six men will never contemplate sleeping with a seventh? Can I afford to sink myself emotionally into a love that might be withdrawn from me as it has been from others? Or should I tell myself, love her while she loves you, love her while you can, let the future take care of itself?

— What does that mean? The future never takes care of itself. You have to take care of your own future if you want one.

— I'm just trying to explain my torment to you. I have a career where I try to make a difference to my own people. I have a daughter whom I want to see make her way in the world. And I have you. Or at least I think I do, but I'm scared.

— You can only have me if you want me, Lucky. If you truly love me.

— I love you, Priscilla. But . . .

— But?

— But there's too much involved. I'm wondering whether I can find the strength to accept that I have to love you enough to let you go.

219

— How can you say that? That's nonsense. How can you love me and let me go?

— I don't know. I only know it would be as painful as amputating a limb. It would mean going round for years afterwards haunted by the ghost of what might have been. And yet, old Oscar put it best: "In love, one always begins by deceiving oneself, and one always ends by deceiving others." I guess I've deceived myself; I had no intention ever of deceiving you. But the more I think of it, the more it seems to me it would be the right thing to do.

— Right by whom? Not by me.

— Right by my family, by Rekha, and by you. You have a wonderful future awaiting you in America. I shouldn't presume to deprive you of it. If I were to say, darling Priscilla, I do not know about our future, I am full of doubt and uncertainty, I love you but I am in torment, I do not want to inflict this on you, take your freedom if you want it — what would you do? What is best for you? Think about it. But please don't doubt my love. Everything I've said comes out of my love for you. Even my willingness to let you go.

— I can hardly believe all that I've heard. Are you saying you want me to be involved with you but you can't leave your wife and daughter? Are you saying you might leave them for me if I hadn't been with other men before? Are you saying you love me but not enough to disrupt your life to be with me? You sound terribly confused.

— I am. When we got involved I began to think nothing else mattered. Not my wife, not my job, not my child, not your past. But I've discovered it all does. That I can't just walk away from it all.

— But you can just walk away from me.

— No, I can't! Don't you see how terrible my torment is?

— But don't *you* see that I can't wait forever for you to end your confusion?

— I know you can't.

— You've come to mean more to me than anyone I've ever known. I thought we had a future together.

— Please don't cry. Here, take my handkerchief.

— I don't understand, Lucky. You tell me I'm the woman you've always dreamed of, I fulfil every desire you have as a man, and when I tell you I feel the same way and I want us to be forever, you withdraw?

— I'm not withdrawing, Priscilla. I love you. I just can't break up my family, destroy my daughter—

— I'd never ask you to destroy your daughter. Can't you take her away from that dreadful wife of yours?

— I doubt a court would give her to me. And with my life, my work, how could I take care of her?

— I'd help.

— But you're not her mother, Priscilla. With all her faults, Geetha is.

— Please remove your arm, Lucky. I'm leaving.

— I don't want you to go.

— No, you want me to stay, so that you can fuck me and then you can go, to your wife. Thanks, but I've had enough of that scenario.

— Priscilla, don't get up, please.

[*Silence.*]

— Priscilla, I love you.

[*Silence. A long silence, followed by the creaking of a door, a sibilant sniffling retreating down the stairs, the rattle of a bicycle chain, and the squeaking crunch of thin tires on the twig-strewn ground, fading into the distance.*]

from Lakshman's journal

August 22, 1989

Words, old Oscar would have said, mere words — but how terrible, how vivid, how cruel. And is there anything so real as the words we use to define our lives?

I remember an old sadhu my parents took me to once, a wizened bare figure whose skin hung impossibly in folds, the hair on his head sparse and unruly, his white beard his only adornment. We sat at his feet for what seemed to me the longest time, but when I began to speak he raised an aged finger to his white-shrouded lips. "Whatever you have to say, my son," he said, "say it in silence."

It is a prescription I forget too often: Whatever you have to say, say it in silence.

With Priscilla now, silence is all I have.

letter from Lakshman to Priscilla

August 25, 1989

My darling Priscilla,

Please try and understand what I'm going through. The last three days since I saw you have been the worst three days of my life. I was shattered when you left like that, and I haven't slept a wink. I feel physically ill. I told you that losing you would be like amputating a limb — they say you constantly feel pain from the place where the limb used to be. In my case, that's my heart.

I feel I've conducted a terrible mutilation of myself in telling you why I couldn't give you the commitment you seek. Watching you cycle away into the darkness last Tuesday was the most wrenching experience of my life.

And yet I have made my own bed and I must lie in it. I'm a desperately sad human being who is suffering terribly, and my suffering is made no more bearable by the fact that it is self-inflicted. I could have said something else to you, but I knew you deserved the truth. I felt I could not do otherwise, my dearest Priscilla, and be true to myself, above all to my obligations as a man and my duty as a father. It was the most difficult choice I've ever had to make, and at one level I still can't believe I've made it.

I can't bear to think I won't see you again at the Kotli. I'll be there anyway tomorrow, as usual. I'll understand if you don't want to come anymore. I'm in too much pain to be anywhere else on Saturday, so I'll go there, even if it is to be alone with my memories.

May the divine Providence in which both of us believes give you strength and happiness, and may some of it rub off on me.

Always your (un)Lucky

from Lakshman's journal

August 26, 1989

She comes to him that Saturday, of course. She leaves her cycle in the shrubbery and walks softly up the old stone stairway to their lair. He is sitting on the ledge, his hair swept back by the wind, looking pensively at the river as darkness slowly reaches out to embrace the horizon. She sees him and her heartbeat catches in her veins like a scarf on a doorknob, so that she stumbles on the threshold and has to steady herself. He turns then, mist in his eyes, and when he sees her the gloom lifts off his shoulders like a veil. He rises and bounds to her, and she is caught up in his arms like a butterfly in a strong gust, fluttering but imprisoned, and he is kissing her so hard that the breath is pushed out of her. She surrenders, feeling his hands running up and down her body as if to reassure himself she is all there. He finds that she is, and his heart is delighted, his eyes sparkling in wordless pleasure as she in turn strokes his face, still silent, and he catches her fingers and kisses them, and before she knows it he is on top of her and inside her and it is as if he is strumming the same tune she has always heard and it has never stopped playing. And afterwards neither of them wants to speak because each is afraid of what the other might say.

And they are right not to speak, for how can either of them explain what has happened? It is a blur in his mind, and yet an indelible blur. He peels off her clothing, the soft cotton skirt with the swirling print, the comfortably loose blouse, as light and flammable as the spirit it sheathes. The hooks of her bra do not resist him this time, her panties slide off like a wisp, and she is naked in his urgent arms, unquestioning in her surrender. He is still kissing her as he turns her around, and she shows no surprise at finding herself on her knees on the mat. He is behind her now, tugging at his belt, and he sees them both in the mirror, that long mirror in which they have

224

so often seen the sunset, except that what it reveals now in the shadows is the paleness of her beneath him on her hands and knees, her face averted, her breasts swaying with each thrust as he takes her from behind. He is transported by his conquest as he watches her in the mirror and beneath him, the curve of her back vividly stretched in her submission, his hands on the soft flesh below her hips as he drives home his message of need and possession. He remembers that this is not supposed to happen, that this is the one thing she will not do, but he has not asked and she has not resisted. He keeps his eyes open throughout, blinking only briefly in climax, and in his wonderment he does not see, or he imagines he cannot see, the solitary tear that drops gently down her love-saddened face.

Geetha Lakshman at the Shiva Mandir

September 2, 1989

Every Saturday I have come here with my daughter to pray, Swamiji, and I have sought your blessings and your advice. Remember how you told me that a devout woman like me should not hesitate to come to you with any kind of problem? Tonight I really need your help, Swamiji.

Yesterday my husband's friend Gurinder told me he had to speak to me. He said he had thought about it for a long time and hesitated but now he felt he had no choice. He made me swear not to breathe a word to my husband about what he was going to tell me. And then he said — aiyo, such a terrible thing. He said my husband was in love with another woman and wanted to leave me. It was the yellow-haired American woman, of course. And he was thinking of leaving my daughter and me and running off with her to America.

Gurinder said he was telling me this because he wanted me to do everything I could to prevent this from happening. He wanted, he said, to save my husband from himself. He was doing this as a friend, because my husband would not listen to his advice that what he was doing was wrong.

What can I do, I wailed. That is up to you, Gurinder said. Plead with him. Love him. Make him feel he must stay. You must fight to keep your husband, Geetha, or you will lose him.

Swamiji, my heart broke. When Gurinder left I rushed to my husband's study, where he keeps all his papers. He is often there, even at night, writing, writing, so much. He gets up at night to go and write there and I pretend to be asleep because I know he doesn't want me to know what he's doing. Sometimes, in the old days, when he went to work I used to sneak in and read what he had written. But it was all very difficult Yinglish poetry that I could not understand. So for a long time I had not bothered to read his writings. Now I knew I had to.

This time it was heartbreaking, Swamiji. What Gurinder had told me is true! He is having an affair with this woman. He has written so many chhi-chhi things about the things they do together. And he has written that he does not love me and he is thinking of leaving me and our daughter. What can I do, Swamiji? I cannot talk to him about this. It would kill me if I had to tell him what I knew! I can only turn to God, Swamiji, and to you. Please conduct a special puja for me to help me keep my husband!

Yes, of course, Swamiji. Beyond a puja? Anything you say. No, no, I don't have to ask my husband for money. My father will send you the money. I don't care about the expense. I don't care how you do it. Use tantra, do the tandava, use anyone and anything you want, Swamiji, but please don't let this foreign devil-woman run away with my husband. . . .

Ram Charan Gupta to Randy Diggs

(translated from Hindi)

October 12, 1989

I shall be frank with you, Mr. Diggs. I don't know whether I am wasting my time talking to you. You foreign journalists and photographers who cover India are only interested in the kind of India you want to see. The horrible, dark India of killing and riots, like this riot that you are so interested in, of course: it is all of a piece with the stories of poverty and disease, of the widows of Benares, the caste system and the untouchables, poor people selling their blood or their kidneys, the slums of Calcutta or Bombay, brides being burned for not having brought enough dowry — how many such stories have you written for your American readers, Mr. Diggs? Of course it is even better if the bad things about India are being set right by kind white Christians — Mother Teresa is a real favorite of yours, I'm sure, especially after she won the Nobel Prize, and isn't a white man making a lot of money these days by selling the pornography of poverty in something he calls "The City of Joy"? I do not deny that these things exist in India, Mr. Diggs, but they are only a part of our reality, and not such a large part of it either. But it is all that you and your cohorts in the foreign press are interested in, and you tell the world that is what India is all about.

You protest, Mr. Diggs? Just because I am speaking to you in Hindi, do not think I cannot read your English-American papers. In fact I will add to my indictment. I have only listed your bad-news stories, and I know you write less negative pieces too. But what are those, Mr. Diggs? Exotic local color. The maharajas and their palaces, their polo games, their fabulous wealth, their lavish lifestyles. You westerners are fascinated by them long after they have lost whatever importance they had in my country. Of course you write about

Rajasthan, its colorful festivals, the Pushkar Mela, the camel fairs, the religious pilgrimages, the beaches of Goa, the erotic sculptures of Khajuraho. I am glad this brings a few tourists in to spend their American dollars in my country, but do not think, Mr. Diggs, that you or they are seeing "India" either.

So what does that leave us with when it comes to hard news, Mr. Diggs? Simplicities. Hindu-Muslim violence; "Hindu fundamentalism"; the secular Congress Party; the westernized pilot Rajiv Gandhi; the fanatic forces of Hindu revivalism. How many dozens of foreign correspondents are there in Delhi, Mr. Diggs? And how many of those have departed from this stale menu? How many have written stories that pay honor to India's great culture and civilization, its history, the complexities and philosophical grandeur of Hinduism? I know of very few, Mr. Diggs. I have no reason to believe you are an exception.

I know you are only interviewing me about this riot because an American girl was killed in it. Tragically killed, I grant you that. But dozens of Hindu youths were also killed, stabbed, wounded, and they do not matter to you. You and your tribe will write of attacks on minorities in India, especially Christians, but you will not mention that minorities — Jews, Parsis, Christians, and even Muslims — have found refuge in this country for two thousand years and have been allowed to practice their own faith without hindrance by Hindu rulers. When will you and your friends in the foreign press give your readers an article on the richness and glory of this ancient country, Mr. Diggs, its varied and profound civilization?

Don't bother to answer me: I know what the truth is. Even before you arrive in Delhi, you foreign presswallahs already have your biases, stereotypes, predilections about India, and they never change with experience. Some of your clichés are romantic ones: John Masters, Gunga Din, the Bengal Lancers, Kipling's innocent Western jungle boy surrounded by the dark animals of the Hindu kingdom — you know them all. But their stories are not my stories, Mr. Diggs. You are writing Western stories for a Western audience and telling them you are writing about India.

And some of your preconceptions are the obvious ones: poverty, the caste system, the untouchables, religious strife. Your norm is a world without any of these, a world that is prosperous, clean, and tranquil. But do you not have Harlem, Mr. Diggs? Or Appalachia? Don't think I do not know about your American poverty. Or your discrimination against your Negroes, your so-called blacks. Isn't that a hundred times worse than our caste system? After all, very often you cannot tell a man's caste by looking at him, but you can always tell black from white at first glance, can't you? And don't you have your own Christian Coalition? How is that different from our Sangh Parivar? Or is religious belief only acceptable in politics if it is Christian, not Hindu?

How many Western lies and distortions about India are we supposed to swallow, Mr. Diggs? The British partition our country, and you put the blame on us. A Christian is killed in a property dispute, and you write that he has been killed because he is a Christian. A politician speaks of rebuilding the most sacred temple of his faith, and you call him an intolerant fanatic.

But then, you don't make any effort to understand Hindus, do you? It is all received wisdom. You portray us as the weak and helpless victims of millennia of invasions, starting with the Aryans three thousand five hundred years ago, the founding myth of British imperialism which sought to portray a weak and dark subcontinent at the mercy of Caucasian power and strength. But when Hindu historians and archaeologists say it never happened, that the Aryans were Indian, living here along the river Saraswati which has since dried up, they are pooh-poohed as chauvinists or fantasists. You are only too ready to trumpet the great achievements of the Mughals, their art and architecture, but in fact they mostly stole from Hindu talent; did you know that the Taj Mahal was really a Hindu palace? You attack the Hindutva movement as fundamentalist, but you say nothing about the thirteen centuries of Islamic fundamentalism and oppression they are reacting to. India is asserting itself, Mr. Diggs, and your readers are told nothing of the resurgent pride of Indians in their own land, their own culture, their own history. Instead all you can see is the threat to "secularism," as if that were some precious Indian heritage. What is this dogma imported from the West that I am supposed to fall on my knees before? Can the word "secularism" be found in the Vedas?

You don't understand. None of you do. But I am not surprised. India is a large and complex country, Mr. Diggs, with our contradictions, paradoxes, inconsistencies all ours. How can you foreigners be expected to understand it? Where else do you have our mixture of ethnicities and castes, our profusion of mutually incomprehensible languages, our varieties of geography and climate, our diversity of religions and cultural practices, our clamor of political parties, our ranges of economic development? How do you understand a country whose population is more than fifty percent illiterate but which has produced the world's largest pool of trained scientists and engineers? How do you cover the poverty and squalor of a land that led a Mughal emperor to declaim, "If on earth there be paradise of bliss, it is this, it is this, it is this"? Everything you write as the truth, I can show you the opposite is also true. You come from a country, Mr. Diggs, where everything is black and white, there are good guys and bad guys, cowboys and red Indians. You can only understand India on your own terms, and you do not understand that your terms do not apply here.

I have not finished. Don't protest. I know that you are not merely writing from your preconceptions — if that is all you did, your editors would fire you, would they not? So you embellish your prejudices by talking to Indians. Not usually Indians like myself, so I pay tribute to you, Mr. Diggs, for having taken the trouble to seek me out. No, you talk to Indians like yourselves — English-educated Indians, people who would not know how to tie a dhoti and are proud they do not eat with their hands. People like the district administrator Lakshman whom you will no doubt go to see. The very people who are anxious to explain their India to you are the ones you ought to mistrust, Mr. Diggs. Because they are too much like you to be of any use. They think they are modern, sophisticated, cosmopolitan, secular. They heap contempt on "Hindu fanatics," laugh at our faith and beliefs, sneer at our traditions. They are embarrassed by the real India, because they are desperately anxious to belong to the world. *Your* world. And you turn to them for insight and advice about *my* country?

231

All you get from the Indians you talk to is the view from New Delhi — even here in Zalilgarh. You foreign correspondents do not realize that New Delhi is not India. At least, not the New Delhi you see and hear, at your diplomatic receptions or businessmen's cocktail parties. *This* is India, Mr. Diggs. I am Indian. Listen to me.

letter from Priscilla Hart to Cindy Valeriani

September 3, 1989

Cin, my dear Cin, I don't know what to do. I went back to him
with everything still unresolved, because I couldn't bear not to. I
went to the Kotli again. And I held him, and he hugged me, and we
made love. Not just as usual. Something happened that day that I
don't really want to write about, but it made me realize how much I
love him, how much I want to give myself to him, how much I'm
sure he is the right man for me. I want to spend the rest of my life
with him, Cin, and it's driving me crazy. I wanted to talk about my
feelings afterwards but somehow the words didn't come and he
didn't want to say anything, didn't really want me to speak either. He
just held me so close against his chest that I couldn't move my lips
even if I wanted to.

So I don't really know where I stand with him, whether I should
be planning for a future with Lucky or packing for my scheduled
return to NY just over a month from now. Or both. God, Cin, I
need your advice.

And there's something else about which I don't know what to do.
Cindy, there's been another upsetting development in the Fatima Bi
business I wrote to you about. Ali, the husband, came back, found
out what she'd done, and beat the hell out of her. Hardly surprising.
He also came charging down to the Center looking for Kadambari
and me. Kadambari wasn't in — she was out on her rounds — and I
had to bear the brunt. He was murderously angry, eyes bloodshot
and red and practically popping out of their sockets, and when he
advanced toward me screaming "I told you to leave her alone!" a
couple of the men in the office had to physically restrain him. "I'll
kill the foreign whore!" he shouted as he was dragged out, flailing
his fists in my direction. Poor Mr. Shankar Das told me not to worry
and asked me if he should call the police. I told him not to. I

couldn't help thinking of poor Fatima Bi and the additional misery she'd suffer if her husband got pulled in by the police because of this. After all, I'd encouraged her to go to the clinic. I know I did the right thing. And I don't seriously believe that, once he's calmed down, Ali will try to do me any harm.

But the whole situation is getting me down. The Center sometimes seems to me a rather ineffective place, and though I write papers for Mr. Shankar Das that he seems to like a lot, I frankly wonder how much difference it makes. My fieldwork is largely done, but it involves doing the rounds with Kadambari, and I'm not real thrilled about that. Kadambari is a peculiar woman, and I'm not enjoying doing my field research in her company. Ever since the Fatima business she's sort of kept her distance from me, as if to signal to everyone that it was all my fault and she wanted no part of it. Well, telling women about their reproductive rights is her job, for Christ's sake!

And then Kadambari's made some strange comments in that sidelong way she has that really gets under my skin. She tells me I've been spotted cycling to the Kotli and that I should be careful, because no one goes there. I ask her why not and she says it's because people believe the place is haunted. I tell her I don't believe in ghosts and she replies, "It's haunted, but not only by ghosts." What's she getting at? I said I've been there a few times and I've never seen anyone else there. She says, well, everyone knows the DM — that's Lucky — likes to go there a lot, and when his car is outside the gate no one dares to venture in, but when he's not there, all sorts of "badmashes" — bad types — use the place. I glower at her and say that whenever I've been there I've never seen the DM either. Kadambari gives me an arch look, can you imagine, and flounces off, muttering, "Don't say I didn't warn you."

Cindy, one thing you've got to promise me, OK? These letters are between you and me. DON'T show them to anyone else, not even Matt. And don't breathe a word about them to my parents if you ever run into them — not that you would, of course. Tell them, I mean. It would just worry them, and it's not as if anyone in America can do anything about all of this anyway. My letters are just a way of

234

sharing everything in my life here with the one person who understands. Assume they're like the phone calls I'd have made to you if I was still in NY, OK? Tear them up when you've read them, as if you've just put the phone down.

Anyway, what does Kadambari think she's warned me about? Lucky? Well, in a small town like this I guess I should have realized that people would begin talking sooner or later. It can't do Lucky much good to be the subject of gossip among the likes of Kadambari. And I don't know how seriously to take her warning to be careful. Does she mean the Kotli's not safe or that I'll be found out? I don't want to ask Lucky because I'm afraid it'll worry him. And because I don't want to do anything that'll jeopardize our meeting there. It's the only place I love in Zalilgarh, and I'd rather die than give it up. . . .

transcript of Randy Diggs interview with District Magistrate V. Lakshman (Part 3)

October 13, 1989

Oh — they're here? Well, their timing isn't too bad. Mr. Diggs, it turns out that Priscilla's parents, the Harts, have shown up to see me. Ah, you know them, do you? Would you mind very much if I asked them to join us? They'll have the same questions as you, and I suppose I could kill two birds with one stone, if that doesn't sound too callous.

What's that? Yes, of course you can tape it, if they don't mind, naturally.

Do come in. Mr. Hart, Mrs. Hart, I'm pleased to meet you. [Scraping of chair.] I'm Lakshman, the district magistrate here. I believe you know Mr. Diggs of the New York Journal? He was just asking me about the events — the tragic events of two weeks ago. Would you mind if he remained here for our conversation and recorded my replies?

You're quite right, Mr. Hart, you're both interested in the truth. Indeed. The truth. You know, that's my government's official motto: "Satyameva Jayate." "Truth Alone Triumphs." It's on all our letterheads — and on this visiting card I've just given you. Truth Alone Triumphs. But sometimes I'm tempted to ask, whose truth? There's not always an easy answer.

Please do sit down, Mrs. Hart, Mr. Hart. Some tea? No? A soft drink? Ah, I'm afraid we have no Coca-Cola here. Would Campa-Cola be acceptable? No?

I do hope you have been comfortable in Zalilgarh. Yes of course, Mrs. Hart, I realize that comfort is not what you're looking for here. Forgive me.

You've seen the Center where Priscilla worked? And spoken to her project manager, Mr. Das? Good.

236

Been to her home? A rather simple place, I'm told. No, I've never been there, Mrs. Hart.

Yes, I knew Priscilla rather well. Or perhaps I should say, my wife and I did. Priscilla was a fairly frequent guest at our dining table. She was such pleasant company, you know. Such pleasant company. And Geetha and I took pleasure in helping her feel welcome in this little town. She seemed to cope with her loneliness rather well.

No, I'm afraid I haven't the slightest idea why she was where she was when she was — killed. Forgive me, I feel a sense of responsibility, really, not merely because I'm in charge of law and order in this town, but because I've been haunted by the thought that perhaps — you see, I think she first heard about the Kotli from me. I was talking to her about the town, and I believe I mentioned it was the one place worth visiting for, shall we say, touristic reasons. I've been there myself sometimes and the sunsets over the river are spectacular. I fear she may have taken my advice.

Yes, of course I can arrange a visit for you there. I'll do so immediately. And you too, Mr. Diggs, if you wish.

I'm afraid we're — none of us is very sure what happened. It seems a group of Muslim troublemakers chose to use the abandoned ruin as a sort of storehouse to manufacture some crude homemade bombs the day before the riot. The day of the riot itself she seems to have stumbled across them, or they across her — no one knows. She was, as you know, stabbed to death. I'm truly sorry.

No, no, there was no robbery or any other kind of assault. It looks like Priscilla simply had the misfortune to go to that place at the very moment her assailants chose to use it. The killers probably thought she'd report them to the police. That they had to kill her to ensure her silence.

No, we didn't find out till nearly twenty-four hours later. It was such an out-of-the-way place that no one really gave the Kotli much thought.

Our energies were focused on the town, and particularly the Muslim quarter. That's where the worst of the rioting occurred. I've been telling Mr. Diggs the details of the story.

What happened is that these fellows brought their bombs into town and began throwing them. We put a stop to that fairly quickly and caught one of the perpetrators. He didn't mention Priscilla in his confession, but he did tell us about their having used the Kotli. It was in a routine follow-up visit to the Kotli that the police found — the body.

No one has confessed to the murder. The bomb makers all claim they never even saw her. Eight lives were lost in the riots, Mr. Hart, including one of a boy who worked in this office. Not one of them is linked to an identifiable assailant. That's how it often is in riots. A confused clamor of hatred, violence, weapons, assaults. In the end, no one is responsible. Or perhaps a whole community is responsible. People pull out bombs or knives, then melt away into the darkness. We are left with the bodies, the burned and destroyed homes, the legacy of hate and mistrust. And it goes on.

I'm sorry I don't have much more to tell you. Perhaps you ought to meet the superintendent of police. I'll ask him to receive you. I'm afraid our rules won't permit him to show you the actual police report, but I'm sure he'll tell you what it says. I'll give him a call and urge him to cooperate fully. We know you've come a long way on this very sad errand.

Would Sunday work for you? Good. I'll try and arrange the appointment and get word to you. No, that's all right, we work seven-day weeks here these days. And of course, we'll organize a visit to the Kotli.

Your daughter was a wonderful person, Mrs. Hart, Mr. Hart. She will be greatly missed here in Zalilgarh.

letter from Lakshman to Priscilla

September 18, 1989

My dearest, most precious Priscilla,

For the first time in my life I genuinely do not know how to say
something I must say to you. I cannot bring myself to say it directly,
to your face, and so I must say it in this letter. We are supposed to
meet tomorrow, Tuesday. I won't be there.

Priscilla, forgive me, but I must end our relationship. I love you
but I cannot leave my wife, my daughter, my job, my country, my
whole life, for my love. I just can't go on giving you the hope of a
future together and returning home to the reality of my present. I
believe it is more honest to tell you that what you want cannot be.

I cannot bear the thought that in writing these words I am
hurting someone who has been nothing but good and loving to me.
I cannot bear the knowledge that I am depriving myself of your
love, which has fulfilled me in ways that nothing else in my life can
ever compensate for. In writing this letter I know I am losing
something I was lucky to have found in the first place — a good,
lovely and loving woman, a chance of a different life, the second
chance that comes to so few in this world.

Then why am I doing it? A dozen times in recent weeks I had
decided to leave my marriage. Yesterday I told myself my decision was
final, that I couldn't live without you. Then last night I couldn't sleep.
I kept imagining what my departure would mean to Rekha. I knew
how Geetha would react — I was sure she would collapse in incom-
prehension and grief; she simply would not be able to deal with the
shock. But Rekha would suffer the most horrendous trauma. I kept
thinking not just that she would suffer the pain of a broken home, but
of the small daily losses she would suffer — that she would not have
her Daddy tucking her into bed at night or reading her an Enid Blyton

story, that she would miss her Daddy at breakfast every day, that she could no longer turn to Daddy with her homework, with her questions about the world, about words, about life: the hundred small interactions that make up the texture of a father-child relationship. And I realized, then, that I could not deny these to her and still feel myself a worthy human being. That having brought her into the world, I had a responsibility, an obligation, to see her through those difficult years of growing up, secure in the environment of a predictable two-parent family structure. And that if I failed to fulfil this obligation in pursuing my own happiness, I would in fact find no happiness at all.

One day she will be grown up and gone, and none of this will matter. But today, now, I cannot do it to her. This is when she needs a father most. But you, understandably, want me to make the break now or never. I respect the way you feel, my precious Priscilla, but I cannot do it now.

I realized, too, during this tormented night, that I could only make you unhappy too, because my guilt at abandoning my family — which is how I would see it — would corrode my feelings for the person for whom I had abandoned them. When you evoke that kind of love, you want to be worthy of it. I could not have abandoned my responsibilities to my daughter and felt worthy of you.

In other words, dearest Priscilla, I was — I am — torn between two kinds of love and the prospect of two kinds of unhappiness. I chose my love for my daughter over my love for you, and the unhappiness of losing you to the unhappiness of shattering her. That is my choice, and I must live with it. I never thought either would be easy: this one is killing me.

I know you will think this proves I never really loved you. That you were a sexual convenience at worst, an escape from a loveless marriage at best. You know that's not true, Priscilla; you've seen what happened the first time I tried to leave you. I still love everything about you, no less than I ever have. I can't bear the knowledge that you are no longer mine, but I want you to be happy. I would do anything for you, short of destroying my family.

In pain, and with love,

Lucky

letter from Priscilla Hart to Cindy Valeriani

September 19, 1989

Dearest Cin, what am I to do? It's over now, he's written me this awful letter, and I've been crying all night. I suppose Mom was right when she said that I see things in people that they don't see in themselves. I saw so much in Lucky — a good man in a bad marriage, someone capable of love who had no opportunity to love until I came along, a man who hadn't seen his own unhappiness fully until he met me. With me I think he realized for the first time that he hadn't truly known love in his life and that he could find happiness loving and being loved. Happiness, of course, at a price. A price that in the end he was not prepared — with his upbringing, his sense of his responsibilities, his inability to escape from Indian society — to pay.

On one level I feel bitterly angry with him. I feel used. And I can't believe a man of his intelligence would be so blind and conventional. And cowardly. In my tears last night, there were moments of deep rage at the way he dumped me. "You two-faced jerk!" I screamed at the letter he'd written me.

And yet, I can't bring myself to hate him, Cin. There's a part of me that wants to, but I can't, I still love him so much. I'm in terrible pain, but I don't want to regret a minute of the seven months we had together. "Had together" — I don't even know if I can say that of a relationship where we were only together two evenings a week, except for those occasional dinners at his home where I was beginning to feel more and more uncomfortable. But yes, "together." Because I loved being <u>with</u> him, Cindy. I saw in him all the things I wanted in a man — not just his looks or his voice, but his earnestness about the world, his desire to make a difference, his easy confidence in his own authority, and his command, quite simply, of India. The India I'd come back to rediscover as an adult, the India that had changed my life so profoundly a decade ago. Loving Lakshman filled every pore of my being; it gave me a sense of attachment, not just to a man, but to this land. Does this sound hokey to you, Cin? I hope not, because I can't explain it any better.

What hurts is that it must have meant so much less to him. I suppose at the beginning he just thought of me as an easy lay. Our relationship must just have been a sexual adventure for him those first few weeks. I know he came to love me afterwards, but I realize now that I'm not someone he would have started off falling in love with. He was attracted to me, sure, but he began it all, that first evening at the Kotli, as just an affair. Through sex he found love, and in love he found confusion, uncertainty, fear. Whereas I loved him from almost the first moment and felt nothing but certainty about him. The sex was just a means of expressing my love, a way of giving myself to the man I loved. I'm not sure that he ever understood the difference.

He used to quote Wilde about hypocrisy being just a way of multiplying your personalities. That was part of Lucky's problem — he had multiple personalities, and they didn't match. The district administrator, the passionate lover, the traditional husband and father, the closet writer who fantasized about a masterpiece he could write one day on an American campus — all of those were him. I couldn't hold on to all of them at the same time. And so I lost him.

But then I borrowed a copy of "The Picture of Dorian Gray" from him, and I came across the actual quote. And guess what, Wilde wasn't talking about hypocrisy at all, you know, but about insincerity! Was Lucky trying to warn me that his love was insincere? I think about these things and it drives me crazy!

It's strange, isn't it, Cin? Ever since Darryl it's been I who walked away from relationships, I who ended every one of them. Poor Winston could never understand why I wouldn't marry him. Nor could my mother. Instead I fell for someone completely unsuitable by Mom's standards — married, foreign, tied to another life — and I've allowed him to dump me. Mom would probably blame it on India. You were overwhelmed by it all, dear, she'd say, this big, hot, foreign, oppressive, unfamiliar place, and you attached yourself to this man as a port in the storm. Once you come home you'll realize he didn't really mean that much to you. You'll get over it.

And that's why I've never been able to tell Mom about Lucky. She'd never understand.

Do you remember, Cin, when we were little and you used to tease me about the amount of tender loving care I gave my Barbie doll? How I'd sit with my little nylon brush and gently smooth down her golden mane, over and over again? "Give it a rest, Prissy," you'd say. "She's a doll. She can't tell whether you've brushed her hair three times or two." And I'd be shocked. "But I'm all she's got!" I'd reply. "If I don't do it for her, who will?" Which of course was totally beside the point you were making. But that's the way I was! And I wonder if I wasn't doing the same thing with Lakshman — stroking him over and over again, oblivious to his reaction? Telling myself I was all he'd got — the only true love he'd ever know? Was I projecting onto him the needs I imagined he must have? Oh Cindy, have I been a fool?

But I have to see him once more. There's something I've got to tell him. And I have to look into his eyes when I say it. Only then will I know if he really ever loved me.

Kadambari to Shankar Das

September 20, 1989

Sir, I am so scared, I am so upset, I don't know what to do, sir. Yes, sir, I will calm down, sir, I just wanted to tell you that that man Ali, sir, the chauffeur, Fatima Bi's husband, he caught me in the street, sir, when I was going to visit one of our IUD cases, and he threatened me, sir. He said he would cut off my — cut off my breasts, sir, because I had told his wife to get an abortion. Sir, I was so scared, I told him it wasn't me, sir, it was the American girl, it was all her idea, and she would be leaving the country soon, so please leave me alone. And he said, sir, you tell that American whore that if I ever lay my hands on her, she won't be catching that plane to America. Sir, I don't know what to do, if I tell her she will just be frightened, but he seems to mean it, sir. What should I do?

Yes, sir, of course, sir. You are right, sir. He is a government driver, he has a job and a family, he will never do such a thing, it is all just talk. Yes, sir, you are right, sir. I will try to forget about it, sir. But sir, please do not ask me to visit those Muslim bastis for a while. Please, sir, let me have another caseload until I am sure he has calmed down. Thank you, sir. You are my mother and my father, sir. Thank you very, very much, sir. . . .

from Katharine Hart's diary

October 13, 1989

Kadambari, who seems to have been assigned by Mr. Das as our
guide to the town, took me today to the women's ward of the
Zalilgarh hospital. It was just as well that Rudyard couldn't come —
he was told it would not be appropriate — because I don't think he
could have handled what I saw.

The hospital is a large, run-down building, dating from
somewhere after the turn of the century, though buildings age so
rapidly in this country that it could be a lot more recent than that.
Decay and rot are everywhere — the bits of chipped-off masonry
visible as you enter, the peeling yellow paint on the walls, the rusty
carts on which dirty orderlies in stained uniforms wheel their
antiquated supplies, the pervasive odor of waste matter and
ammonia. A public hospital in small-town India is a far cry from the
luxury hospital in Delhi in which Lance had his appendix removed;
the only thing the two places have in common appears to be the
profusion of people — people waiting to be seen, people bustling
about the corridors, people standing around aimlessly, people lining
up outside the dispensary and the lab. But they're a different class of
people. I knew before I stepped into the hospital that this was where
the really poor came; the somewhat better-off would frequent one
of the two private "nursing homes" that have sprung up in the
town, while the rich would simply go to Delhi. But even then I was
not prepared for the horror of the women's ward.

We entered it from a dank corridor, dimly lit by a flickering neon
tubelight. The ward was essentially a single long room, and I was
drawn short by the sight as soon as I stepped in. The narrow metal
cots were all occupied, and there were women on the floor as well,
some on thin beddings, some stretched out on their own faded
cotton saris. Overflowing refuse-bins spilled onto the floor, where

bloodstained rags already lay, so that I had to pick my way over garbage while avoiding stepping on bodies, and vice versa. It was hot, and there was no fan; perspiration dripped down my arms, and the stale smell of sweat from dozens of bodies mingled with the chemicals in the air to make me gag. Many women moaned in pain; only a few seemed to have IV's on their arms, dripping morphine into their veins. Some stared emptily at the ceiling, where darting lizards and geckos provided the only distraction.

I was there because Mr. Das thought I would be interested to see some of the kinds of women Priscilla was trying to help: women who had had difficult childbirths, women whose ill health did not permit them to bear or look after more children, women recovering from botched self-induced abortions, the whole female chamber of horrors in this overcrowded and desperately poor country. But after a few perfunctory minutes with such women, exhausted figures who responded listlessly to my inarticulate questions, I moved numbly on. Kadambari wanted me to meet someone else altogether, someone whom my daughter had had nothing to do with.

She lay wrapped like some grotesque mummy on a cot in the darkest corner of the room, moaning involuntarily with every second breath. "Sundari," she said briefly. "My sister. She has burns over seventy-five percent of her body. She is not yet nineteen years old."

Sundari opened pain-wracked eyes when she heard her name, and smiled weakly to acknowledge her visitors. "Sundari, you know, means beautiful," Kadambari said. "She is very beautiful, my sister." And indeed, what I could see of her face seemed quite unlike Kadambari's, with a delicately lovely nose and lips, but from under the swathed bandage, I caught a glimpse of the warped dry burned skin of her neck.

"Tell her your story, Sundari," Kadambari said, her voice un-gentle, commanding.

"No, it's all right, don't bother her," I protested, but Kadambari was insistent. Sundari looked at me without moving her face, her eyes raking me with a regard that combined defeat with yearning, as if she wished I could reach out to her and pull her out of the quicksand into which she was sinking.

"I got married last year," she said in a feeble voice, her bluish lips barely moving. "Kadambari helped arrange it. My father had to take a loan to pay for the wedding. He gave the boy a Bajaj scooter. Rupesh. That is his name. He is — he had a job, as a peon in an office. A few months after the wedding, he lost his job.

"We were living with Rupesh's parents. His father is old and sick. His mother ran the house. I had to do whatever she told me to do. Help her cook the food, chop the vegetables, clean the kitchen, empty the garbage. And more. Massage the old man's feet. Help clean him. He could not even get up to go the bathroom. It was disgusting.

"I had never done some of these things before. Rupesh seemed to like me. He kept telling me at night how beautiful I was. So I asked him, couldn't we go away? Live by ourselves somewhere. He was shocked. He said his duty was to his parents and so was mine, as his wife. His mother overheard us and slapped me. I looked to Rupesh to protect me but he just turned his back and let her slap me again. From that day I realized I was alone in that house.

"Every day the beatings got worse. Nothing I did around the house was good enough for my mother-in-law. She was screaming at me all the time. If the floor wasn't clean, she beat me. If anything was unsatisfactory about the food, the plates, the way the bed was made, it was my fault. If I didn't run to my father-in-law every time we heard him hawking and spitting in the next room, I would be called a lazy and ungrateful witch and beaten again. Rupesh learned to turn his eyes away from me. He told me I had to obey his mother at all times.

"When he lost his job they treated me even worse. They said I had brought bad luck upon my husband and his family. They said I was born under an evil star, and that my parents had bribed the jyotishi to alter my horoscope so that it seemed to match Rupesh's. Then they started complaining about my dowry. How little it was, how it was less than my father had promised when the marriage was arranged. None of this was true, but if I said so they screamed at me for talking back to them and beat me more."

I looked around for some water to give the poor girl, whose dry lips barely moved as she spoke, but I could see none. She struggled on. "I was miserable, crying all the time, unable to sleep. When Rupesh came to me at night he no longer said I was beautiful. He did not stroke my cheek as he used to. He took me by force, very roughly and very quickly, and turned away.

"One day I threw up in the morning and was beaten for that too. But in a day or two it became clear I was not sick, but pregnant. For a few days the beatings stopped. Rupesh's mother even began talking of the son her son was going to have. Then a new nightmare began.

"Rupesh's mother had a relative who worked in one of those new clinics that do amniocentesis. He slipped me in without my in-laws having to pay anything. The doctor inserted a big needle into me. It hurt a lot. A few days later Rupesh came to the house looking as if he had been whipped. My sample had tested positive. The baby was going to be a girl.

"The beatings started again. My pregnancy was no longer an acceptable excuse not to do the chores they wanted me to. Rupesh looked more and more woebegone by the day. And his mother started saying, 'What use is this woman who does no work around the house and cannot even produce a son?'

"One day last week I was working in the kitchen rolling the dough for chapatis which my mother-in-law was making at the stove. I remember Rupesh coming in with a can of kerosene for the stove, and my mother-in-law picking up a box of matches. I turned back to my dough when I felt a splash on my sari. The next thing I knew my whole body was on fire. I screamed and ran out of the kitchen and out the front door. People came running. If I had run the other way, into the house, I wouldn't be here today."

Her dry lips parted in a sad and bitter grimace. "Perhaps that would have been better for me than — than this." Her eyes, the only mobile part of her face, took in the room, the bed, the other patients, Kadambari, and me. "Why did my neighbors bother to save my life? What did they save me for?"

I turned to Kadambari. "And Rupesh and his mother? Have they been arrested? What are the police doing about this?"

"They say it was a kitchen accident," Kadambari replied. "There are a few dozen 'kitchen accidents' like this every year in Zalilgarh. What can the police prove? It is her word against theirs."

I looked sadly at the young girl, knowing she will be disfigured for life, and worse, that she will either have to go back to live a pariah's existence in the very family that tried to kill her, or return to her own parents, who will feel the disgrace of her broken marriage and face a mountain of unpaid debts from the wedding and the hospitalization of their daughter.

"The baby?" I asked. Sundari closed her eyes; it was the only way she could avert her gaze.

"She miscarried, the day after the burning," Kadambari said.

Kadambari spoke into my silence. "She was a good student and wanted to go to college," Kadambari said. "But my parents felt she had to marry before she became too old to find a good husband."

"A good husband," Sundari whispered from the bed.

When we left the ward Kadambari was strangely more communicative than she has been so far. "You see, Mrs. Hart," she observed, "<u>this</u> is the real issue for women in India. Not population control, but violence against women. In our own homes. What good are all our efforts as long as men have the power to do this to us? Your daughter never understood that."

I wheeled on her then. "You're wrong, miss," I said in my most schoolteacherly manner. "Priscilla did understand. Her whole approach was based on her belief that women need to resist their own subjugation. That when they are empowered, they will no longer have more babies than they can look after. She wrote that to me very clearly. I am surprised you could have worked so closely with her and not understood what my daughter believed in."

Kadambari looked unabashed, even defiant. "A lot of people," she said slowly and softly, "did not understand what your daughter believed in."

She would not explain what she meant, and the rest of our journey back to the guest house passed in a strained silence. When we arrived I thanked her for having introduced me to her sister. Rudyard emerged at that point and insisted she stay for a cup of tea. He always had a tin ear for my signals. In the circumstances, I could scarcely excuse myself. So I sat down in one of the rattan chairs in the guest house's verandah, and while the tea was being made, I told him what had happened.

"God, that's terrible," he said. Then he turned to Kadambari. "Tell me, this sister of yours. Will she get well?"

"The burns will take a long time to heal," Kadambari replied, "but the doctors say she will live."

"She won't have much of a life, Rudyard," I began. "Her—"

"I understand all that," he interrupted me. "My question to you, Miss Kadambari, is: Would she be able to go to college?"

"My parents can't afford to send her to college," Kadambari said. "They live on what I earn at the HELP project."

"That wasn't my question," Rudyard said with that note of impatience that executives so often mistake for efficiency. "If she could go, would she want to? Would she get in? Would she be able to cope?"

"She was the top student in her high school class," Kadambari said.

"Great," Rudyard said. "Now here's what we'll do. I'm going to sign over a thousand dollars worth of traveler's checks to you tomorrow. That should be more than enough to cover your family's expenses while she's in hospital. And for every year that she's in college, I'll set aside money for her tuition fees, books, and living expenses."

Kadambari seemed stunned, but even she could not have been as stunned as I felt. This was not a gesture I would have thought Rudyard capable of.

"Your sister's going to have a future, young lady," Rudyard said. He left unspoken the thought, Unlike my daughter.

"Rudyard, that's a wonderful thing to do," I said, a new respect for him in my eyes.

"It's what Priscilla would have wanted, Kathy," he replied.

It was the first time in years that he'd called me Kathy.

note from Priscilla Hart to Lakshman

September 29, 1989

As you know, I'm leaving town on Tuesday morning. My flight back home from Delhi is on Thursday. I guess I'll never see you again.

It's been so hard, Lucky. There are a hundred things I've wanted to say to you, to ask you. But you've never given me the chance, and we may never have the chance again.

I'm going back to the Kotli for the very last time tomorrow. How many Saturday evenings I've spent there with you! Do you remember, last month, when you wrote to me and said you'd be there after I'd walked out on you — and I came to see you because I couldn't bear not to? That all seems a hundred years ago now, Lucky. But it's now my turn to ask the same thing. Will you come tomorrow, for old times' sake? I just want to see the sunset one last time with you, and to say goodbye properly. I don't want to leave Zalilgarh feeling that the last word I had from you was that awful letter.

I'm sure you can do it if you want to. I know your wife and daughter are usually at the temple Saturday evenings. It's not much to ask, is it, Lucky?

Don't let this note put too much pressure on you, Lucky. If you think it's too painful for you, or disloyal to your family, or whatever, don't come. Think about everything and decide for yourself. I'll be waiting.

I know you're a decent and honorable man. Whatever you do, I know you'll do the right thing.

Yours as ever, P

from Lakshman's journal

October 3, 1989

I haven't slept for three nights. The riot is over now; tensions are calming, though God knows when they will erupt again. I have abandoned the camp cot in the police station and returned to what I know as my home. But the horrible finality of Priscilla's death keeps me awake in my own bed.

I <u>completely forgot</u>. It is as simple as that. I read her letter; I mentally upbraided her for having been so oblivious to the real life of Zalilgarh that she forgot there was a major Hindu procession on Saturday; but I planned to go to her afterwards. There was never any question in my mind that I would go to her, for that one last embrace, the final goodbye. But of course I didn't plan on a riot, and once it began I forgot everything else, even her, waiting for me at dusk at the Kotli.

When Guru came to give me the news I doubled over as from a blow to the stomach. If I had had any food in me I would have been sick, but I experienced a retching of my soul instead. He put a hand on my shoulder and thrust something at me with his other hand.

"We found it by her body," he said gruffly. "It's not entered in the log. You can have it."

I looked stupidly at the foolscap volume, spattered with her blood. Priscilla's scrapbook.

It was the only thing of hers that I'd ever have. I clutched it as a drowning man clutches a floating plank from his unsalvageable ship. "Thanks, Guru," I managed to say.

And then, for the first time since my father's death, I wept.

Katharine Hart and Lakshman

October 14, 1989

KH: I'm really sorry to bother you again, but it was important that I see you alone. Without — the others.

VL: Of course. How can I help you?

KH: There's something about Priscilla's life here that's not very clear to me. That bothers me.

VL: Yes?

KH: Well, I may as well plunge right in. In one of her letters to me she mentioned that she'd met someone she was quite — attracted to. Someone in a position of authority here.

VL: And?

KH: I wondered if it might have been you.

VL: Good God, Mrs. Hart! I'm flattered, I suppose. But I'm overworked, overweight, and married. It couldn't have been me.

KH: I'm sorry if I've been impertinent in any way. Rudyard — Priscilla's father — doesn't know about any of this. Nor does the journalist, Mr. Diggs. I'm not trying to embarrass you, Mr. Lakshman. I just want to understand everything I can about my daughter's death.

VL: I wish I could help you, Mrs. Hart. But there was nothing between us. If you will permit me to say this, sometimes it is best not to assume we can know everything. Your daughter led a good and admirable life. She worked for others; she was popular and well-respected. She died a tragic, senseless death. You know the old Greek adage, the good die young. That was all there was to it.

KH: But there was more. There was something else, something that might explain why she was there, in that out-of-the-way place. Perhaps it had to do with some aspect of her life we don't know about.

VL: Perhaps. But does it matter what we do not know? Any attraction she may have felt to anyone did not kill her. Communal passions that she had nothing to do with, did.

KH: I suppose you're right.

VL: I am, Mrs. Hart. And now, if you'll excuse me, I have work to do. I wish you a safe trip back home.

Gurinder to Lakshman

October 15, 1989

Why the hell did you saddle me with that bunch, yaar? Bloody demanding Americans. They want this, they want that, they want to see the exact spot where we found her, what are the details of the police report, why did the postmortem omit this or that. I'd already given the journalist Diggs more than enough of my time. Then the fucking Harts on top of it, it was all too much.

And that mother of hers! Went on and on about the missing scrapbook. She knows it exists, she says. Well, ma'am, perhaps it does, I respond, but it's not up my fucking ass. No, I don't really say that. But I finally have to show her the whole pissing inventory in the bloody logbook of every item found at the murder scene. No scrapbook. That quieted her.

We've already spent more time on this visit than on everything to do with all the other riot victims, dead and injured. What is wrong with us, that we give so much importance to a bunch of foreigners? I'm glad they're leaving tomorrow, I tell you.

That bloody Hart, with his patronizing airs, as if he knows India so well from having tried to sell his bloody Coke here. What has he ever done for India, or for a single Indian? We don't need your pissing soft drinks, I nearly told him. We've had lassi and nimbu-paani for a thousand years before anyone invented your bloody beverage. Just as well we kept you out. The frigging East India Company came here to trade and stayed on to rule; we don't want history to repeat itself with Coca sucking Cola. We don't need you, mister. We can get pissed on our own, thank you bloody much.

And Diggs. Poking around the bloody embers of the riot like a bloody commission of enquiry. All for some thousand-word piece in which he'll use two sentences of the two hours I gave him. I liked him at first, even took him home for a drink last night, told him some things I haven't told anyone from the press before. Off the frigging record, of course. Feeling a bit ashamed of my garrulousness now. Why are we so sucking anxious to oblige these bloody foreigners, Lucky? Some flaw in the national character? I wouldn't have given an Indian journalist a fraction of the stuff I gave this man, and he won't even use it. Maybe that's why.

Anyway, you'll want to know what I told them. I told them what seemed to have happened. The Muslim bomb-chuckers, running away from the house where I'd fired at them, came back to the Kotli to seek refuge — all except the motherlover we'd caught. They found Priscilla there — or she found them, it's not clear. They killed her to protect themselves.

Of course, none of them will admit it. They swear her body was there when they arrived. And of course we didn't catch them there. When the interrogation of the other fellow revealed their use of the Kotli, we went there the next day to look for evidence of bomb making, and found Priscilla as well. The others weren't there; we rounded them up from their homes on the arrested bugger's evidence. At least one of them, the municipal driver, Ali, looks like he's capable of anything.

And in case you're wondering, I didn't offer them any speculation on why she might have been there.

I see you don't want to talk. Just one thing. I'm glad you listened to me and shut up about your precious Priscilla. The last thing you needed for your career, not to mention your marriage, was an article in the New York fucking Journal about the slain American girl having an affair with the district buggering administrator. The dung would truly have hit the punkah then, Lucky, and you could have kissed goodbye to your future. You might as well have resigned and run off with Blondie the way you nearly did.

Okay, okay, I'm sorry. I just don't get it, but I know she meant a lot to you. So does this country, Lucky. You've got work to do here. The riot's over. She's gone, as she would have been gone anyway. It's time to turn the page.

Ram Charan Gupta to Kadambari

September 25, 1989

How very interesting, young lady.

So our do-gooding district magistrate is having a little fling on the side, is he? With this white woman, you say? That could be very useful information indeed, my dear. Tuesdays and Saturdays? My, you are thorough. Very diligent of you.

You are a good girl, Kadambari. A good Hindu girl. Here's a little something for your trouble. No, that's all right, my dear. I insist.

Mohammed Sarwar to Lakshman

October 14, 1989

Well, I got more than I bargained for on this visit. A full-scale riot. Two people killed on my street. And firsthand evidence of police excesses committed during house-to-house searches in the Muslim bastis. My uncle, Rauf-bhai, is the sadr of the community. He's helped you manage this riot, keep the peace. Even he wasn't spared, Lakshman. His house was broken into and trashed by the police search team. They took the TV and radio, poked holes in the mattresses, smashed some furniture. I live in the house; my research notes were picked up, scattered, trampled upon. Randy Diggs, the New York Journal–wallah whom I know from Delhi, wanted to meet me, and I couldn't even invite him home. How ashamed I feel. Of everything. Of everything that we are.

Of course you'll take action, Lakshman, I have no doubt. But how could you allow such a thing to occur in the first place? What kind of country are we creating when the police response to a riot simply sows the seeds of the next one?

Iqbal said it best, as always: "Na samjhogey to mit jaogey aye Hindostan walon / Tumhari dastaan tak bhi na raheygi dastanon mein." "If you don't understand, O you Indians, you will be destroyed. Your story will not remain in the world's treasury of stories."

Ram Charan Gupta to Makhan Singh

September 30, 1989

The bastard. This is the way that Lakshman treats us, after what the Muslims did to us last night? Makhan, I am so angry about what has happened to your son Arup. Such a handsome boy, too, and just before his wedding. But don't worry, Makhan. We will have our revenge. On the Muslims, and on the bastard who gives them such free rein.

Yes, we will revenge ourselves on Lakshman too. I understand your rage. It is these Muslim-lovers who make such attacks on our good Hindu boys possible.

But don't do anything foolish and hotheaded. He is the DM, after all. Do you want the wrath of the entire government on your head? No, there is a simpler way. You can catch him with his pants down. Literally.

Apparently he has a secret assignation every Tuesday and Saturday evening. At the Kotli. He is alone there. With a woman. The American woman we have seen cycling around town. But he's completely alone, in a deserted place. No guards to protect him.

That would be a good place to teach him a lesson, Makhan. And his woman too.

And you know what day it is today? Saturday! March in the procession, visit Arup in the hospital, have your bath, perform your prayers, and go to the Kotli when the sun sets. Revenge is sweeter when you have had time to savor it.

from Katharine Hart's diary

October 16, 1989

I am sitting next to Rudyard, yet again, on a plane, for the last time. He has been both diminished and redeemed by this trip, manifestly dwarfed by the complexity he encountered in India, humbled by the memory of his own failure there, and yet that deeply compassionate gesture. I felt sorry for him as he stumbled about trying to cope with his grief and his inadequacy, and I realized I've never felt sorry for him before. I find it curiously liberating.

I had to see Lakshman. It was him, of course. He confirmed it out of his own mouth. That phrase from Priscilla's letter — "in his own words, he's overworked, overweight, and married." He couldn't resist using it again. But I could see what Priscilla might have seen in him. And he's not that overweight either.

I suppose I can understand why he feels he can't afford to admit it. I wonder how much she meant to him. Or he to her, since she was leaving India, after all. The last love of her life . . . It doesn't bear thinking about.

I'll never know what happened to my poor baby. Perhaps it's just as the officials said it was, and she was surprised by criminals, or surprised them in the act. They must have thought it was her life or theirs. But what was she doing there? It doesn't make sense.

Except, perhaps, in the terms India believes in: Destiny. Fate. Karma.

Maybe it was God's will, and all one can do is to accept it. She died where she would have wanted to have lived.

Gurinder to Ali, at Police Thana Zalilgarh

October 5, 1989

Come on, you misbegotten sonofabitch, tell me the truth. What happened at the Kotli?

Don't give me that shit. You were there, you know it. You and your fucking friends, with your stupid bloody soothli bombs. Go on, turd-eater, tell me. You made the bombs, took them to town, tried to use them. Then I came along and started firing and you crapped in your pants and ran. We caught the young bugger, but you'd made it out by then, you and your cohorts. You didn't know where to hide in the middle of a fucking riot, so you buggered off back to the Kotli, expecting to spend the night with the rest of your frigging bomb-making ingredients. And what did you find when you got there? A bloody American woman, that's who.

And not just any bloody American woman, right, Ali? Somebody you had a fucking strong reason to dislike. Somebody you'd threat-ened more than once. There she is, you're fucking scared, your adrenaline is pumping like crazy, she recognizes you, you know you're done for, so you go at her, don't you, Ali? Don't you? Tell me, sisterlover! There's worse for you if you don't talk! What did you do with the fucking knife, you sonofabitch?

Forget him, Havildar. This bastard won't talk.

Maybe he's telling the truth. Maybe he didn't do it. But he did enough to get him put away for a long time. He won't be beating his pissing wife for a while.

Ram Charan Gupta to Makhan Singh

October 3, 1989

I don't want to know. Don't tell me anything, Makhan. Perhaps you went there after your bath, your prayers fresh in your mind, looking for the DM to teach him a lesson. But he was in Zalilgarh, putting down the riot. Instead, perhaps you found his woman, sitting there, waiting for him. Perhaps she started running away from you, and you caught her, and perhaps she fought too hard and you used your knife. Perhaps you thought of Arup, scarred and disfigured for life because this woman's special friend won't let us deal with these Muslims once and for all. It doesn't matter. I don't want to know.

After all, perhaps you didn't go there at all. Perhaps you finished your prayers and found the curfew made movement impossible, so you stayed at home. Don't say a word! Or perhaps you went there and found the Muslim criminals already there, and you found discretion the better part of valor and turned back. So many possibilities . . . But I really don't want to know, Makhan.

Sometimes, when you are in the position I am in, ignorance is bliss, Makhan. And I am a blissful man tonight.

Rudyard Hart to Katharine Hart at the PWD guest house, Zalilgarh

October 15, 1989

Katharine, Kathy, goodnight. No, wait. I don't know how to say this but I must. When we went to that Kotli place and saw the room where she was killed I thought I would burst in pain. But then something miraculous happened. I saw you. I saw the strength in you, the inner calm you've always had. When you knelt to touch that bloodstain on the floor of the alcove, the screaming inside my heart stopped. And a sort of peace descended on me.

Wait, I haven't finished. I don't know what exactly I was looking for when I decided to come here and talked you into coming too. Closure, I guess. Some way to come to terms with the finality of Priscilla's — of the knowledge that she was gone. I don't know if I've found that. I've found something else, though. A way of seeing into myself.

Coming back to India has taught me a lot about my first time here. When I was here last, Kathy, I saw a market, not a people. At my work, I saw a target, not a need. With Nandini, I saw an opportunity, not a lover. I took what I could and left. And now India has taken from me the one human being who mattered most to me in the world. Except that she didn't know it. And I didn't fully realize it myself until it was too late. . . .

There are a lot of other things it's too late for. But there's one thing I should have said to you a long time ago. A very simple thing: I'm sorry.

It's never too late to say you're sorry, is it, Kathy?

Geetha at the Shiva Mandir

October 7, 1989

Every Saturday I have come here to pray with my daughter, and I have sought your blessings and your advice, Purohit-ji, as well as that of the Swamiji.

I want to tell you this evening that my prayers have been answered.

Here is my offering for a special puja. That's right. For my husband's health, happiness, and long life.

from Lakshman's journal

October 4, 1989

I leaf through her scrapbook, and my grief blurs the lines on each page. I try not to imagine her death, but I cannot help myself.

The Kotli, at dusk, as the trees make a sieve of the fading light, and the air is still. She goes to our usual place, for the last time. Behind her, Zalilgarh is burning, but she is oblivious of it, forgetting the world in her desire to see me. Her body is full of sentences waiting to be spoken, of moments yet unlived, soft and heavy as if awakening from a sleep of lingering dreams. She waits, as the darkness gathers around her like a noose.

There is a scurry on the stairs, a stab of fear in her heart. Night falls on her like a knife.

Her assailant — assailants? — would not have had an easy time killing her. She would have fought furiously. She had one more reason to want to live.

I know now why it was so important for her to see me one last time. She had something to tell me, something that she thought might yet change my mind.

One more detail Gurinder had to suppress in the postmortem. She was carrying my child.

AMERICAN DEATH IN INDIA

Continued From Page 5

tempers dangerously.

"There was nothing we could do to stem the raging flood of communal hatred," admitted V. Lakshman, 33, the district magistrate, or chief administrator, of the town.

As the seemingly endless procession wound its way slowly through the narrow lanes, Lakshman and his superintendent of police, a convivial Sikh named Gurinder Singh, patrolled the throng with their officers, hoping to head off violence before it erupted. The two men described a scene of stamping feet and shouted slogans, with processionists spewing vitriol and flashing blades in the hot sun. Twice the marchers came close to attacking the town's main mosque, and twice they were headed off. Just when it seemed that the march would proceed without serious incident, a bomb attack occurred on the procession. Shooting followed, the crowd ran amok, and Zalilgarh soon had a full-scale riot on its hands.

Eight people were killed in the disturbances, forty-seven injured, and hundreds of thousands of dollars of property damaged. By the standards of some of the riots that have been sweeping northern India

in the wake of the Ram Janmabhoomi agitation, Zalilgarh's was a modest affair. What made it unusually tragic was that it took an American life, one that was neither Hindu nor Muslim: Priscilla Hart's.

Ms. Hart had friends in both communities, and they are united in expressing shock and grief at her killing. "She was so special," said Miss Kadambari (who uses only one name), an extension worker at the project who worked closely with Miss Hart. "No one could have wanted to harm her." Her project director, Mr. Shankar Das, recalled her as a "sweet person" who "made friends very easily." No one in Zalilgarh could explain why anyone would want to kill Priscilla Hart.

"In riots, all sorts of things happen," said Gurinder Singh, the policeman. "People strike first and ask questions later."

For Priscilla's parents, Rudyard and Katharine Hart, who traveled to Zalilgarh to understand the reasons for their daughter's death, the questions will never cease. The Zalilgarh police have arrested a number of Muslim rioters, some of whom they suspect of involvement in Ms. Hart's death, but they have no clues and no confession. As is often the case in riot-related killings, the real murderers of Priscilla Hart may never be apprehended.

"It is hard to escape the conclusion," a U.S. embassy spokesman said, "that she was simply in the wrong place at the wrong time."

Mr. Lakshman, however, questions whether there is such a thing as the wrong place, or the wrong time. "We are where we are at the only time we have," he said. "Perhaps it's where we're meant to be."

AFTERWORD

On December 6, 1992, a howling, chanting mob of Hindu fanatics, armed with hammers and pickaxes, demolished the Babri Masjid in Ayodhya, vowing to construct the Ram Janmabhoomi temple in its place. In the riots that followed across the country, thousands of lives, both Hindu and Muslim, were lost. These events marked the worst outburst of communal violence in India since Partition.

The consecrated bricks gathered in the Ram Sila Poojan program of 1989 are still gathering dust. Though, at this writing, the Hindutva-inclined Bharatiya Janata Party (BJP) is in power at the head of a coalition government in New Delhi and also runs the state government of Uttar Pradesh, the temple has not yet been built.

Various affiliates of the Sangh Parivar family of Hindu organizations have announced plans to proceed with the construction of a Ram temple on the site, in defiance of court orders. At the great Maha Kumbha Mela pilgrimage on the banks of the sacred river Ganga in Varanasi in January 2001, they displayed an impressive model of the temple they intend to build, and declared that they would commence construction on March 12, 2002, whether or not the government granted its consent. Prime Minister Atal Behari Vajpayee, however, has declared that the matter can only be resolved in one of two ways: through the judicial process, or in a negotiated agreement between Hindus and Muslims. Neither method has made much headway in the last five decades.

We live, the late Octavio Paz once wrote, between oblivion and memory. Memory and oblivion: how one leads to the other, and back again, has been the concern of much of my fiction. History, the old saying goes, is not a web woven with innocent hands.

May 2001

ACKNOWLEDGMENTS

I owe a special debt of gratitude to my dear friend Harsh Mander, IAS, on whose hitherto unpublished account of a riot in Khargone, Madhya Pradesh, I have based some of the details of the Zalilgarh episode. As this book goes to press, I have learned that the story of the Khargone riot is being published in 2001 by Penguin India as part of a debut collection by Harsh Mander, *Unheard Voices: Stories of Forgotten People,* which I warmly commend. With Harsh's permission I have used many of his basic facts about the management of the riot and, in a few places, his own words, and I remain deeply grateful. Readers should know, however, that no foreigner was killed in Khargone; all the key details as they relate to the characters in this novel — and in particular all the personal relationships, character elements, beliefs, and motivations depicted herein — are, of course, completely fictional.

The research by "Professor Mohammed Sarwar" on Ghazi Miyan is based on the actual work of Professor Shahid Amin of Delhi University, another old friend to whom I am grateful, though every other detail relating to the character, including the views expressed by him, are solely my responsibility. The efforts of "Rudyard Hart" on behalf of Coca-Cola in India were in fact undertaken by Kisan Mehta, for whose kindness, recollections, and insight I offer my thanks.

My friend and publisher in India, David Davidar, and my literary agent in New York, Mary Evans, offered valuable suggestions on the text, which have helped me improve it immeasurably. Jeannette and Dick Seaver at Arcade Publishing, and the diligent Ann Marlowe, have been terrific in their support for *Riot* and its author. My sisters, Shobha Srinivasan and Smita Menon, read the manuscript with devotion and insight; they have each left their mark on the characters and events of this novel in more ways than one. To them all I offer my thanks, and my love.

For help in various ways as this book was brought to completion, I am also grateful to Rosemary Colaco, Sujata Mehta, and Vikas Sharma. My thanks, too, to Sreenath Sreenivasan for creating a Web site for me and to Ambassador A. K. Damodaran, for a verse about John Knox.

This novel was completed during a difficult time in my life, when it would have been impossible without the maturity, large-heartedness and strength revealed by my sons, Ishaan and Kanishk. To them, for being themselves, I shall always be eternally grateful.